PRAISE FOR

“Everything a cozy fantasy book should be. Diamanti weaves together a heart-warming tale of healing and self-discovery. With just the right balance of cozy and impact, this is definitely one of the best cozy fantasy books I've read.”

- Herman Steuernagel, Author of *The Bartender Between Worlds*

"An emotional journey that perfectly blends cozy fantasy, healing, and growth!"

- Liz Delton, Author of *Seasons of Soldark*

“Guard in the Garden is a cozy fantasy set in deep soil. Diamanti pulls at your heartstrings in this slice-of-life tale of a battle-wounded soldier adapting to civilian life while navigating personal relationships and gardening.”

- Andrew D. Meredith, Author of *Quaint Creatures: Magical and Mundane*

“Guard makes you feel like you’re strolling within the gardens of the Garome district. Leisurely, delightful, and emotional, with plenty of heart-warming characters and mouth-watering meals to boot.”

- R.K. Ashwick, Author of *The Stray Spirit*

“Guard in the Garden is such a lovely, soft story about the struggles of PTSD and finding a new place for yourself in the world.”

- J. Penner, Author of *A Fellowship of Bakers & Magic*

"This story reminds me of all the best things about Legends and Lattes, but also reads as a unique story. There’s something truly special about a character trying to be useful when he feels he can no longer live up to his previous self. A beautiful, well told story of healing. Amazing!"

- Jennifer Kropf, Author of *Welcome to Fae Café*

ALSO BY Z.S. DIAMANTI

STONE & SKY
STONE & TIDE
STONE & RUIN
STONE & SKY PRELUDES COLLECTION

GUARD IN THE GARDEN
WAGONS & WYVERNS

FREE PRELUDES

AT

FreeFantasyFiction.com

GUARD IN THE GARDEN

FABLES OF FINLESTIA

FABLES OF FINLESTIA

GUARD IN THE GARDEN

Z.S. DIAMANTI

GOLDEN GRIFFIN

For Joe,
And all my other fellow veteran brothers and sisters
who know what it's like to fight a war one day
and fight yourself the next

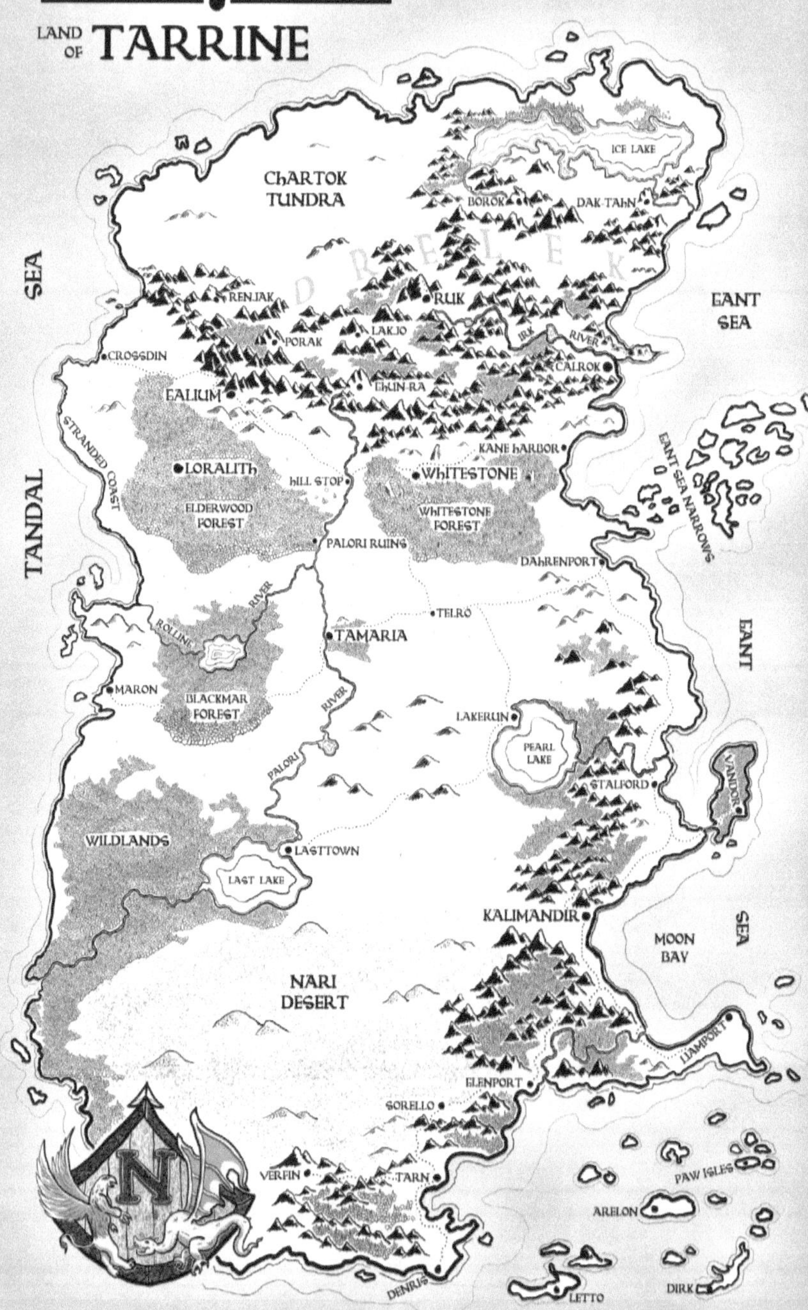

FINLESTIA
LAND OF TARRINE

SEA

TANDAL

STRANDED COAST

CHARTOK TUNDRA

ICE LAKE

BOROK
DAK-TAHN

DRELEK

RENJAK
RUK

LAKJO

PORAK

CROSSDIN

CALROK

IRK RIVER

EALIUM

ELIN-RA

EANT SEA

KANE HARBOR

EANT SEA NARROWS

LORALITH

HILL STOP

WHITESTONE

ELDERWOOD FOREST

WHITESTONE FOREST

PALORI RUINS

DAHRENPORT

RIVER

TELRO

ROLLINI

TAMARIA

EANT

MARON

RIVER

BLACKMAR FOREST

LAKERUN

PEARL LAKE

VANDOR

PALORI

STALFORD

WILDLANDS

LASTTOWN

LAST LAKE

KALIMANDIR

SEA

MOON BAY

NARI DESERT

LIAMPORT

GLENPORT

SORELLO

PAW ISLES

VERFIN

TARN

ARELON

DENRIS

LETTO

DIRK

N

LAND
OF **KELVUR**

SEA

EANT

CRAG
WASTES

GRAES

ZORS

FELL KEEP

VENTOHL

DUSKWOOD

EASTERN
KNOLLS

LAKE KNOLL

DORANTOWN

THE PALISADE

AIDEN'S DELL

THE SHOALS

ANTALON

ZOR LEDI

FOREST OF
WIRRA

ZOR TOREIS

ZOR VELNIS

SEA

ELAIN'S SHOULDER

TALVIN

LAKE TORI

LOD MORAZ

SOLREH

ZOR PLEDIR

LOD ZIM

LAKE
NEL

LORNASH POINT

ZOR LANTI

LOD KELPIO

FAR

FAR
COVE

LOD POINT

LOD
LAKE

LOD METO

LERIAN SEA

PROLOGUE

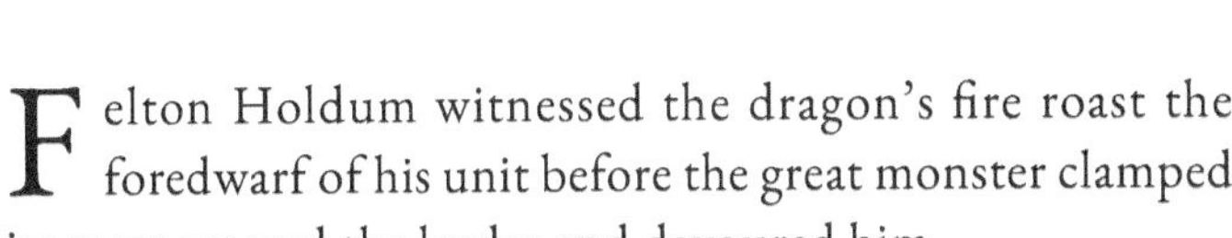

Felton Holdum witnessed the dragon's fire roast the foredwarf of his unit before the great monster clamped its maw around the leader and devoured him.

A realization sent a rushing wave of fear crashing over the dwarf. Their plan had failed. The orc army of Drelek had arrived at the gates of Galium intent on wiping the dwarven city off the map. As he assessed the chaos around him, Felton feared the enemy would achieve their goal.

He gripped Honor's sleek neck, the black fur of her coat slick with sweat. The garvawk's panther-like body drooped underneath him as she beat her bat-like wings.

"Easy, girl," Felton said to her.

They'd suffered a swipe from the dragon's thrashing tail while the garvawk warriors attacked the beast from the mountain's shadows. His unit had flawlessly performed their initial surprise attack—the only play their far smaller garvawks could make against the mighty dragon.

The orc wyvern squadron that accompanied the dragon rider chased and engaged Felton's fellow warriors. The garvawks' ability to flit in and out of the shadows cast by the immense Drelek Mountains beneath the silvery moonlight complicated the orcs' endeavors.

Felton patted Honor's head, hoping she was ready to rejoin the fight. When the dragon's tail had hit them, the dwarf had nearly been thrown from the dazed and spiraling garvawk. Thankfully, the saddle held him fast, and Honor managed to right herself before they crashed into the mountainside.

A nearby screech startled them, and Felton heeled Honor into motion. A wyvern-riding orc barreled at them, the wyvern's wicked maw salivating at what it deemed an easy kill. The orc looked no less bloodthirsty.

Honor tucked her wings and dove. Wind whipped around Felton's ears as they rushed toward the sloping ground of the front range. Out of the corner of his eye, the dwarf noted the ground battle continued to wage with unrelenting fury.

Another screech from the angry wyvern behind them made Felton tense and press closer to Honor's back. She outstretched her wings, slowing their descent until she could kick off the boulders and alter direction. Her maneuver was so quick, Felton heard the orc behind them roar in frustration.

Honor flapped her wide wings quickly as they disappeared and reappeared in the starkly contrasting shadows. The garvawk tucked her wings and plunged the duo into a dark crevasse. She landed them on a boulder, well-hidden in the darkness. Her body heaved with her lungs as she tried to catch her breath.

Felton took stock of their situation. He was down two throwing axes—only one remained. He was also down to his last two knives. Once those were gone, he'd have to rely on his battle axe. He did not relish the idea of having to get close enough to use it on the wyvern-riding orcs.

All his life, Felton had been a warrior. Before he was chosen for the honor of being a garvawk warrior of Galium, he'd spent many years in the warhog cavalry, up close and personal with their enemies. Garvawks were fierce creatures, also familiar with battle. Honor would fight tooth and claw against any wyvern.

Felton worried about their chances, though. Since the dragon's tail hit them, Honor had not been quite right and displayed the effects of being stunned.

He heard the battle cry of another dwarf just before the clanging ring of metal on metal. His brothers needed him.

"Come on, girl," he said, gently stroking her neck. "They need us."

Felton heeled her, and Honor catapulted into the sky.

Ahead of them, an orc flew to aid one of his friends against one of Felton's. The dwarf threw a knife, sticking the orc in the arm as he reached up to shield himself. The injured orc roared and kicked his wyvern, turning the beast toward Felton and Honor.

Honor flapped her wings and dodged as the orc loosed a throwing axe at them.

"I've got one of those, too!" Felton hollered as Honor flapped into a charge. The dwarf reared back and hurled his throwing axe. It blasted into the orc, sending him toppling from his mount to the ground far below.

Honor crashed into the wyvern, viciously clawing and biting. The two furiously snapped and scratched at each other, nearly launching Felton out of his saddle before the wyvern's teeth clamped onto the garvawk's leg.

The dwarf held tightly with one hand while he struggled to pull his battle axe from the saddle loop. When he finally pried it loose, Felton lifted it with both hands above his head and brought it down on the wyvern's skull, instantly killing the creature.

Honor cried out in agony as the wyvern's teeth ripped away from her leg on his heavy plummet from the sky. Felton took the momentary reprieve to inspect the damage to his partner.

But the reprieve was short-lived.

An arrow struck Felton's leg. He roared in anguish, prodding at the shaft protruding from his flesh. By the time he looked up to see where the attack came from, it was too late.

A spear struck Honor, and the pair fell from the sky.

Honor crashed into the mountainside, and Felton was flipped onto a nearby boulder.

The dwarf pawed at his head, and blood covered his hand. He blinked, struggling to focus on the dragon in the distance through the growing heaviness in his brain. The beast passed over the city of Galium, spewing its wretched flames upon Felton's people.

As the dwarf's head lolled sideways, the last thing he saw was the amber glow of dragon flame illuminating the night sky.

SUMMER

CHAPTER 1
EMPTY ROOMS

Felton hoisted himself from his bed in the healer ward. As he did, a groan escaped through his clenched teeth.

The few months since the Battle of Galium had been painstakingly frustrating for him. For the first few weeks, he'd been bedridden alongside many others, as they healed from various battle wounds.

Lying in bed while the healers checked on him each day had been more painful in his mind than his physical pain. Day after day, he'd lain there waiting for the healing to make him whole again. His inability to speed up the process grated on him.

When the pain began to ebb, Felton spent much of his days in utter boredom. He replayed conversations he'd had while bedridden, unable to shake their memory.

"Our allies slew the dragon in the end," Lotmeag Kandersaw, a fellow garvawk warrior, had told him. "They used some sort of magic that even King Thygram's mage adviser doesn't fully comprehend. And then, more allies arrived from Whitestone just in time to finish the battle and save the city from total destruction."

Other news lingered bitterly in Felton's mouth.

"When we found you on the mountainside, we found Honor as well ..." Lotmeag had said.

A spark of hope flickered in Felton's chest, but his friend's hesitance and downcast gaze squelched it quickly.

"So, she's gone ..." Felton barely uttered.

"Aye," the other dwarf said softly. "I'm so sorry. From what we could tell, she positioned herself as best she could during the crash to spare ye. Whatever she did, only just worked. Ye were near dead when we found ye."

Felton hadn't been with Honor long, but the loss devastated him. He'd spent his whole life training and becoming an elite warrior so he could be paired with a garvawk. And like a breath blowing out a candle, it was gone. His partner, his teammate. She was gone. And with her last act, she'd saved him? It was too much to bear. He'd cried quietly many nights, trying to muffle his sorrow to avoid waking the others in their beds, lining the healing ward.

Lotmeag also informed him that they'd lost numerous members of the unit, not least of whom was Bendur Clagstack, the foredwarf of the garvawk warriors. Lotmeag had taken over the unit's leadership as foredwarf and, as such, had visited Felton several times.

The new foredwarf filled him in on the current state of their unit. Many had fallen, but Felton was the only one of them who had survived.

Lotmeag's visits became infrequent, as he was pulled away to his new duties. Felton couldn't help but feel a little abandoned and a stubbornness he'd always been told he got from his mother began to take root. It was better not to have visitors seeing him in that state. He could wallow in his frustration at the slow healing process, and no one could say anything to stop him.

Except Healer Gembeck. The old dwarf didn't take any stubbornness from anyone, and Felton was surprised that his hereditary penchant for the trait wasn't strong enough to resist the healer.

After weeks in bed, Healer Gembeck and a few others helped Felton onto his feet. The task of retraining his body to function normally again began. On his first attempt to walk, he'd collapsed in a heap on the floor, unable to steer his legs after the long weeks of stagnation.

"Shave me!" Felton had cursed himself.

"Patience," Healer Gembeck said, kneeling next to him and helping him sit up.

"I've been in bed for weeks," Felton grumbled. "I thought it was supposed to make me better. Now, my legs don't even work!"

"Healing is an art," the elder dwarf said. "It takes time and persistence. And sometimes the painting looks all wrong before it finally looks right. Every part of the process is necessary. Every seemingly random stroke of the brush a part of the completed masterpiece."

"Great ..." Felton moaned. "Are you a poet or a healer?"

Healer Gembeck's wrinkled face creased with mirth. The crow's feet carving deep well-used canyons in the corners of his eyes.

Every day after, Felton slowly worked up to more time on his feet, while the healers begged him to slow down. Felton couldn't. The sooner he renewed the strength in his legs, the sooner he'd be able to return to the fight.

Felton watched dwarf after dwarf recover from their ailments and leave Galium's healing ward. The weeks stretched painfully onward for him, and he realized something was terribly wrong. His leg that had been struck by the arrow wasn't improving. He felt stronger everywhere else, though. Why wasn't his leg getting any better? The healers could not determine what was stalling his progress.

One particularly frustrating day, Felton got the notion in his head that if he willed his leg to work properly—forced it into a make-or-break scenario—he could push past the pain. While none of the healers were near, Felton lifted his cane and balanced tentatively. He pressed his foot into the stone floor a few times, testing its strength. He winced as pain shot up his leg and into his hip. Out of rage-fueled determination, Felton resolved to run.

He made a long stride and launched himself into a sprint with his good leg. When his other foot hit the ground, a jolt of pain shot through him. He lurched forward, sprawling onto the floor. His whole body slid, and his cane clattered away.

A boot halted the cane's slide.

"Felton!" Lotmeag Kandersaw said in shock. "Are ye alright?"

Felton pressed his face away from the floor and looked up. Tears streaked his face, and he quickly wiped them on his sleeve. He cursed his muck luck—of all the days for the foredwarf to visit him!

"No! Go away!" Felton cried as Lotmeag went to help him up.

"Let's get ye up and—"

"No!" Felton growled. "I can do it myself. Just go away."

Lotmeag stared at him for a long time. Felton could feel it, even though he couldn't bring himself to make eye contact with the foredwarf. How could he? Sprawled on the floor. He didn't want his foredwarf to see him like this.

"I just ..." Felton began. "Just don't worry about me. I'll come to see you when I'm better."

Lotmeag hesitated for a moment, but when Healer Gembeck drew near and gave him a nod, the foredwarf only said, "Ye do that. I'll see ye in no time, I'm sure."

A few more weeks passed, and Felton regretted his words. He'd been so angry. So foolish and thick-headed.

Unfortunately, no matter how hard he tried, Felton's leg never seemed to improve. He skillfully maneuvered around the healing ward with his cane—helping where he could. He could do nothing without the cane, though. He grew to hate the way it felt in his hand, despising it as though the cane itself had been the arrow that had damaged his leg.

Despite his internal turmoil, Felton had left a positive outward mark on others. He'd helped with new patients that came in with injuries sustained during the reconstruction of their city. By the time Felton left the ward, many of the healers were sorry to see him go, especially Healer Gembeck, who'd grown rather fond of the warrior. In truth, despite his initial frustrations with the old healer, Felton respected him greatly, having seen Gembeck's compassion in action for so long.

"You're going to need to be patient," the old healer dwarf said on the day Felton left.

"I've been patient for months," Felton said.

Healer Gembeck chuckled. "You have been a stubborn patient but not *patient*."

Felton sighed deeply. "I don't have time to be patient. I need to get better. I need to get back to the fight."

The older dwarf stroked his long white beard and studied Felton. Carefully, he said, "From what I hear, the fight is over for now. A time of peace is the perfect time to be patient. I think time is what you need more than anything right now."

Felton clenched his teeth. How could he take time to be patient? He'd lost friends, and even then, more of his friends were training and preparing for the next threat. How could he do any less?

"I'll do my best," Felton said.

"That's all any of us can do," Gembeck replied.

The wounded dwarf bid the old healer goodbye, his cane clacking as he exited the building.

The garvawk warriors had their own hall deep within Galium's castle. Known by its members as Bannett Hall, the area was named after the first foredwarf of the garvawk warriors when the unit had been established centuries before.

Felton's cane clicked softly but echoed through the stone hallways of the main keep. Dwarven craftsmen had expertly designed the entire castle to be built straight into the mountainside. Felton gazed up as he entered Bannett Hall, one of the largest halls with a high ceiling. A singular stairway rose at the end and split to either side.

At the top of the stairs was another room where the garvawk warriors spent much of their time. There they shared meals and discussed tactics, patrol assignments, and various stratagems. With no dwarves training in the main section of the hall, Felton assumed they were in the gathering room.

As he approached the stairs, he slowed. He shot tentative glances to the railings above on either side. On the second floor, garvawks in their stone forms perched on the edges. To outsiders, they might look like menacing statues of barbaric creatures. A garvawk warrior knew better.

Felton sniffed the air, breathing in the memory of the place. Having been the newest member of the garvawk warriors prior to the Battle of Galium, he'd yet to move his belongings from the barracks at the warhog station. The garvawk warriors had a full company before the battle and planned to expand the quarters of Bannett Hall. Due to the irregular and unpredictable nature of procuring new garvawks, they didn't know when they would need more rooms until Felton bonded with his garvawk. It had been the fullest fighting force of garvawk warriors ever. Until the devastating battle ...

The dwarf lingered at the bottom of the stairs. Too many of the garvawk perches were empty. Each stone garvawk sat regally in front of the door to their rider's room. The empty perches were a stark reminder of the empty rooms of his fallen brothers.

Felton's face hardened behind his great brown beard as he gazed determinedly toward the gathering room doors. He gingerly tested the first step and then the second, leaning on his cane for added support. "Mud and shale," he cursed under his breath. This was going to be harder than he anticipated. Awkwardly, he hefted himself up, planting both feet firmly on the step before attempting the next. Step-by-step, the indomitable dwarf worked his way to the top.

When he walked through the door, the raucous laughter of his kinsmen enveloped him. He'd just missed the joke, something the dwarves were fond of sharing. Seeing fellow warriors' merriment brought warmth to his heart.

One of the dwarven warriors, refilling his mug from the barrel of mead, noticed Felton by the doorway.

"Felton!" Kel spouted. "By my beard!"

The room's merriment turned toward their returned brother. Shouts of pride and swears that there was never any doubt resounded among them.

A wide grin split Felton's face as he hobbled toward the mead barrel. The raucous sounds ceased as the unit watched him work his cane to propel himself along. Lotmeag stood from his seat at the head of the long table and strode to meet Felton before the wounded dwarf could reach the mead barrel.

The foredwarf caught him and whispered, "Felton, what are ye doing here?"

"I'm back," Felton said earnestly. "I'm ready to get back to the fight."

Lotmeag's eyes narrowed as he looked the dwarf up and down. Felton's heart dropped. He'd seen that look on the faces of the healers for weeks—sympathy.

"Felton ..." Lotmeag said gently. The foredwarf chose his words carefully. "Let's step outside, yeah?"

Lotmeag walked slowly beside Felton, ushering him from the gathering room. A few dwarves called out, "See you soon, Felton!" Their words of encouragement lacked any zeal, though.

As the doors closed behind them, Felton expected to hear the boisterous laughter resume, but the gathering room had fallen into a solemn silence. The echoed clunk of the iron door handle produced the only sound.

"Felton," Lotmeag started again, "I thought ye were going to come see me when ye were better."

"It's just my leg," Felton assured him. "It won't be much trouble, especially if I have a new garvawk. Riding garvawk doesn't take too much leg strength."

"Ye and I both know that's not true ..." the foredwarf said. "And at any rate, we don't have another garvawk right now. Nor do we have any prospects. Ye know better than anyone how hard it is to capture a new garvawk, even when we've found one."

Felton did know. Only a few months ago he'd been granted the honor of becoming part of the garvawk warriors. He remembered his *glendon* team well. They'd gotten news from the miners in one of the western valleys that they'd spotted garvawk sign as they opened a new cavern.

Lotmeag had led the team. The *glendon*, roughly translated from old dwarvish to mean "the hunt," was the traditional way to catch a garvawk and bring it into the unit. Several warriors and a mage were required to complete the process. Most of the time, they were terribly dangerous missions. Felton's had been.

When they'd attempted to catch the garvawk in their weighted and hooked nets, one warrior's net became tangled and the garvawk had nearly escaped, slashing Felton in the shoulder with her savage claws. He'd joked that Honor was only marking him because he was going to mark her.

Once they'd netted her, their team's mage performed the magic spell to turn Honor to stone. He marked her shoulder like they did every new garvawk, and Felton spoke the bonding words to awaken her from her stony state.

As he remembered the moment Honor had first laid her great cat eyes on him, Felton's own eyes glossed.

"Felton?" Lotmeag said, drawing him back to the present.

"I ... I'm sorry," Felton stammered.

"Ye know, I can't make a garvawk magically appear. It could be weeks or months or even years before the miners find sign of garvawk in their tunnels."

"I know," Felton said, slumping into his cane.

"I'll do whatever I can, but ye need to get yerself healed up. Spend some time with yer aunts. Get better, and when the time is right, we'll find a new garvawk."

Lotmeag's tone was encouraging and he sported a smile, but the pity in the foredwarf's words constricted Felton's chest.

"Aye," Felton said quietly, nodding his head and staring at the stone floor under his boots. "You know I'll be ready for the call."

"I know ye will," the foredwarf assured. "That's why ye were chosen the first time." Lotmeag's wide hand patted the dejected dwarf on the shoulder.

Felton turned and worked his way down the stairs. He didn't hear the doors to the gathering room reopen and knew the foredwarf watched him. He walked as straight as he could—a show of pure will and effort to avoid showing weakness. He couldn't bring himself to look back over his shoulder, for fear of meeting the foredwarf's pitying eyes again.

As soon as he turned the corner into a corridor with no line of sight from Bannett Hall, Felton slumped into the stone wall and slid to a seat. Tears fell from his eyes, disappearing into his thick brown beard. As much as he could no longer hold himself upright, he could also no longer hold back his sorrow.

CHAPTER 2
BACON HASH SCRAMBLE

s Felton's panic snapped him out of sleep, the salty aroma and the sizzling sound of bacon grounded him in reality. He'd had another rough night, tossing and turning between startling wake-ups. He dreamed of matters beyond his control. Night terrors often put him in situations where he needed to do something to save someone, but he couldn't. His blasted leg always held him back.

A sing-song voice from the kitchen told him that Aunt Cleary was cooking breakfast. If there was one good thing about sleeping on his aunts' couch, it was the good eating that followed.

He slowly sat up on the couch, scratching at his long beard. He rubbed the scar above his right eye. Hitting the jagged rock on the mountainside had left him with a nasty scar, but at least he still had sight in his eye.

Felton was surprised to see his Aunt Gael sitting nearby, working her needles as she knitted a colorful lump of something Felton couldn't identify. Aunt Gael stared at him through spectacles that magnified her eyes and made her look like a dwarven insect.

"Good morning," she said, her hands a flurry. Felton wasn't sure how she could continue knitting without looking at her project.

"Morning, Aunt Gael," he said through a yawn.

"Another rough night for you," she stated, not slowing her needles.

"Aye," Felton agreed.

He'd been staying with his aunts for several days, hoping his leg would feel better with some rest. Instead of experiencing improvement, he found himself stir-crazy, dying to do something—anything.

"You going to get off that couch today?" she asked.

"Aye," he said. "What you cooking in there, Aunt Cleary?"

He turned over the back of the couch, his beard dangling. Aunt Cleary was the spitting image of Aunt Gael—the only distinguishing mark between them being Aunt Gael's bespectacled face. His father's dwarven twin sisters did their hair the same and even dressed alike. Their sing-song voices were so similar that Felton thought it would be easy to mistake them for each other. He'd often considered the possibility that they had traded places on occasion to mess with him, but Aunt Cleary was adamant that she never needed spectacles and, even in her old age, could see as well as a giant eagle.

"Bacon hash scramble," she sang.

"Smells right savory," he commented.

"I'm using a new mix of spices. It's almost ready," she added.

Whatever she was using, Felton trusted her completely. He'd never met anyone who cooked as well as Aunt Cleary. She was prone to experimentation, which resulted in some surprisingly spicy meals on occasion. But nine times out of ten, he'd take her cooking over anything he'd been fed at the warhog barracks.

He'd spent years with the warhog riders, eating the food at the dining hall. Although all the meals were stomachable, a hearty constitution was necessary to maintain such a diet. The cuisine he'd enjoyed with the garvawk warriors for the couple of weeks before the Battle of Galium also put the barracks menus to shame. The elite unit ate meals prepared by the castle staff. Even so, he preferred his aunt's culinary concoctions.

Felton lifted himself from the couch, pressing his cane into the floor for leverage. He kissed Aunt Gael's cheek before heading into the kitchen to see how he could help.

"Oh, no bother. No bother," Aunt Cleary said, shooing him.

"At least let me grab a few plates," he begged.

"Aye. Fine." She relented.

Felton leaned over her shoulder to peek in the pan. He breathed in the scrumptious smell as he eyed the browning potatoes Aunt Cleary had shaved into the pan. They sizzled alongside bacon, onions, peppers, and eggs she'd scrambled.

Aunt Cleary caught him hovering and elbowed him in the ribs. "No snooping. I know you're trying to sneak a taste."

"I wasn't sneaking a taste." Felton shrugged innocently, holding up an empty palm and shaking his cane with the other.

"Smell is half the flavor," she scolded, shooing him to the cupboard where they kept the plates.

He moseyed on, awkwardly grabbing the plates in one hand. One of the clay plates slipped from his grasp and crashed to the floor, shattering and sending pieces skittering.

"You alright?" Aunt Gael called from her chair in the sitting room.

"Fine," Felton growled.

"Oh, deary," Aunt Cleary said. "You go on and leave that to me. I'll sweep it up after I'm done cooking."

"No," Felton waved her off. "I'll take care of it."

He maneuvered around the table and found the broom and dustpan, only to realize he wasn't sure how he was going to sweep and walk.

"Mud and shale," he cursed.

"What's that, deary?" Aunt Cleary called from beside the sizzling pan.

"Nothing," Felton said quickly.

He worked slowly, leaning his cane against himself while he shifted his weight to his good leg and swept. It was painfully slow work, and he only swept a tiny spot before Aunt Cleary announced breakfast was ready.

As they sat around the table, enjoying the delightful bacon hash scramble Aunt Cleary had whipped up, the twins prattled on about the latest happenings in the Garome District of Galium. The area was named after one of the founders of the great dwarven city, and Felton wondered if he wasn't much liked.

The Garome District, to his recollection, had never been one of the more prosperous districts of Galium. The people had always seemed quaint, and the ones he'd met growing up hadn't impressed upon him that they had a sense of determined discipline.

"So, Roey says to me that the old tackle shop isn't going to reopen, even though they've been repairing the miller's shop it was attached to. Says Jenbo moved out to Crossdin to restart there," Aunt Cleary said with a skeptical glance to her sister.

Felton squinted. He wasn't sure how often his aunts were apart and wondered if Aunt Gael had been there for the conversation also. His aunts were a little odd sometimes.

"Aye," Aunt Gael said, shaking her head. "A terrible shame that is. Couldn't afford to rebuild after the dragon fire."

"Roey said Arth was willing to help, but Jenbo declined the miller's offer."

"Aye. Jenbo was always a stubborn halfling. Would give Felton a run for his coin," she said with a snicker.

"Hey ... what did I do?" Felton asked defensively.

"You're just upset because Jenbo was so bad at Castle Brick," Aunt Cleary said.

"He was an easy mark," Aunt Gael said with disappointment. Felton considered her tone rather disconcerting. She chuckled. "He was always throwing away his coin."

"There are plenty of others coming around the district with all the reconstruction efforts," Aunt Cleary assured her sister.

They sat for a long while, munching in silence.

"You going out today?" Aunt Gael eventually asked, eyeing her nephew.

"Aye," Felton said before he thought it through. In truth, he had no plans to do so, but he couldn't imagine sitting around their apartment all day again either. "I was ... planning to go for a walk."

"A walk, deary?" Aunt Cleary asked, her face scrunching with concern.

"Aye. I need to stretch my legs," he said, though her look pierced him. "Just like practicing anything. The more practice, the better it'll get."

"You should go by the garden," Aunt Gael said before shoveling another bite of bacon hash scramble into her mouth. As she chewed, her thick spectacles glinted in the sunlight that poured through the kitchen window.

"The garden was half-burned in the dragon fire, too," Aunt Cleary noted.

"Sure," Aunt Gael said through her bite. She swallowed and continued. "But it's such a lovely place to walk."

Aunt Cleary didn't look convinced, but she didn't argue. "Felton, would you pass me the parsley?"

Felton looked at the small jars on the table near him. They were filled with a variety of herbs and spices, but he couldn't seem to find the parsley. He realized it was sitting right in front of Aunt Cleary.

"It's right there in front of you," Felton said, concerned she hadn't seen it.

"Oh!" she said, surprised. "Thanks, deary."

Aunt Gael pushed her spectacles up on the bridge of her nose and shook her head with a sigh.

CHAPTER 3
THE GAROME DISTRICT

The sunlight and fresh morning air brought a revitalizing energy to Felton as he left his aunts' apartment. He peeked back at the Holdum sisters' place, looking far less cozy from the outside. In truth, it looked very much like a shack squeezed between two larger buildings.

The one on the left was a charred remnant of a tanner's shop. Though he was sad to see someone's livelihood destroyed, Felton had to admit that the smell in the area had improved. The building on the right was the local tavern, one of the largest buildings in the Garome District.

Their apartment was attached to the backside of the tavern. Felton walked around the corner and saw the wooden sign scrawled with the words, *Roey's Tavern.* Aside from serving as a staple establishment for people to grab a bite to eat and a beverage to quench their thirst, *Roey's* often hosted community meetings and various events.

Roey herself emerged from the front door, discussing some matter with a young human boy. He was tall for his age and stood a head above the halfling tavern owner. Her eyes darted toward Felton, and she quickly concluded her conversation. She turned toward the dwarf with a determined step.

The boy shouted over to Felton, "Good morning, good sir! There will be a Castle Brick tournament at *Roey's Tavern* on

Finday's eve. If you're so inclined to o … o … oblige us with your company, there will be a coin purse for winners and—"

"Laen." Roey stopped and glared over her shoulder at the boy. "Can't you see, I'm walking right to him? You don't think I could share that with him in conversation?"

The boy scuffed his boots on the cobblestone road, looking sheepish. "Sorry, Miss Roey."

"I like the enthusiasm, my boy. Save it for when those construction workers come through for lunch."

"Yes, Miss Roey," he said.

Roey turned back to Felton and shook her head with a sigh as she strode the rest of the way to him. Felton pressed his lips together in a smile. He wasn't particularly in the mood for a conversation, but he knew he couldn't outpace her to escape.

She was a round halfling—a good sign for a tavern owner. Felton wasn't sure he'd trust the food if the tavern owner were scrawny. Roey sported a wide smile, and her curly mop of brown hair bobbed on top of her head as she waddled toward him. The hair on her toes matched that on her head but looked more like birds' nests on her feet. Though Felton wasn't a tall dwarf, he still stood head and shoulders above her.

"Hello there, Felton," she said kindly. "Your Aunt Cleary mentioned you were back in the district. Said you'd be staying longer than your previous visits."

"Aye," Felton managed to reply, though he would have to talk with Aunt Cleary. He wasn't keen on her sharing his depressing tale with everyone in the neighborhood. "Maybe for a little while, but I'll have a new assignment in no time."

"I see," Roey said. She inspected him for a moment, not saying anything until, "Well, you're more than welcome at the tavern any time. Folks around here wouldn't mind seeing you, too. First pint is on me."

Felton grunted. "Thank you. I suppose I shouldn't let a deal like that pass me by."

"I shouldn't think so," she laughed. "And if Laen's announcement wasn't clear, we've got a tourney going on this weekend. I know your aunts will be there."

Felton hemmed, "I'm not much good at games—never quite understood the draw to them."

"Well, you're welcome to come nonetheless," Roey said with a bright smile. "Where you off to now? I could pour you that pint, if you're not busy."

"Ah, I can't," Felton lied, knowing he had no plans.

"Soon then," Roey said.

"Soon," Felton agreed, though his idea of soon probably didn't match the one she had in mind.

Roey smiled and nodded before turning and scuttling back through the doors of her tavern.

Felton walked on, his cane clacking on the cobblestones as he moseyed the length of the Garome District's main street. Many of the buildings showed charring from the dragon fire, while also sporting replacement planks or stone bricks. Felton thought the district might have looked pretty when it was first built, when all the architecture matched. As bright and sunny as that day was, the light emphasized all the mismatched quirks.

He meandered past the miller's shop and spotted the old tackle storefront that Aunt Cleary had mentioned. It didn't look to be in great shape, but it also didn't seem irreparable. A bit of hard work could bring the place back to life. He guessed that old Jenbo had moved on for some other reason. Felton couldn't blame him. Jenbo was less likely to run into a villainous dragon-riding orc in Crossdin.

As Felton passed the smithy, he noted a lanky human boy of 13 or 14 years old. The dwarf thought it funny how humans tended to look like willowy trees or newborn deer when they hit their teenage years. When the boy looked over, Felton gave him a friendly nod. The boy waved a contraption of metal that didn't resemble anything Felton had ever seen.

What in Finlestia ... the dwarf thought.

The blacksmith stepped near to the boy. Judging by the tall man's equally dark hair and skin, he was clearly the boy's father. He scolded his son for something, and the boy tried explaining what he was working on. Felton didn't want to linger or watch the boy's trouble, so he moved along.

He did find the sight strange. Not many humans worked as blacksmiths in Galium. Dwarves had a certain pride for metal and stonework that didn't leave much room for outsiders. Galium had originally been a dwarven city, and in many respects, it still was. Over the centuries, many races had arrived to dwell there, and generations had passed since the city was populated by dwarves alone.

Before Felton could give the human smiths any more thought, the warm scent of freshly baking bread drew his nose toward the other side of the street. *Bend's Bakery* pumped out an intoxicating aroma. The dwarven baker's shop appeared to be in decent condition, seemingly having escaped most of the dragon's wrath. Felton couldn't pinpoint any rhyme or reason for the area's destruction. It seemed that, in the dragon's wanton rage, the flames had sprayed and landed indiscriminately about the district.

"Mr. Felton," came the baker's voice nearby. Felton had wandered closer than he'd realized, drawn by the enticing fragrance. "It's good to see you," he said.

"Aye," Felton grunted, cursing himself for blindly following his nose and getting caught in yet another conversation. "How are you, Mr. Bend?"

"Right well, myself," he said cheerily. "Beautiful summer day like this, plenty to be well about."

"Aye," Felton whispered, though he wasn't sure he was in an agreeable enough mood to mean it. "What are you baking?"

"Oh," the baker laughed excitedly, as he stepped out the front door and strode toward the grumpy warrior. He leaned in conspiratorially, as though he were about to reveal some great secret to Felton. "I've been preparing some loaves with a new combination of herbs. Got some basil, some oregano, some garlic and—" He stopped abruptly, and his eyes widened. He smiled over his tightly braided beard. Even though the baker kept his beard well-wrapped, it was still covered in flour. "Well, what am I telling you all about it for? Come in, I'll let you try some. Hot out of the oven."

"I really can't." Felton raised a hand to dissuade the baker, though his mind berated him for turning down the bread that smelled like it came straight from the Halls of Kerathane.

"Nonsense," Bend said. "I'll even send you home with a loaf for you and your aunts."

"I really can't," Felton said again. He shrugged in the general direction of the inner city. "I have to be going."

"Oh, I see. Important garvawk warrior business, no doubt," Bend said, pursing his lips and nodding. "You come back by when you're done, and I'll wrap you a loaf to take to your aunts then."

"I will," Felton agreed. "It smells delicious."

"Wait until you taste it," the baker said with a starry look in his eyes.

Bend spun and disappeared through the doorway, returning to his work.

Felton chose another street to walk down, thinking it would be quieter and easier to avoid more unwanted conversations. He hobbled along, his wooden cane emanating the muted sound of wood on stone. The street was indeed quieter, but it made the click of his cane more irritating to his ears.

As the Garden of Garome came into sight, the stone walls seemed to be mostly intact, and the small house to one side didn't appear to be charred or disfigured. Rather, it looked cozy and welcoming. Vines and trees painted the scene verdant.

Felton approached the garden entrance, a wide arch in the wall. He hoped to step inside and find a bench to perch on for a while.

As he rounded the entryway, he discovered a large tortoise standing in the middle of the walk as though he were guarding the place. Felton chuckled at the sight. The tortoise was large, with long limbs lifting his heavy frame from the ground. The creature looked at the dwarf with an emotionless face. His long neck brought his head almost to the height of Felton's chin.

The tortoise stared at the dwarf for a long while, unmoving. Felton watched the creature back. When the tortoise didn't make any moves, the dwarf turned to the side, thinking he may have gotten in the creature's way.

"My apologies," he said to the tortoise.

The creature didn't move but continued to stare at the dwarf.

"Okay ..." Felton muttered.

He looked past the tortoise, scanning the garden inside. While patches of plants were in their full summer growth, large swaths of the place had been charred and laid bare.

Some of the dragon fire must have hit the place after all, Felton thought. Someone had been quick on their feet, though, putting out the fires to save the rest of the garden. *Most likely the garden keeper,* Felton assumed. *Mighty brave.*

Felton nearly jumped out of his skin when he looked back to the tortoise. It had drawn nearer to him without the dwarf noticing and appeared to be glaring at him. He eyed the creature cautiously, wondering if the tortoise was really leering at him or if he was imagining the stink eye.

The humming of a lovely tune danced on the light breeze and tickled the dwarf's ear. He glanced around to catch sight of the hummer but guessed it came from deeper within the garden. He decided to enter and look, but when his gaze returned to the tortoise, the creature's bald head was only a foot from him.

Felton jumped. "Shave me," he cursed under his breath.

The creature continued to eye him, so Felton slowly moved backward and away from the garden. He could always come back another time and see the place. Maybe the tortoise wouldn't be there then.

As he rounded the corner to another street, the dwarf took one last look back. The tortoise stared unswervingly at him.

Felton shuddered and hurried his hobbling.

CHAPTER 4
A KIND WAGONER

Step by agonizing step, Felton walked onward. The road on which he trod was a well-traveled one. Folks from all over the city traversed it, heading wherever they needed to be. Felton grumbled to himself as he watched folks speedily pass him.

A young dwarf passed him, pulling a cart full of barrels. Felton could tell it was a heavy load as pebbles skittered away under the wheels. The weight didn't seem to slow the lad.

As the day shifted into evening, the traffic along the street slowed, leaving Felton to walk the road alone. The sun was setting behind him, painting the sky and the mountains with oranges and pinks. It might have been a beautiful sight, had his mood not been so sour.

The clopping of horses behind him forced him to sidle to the edge of the street. His leg wouldn't get any better if he got himself run over. The horses slowed, and the wagon they pulled matched his tedious pace.

"Hello, there," a kindly voice called from the driver's box. "Where you headed there, friend?"

Felton looked up to see a halfling wagoner with a golden brown mop of hair and a pipe clenched in his widely smiling teeth.

"To see some friends," Felton said shortly.

"Oh, good," the halfling said. "Whereabouts are they? I could give you a ride. I'm just getting back from a trip to Crossdin. Already hit the wagon depot and was on my way home to my lovely wife and my daughter, Button. No two prettier ladies in the world, I'd wager."

"No thanks," Felton said. "I'll manage fine on my own."

"Oh, I have no doubt, sir," the halfling said, his wagon still moving at Felton's slow pace, "but I was thinking, it's going to be dark soon. If you're going to see your friends, it's not polite to be arriving after dark. Not that I question your manners, of course. I was just thinking if you get there a little faster, you'll have more time to spend with them before it gets late. Always good to have more time with friends."

Felton stopped and leaned against a low stone wall. As much as he hated to admit it, he was spent. He'd been walking all day, except for the moments he'd taken to stop and rest—which had been frequent. The wagon slowed to a stop as well, and the halfling looked down at him.

"Where you headed?" the halfling asked, compassion rimming his face.

In that moment, Felton welled with anger. His frustration boiled and confused the compassion for pity. "I don't need your pity," he grumbled through clenched teeth.

"No pity to be had, my friend," the halfling said. "Just a short ride."

Felton squeezed his cane in his fist, turning his knuckles white. He didn't want to give in. He was no quitter. But his body was tired, and he wasn't even sure where he was going. He said the only place he could think of. "Can you give me a ride to *The Hungry Hog*?"

"The tavern by the warhog station?" the halfling asked to clarify.

"Aye," Felton conceded. "That's where I'm meeting my friends."

"Of course," the halfling said cheerily. "I'll get you there in no time. Come. You can sit with me here."

It took some effort on the part of the halfling—as much as Felton—to hoist the dwarf up into the driver's box. Felton groaned as the halfling pulled him up but found the bench quite comfortable once he was seated.

The halfling snapped the reins and spurred the horses into motion. The wagon lurched behind them.

"Just got the seat re-cushioned." The halfling laughed, poking at the material. "I was thinking, it makes a lot of sense to make this seat as comfortable as the riders' seats in the back. Sometimes not everyone fits back there and someone has to sit here with me. Making this seat comfy is all part of the wonderful journey experience," he said with gusto. "If passengers have a good ride, they ask for you by name the next time they're at the wagon depot," he added with a wink and a pop of his pipe. "Which reminds me, Tobin Keeland, at your service."

"Felton Holdum, at yours."

"Splendid to meet you. Just splendid. Are you a warhog rider then? Just headed back to the station to meet up with your mates? As much as I love my horses, I've often wondered if warhogs would make good wagon haulers—big tough brutes like them. Something I wouldn't mind trying sometime." One of the horses snorted, and Tobin laughed. "Oh, Wendra. Only teasing, my love. She does get so jealous, that one. Does your warhog do that too?"

Felton could hardly formulate a thought. He'd tried to answer the halfling's earlier questions, but Tobin hadn't taken a long enough breath for the dwarf to get a word in. As the halfling drew a puff of his pipe, awaiting a response, the dwarf answered the last question. He appreciated that Tobin assumed he still had a warhog and didn't immediately dismiss the notion because of his bum leg. "I don't have a warhog anymore."

"Oh, no. Terribly sorry," Tobin said. "Lost him in the battle then?"

"No," Felton said. "My warhog was reassigned to a new rider when I joined the garvawk warriors."

"The garvawk warriors, you say?" Tobin asked excitedly. "I just so happen to know the foredwarf. You know Lotmeag Kandersaw, yeah?"

"I do; he's a good dwarf."

"Agreed. One of the most honorable, I'd wager. Also, the uncle to my little Button." Tobin laughed and shook his head. "Well, also the brother to my beautiful wife, Lenor. I suppose he was her brother before he was our little Button's uncle. Funny that. I'll have to tell Lenor about that later. She's probably making supper as we speak."

"Oh! Well," Felton started, "don't let me make you late for supper. You can drop me off here. I can make it the rest of the way."

"No worries, at all," Tobin said, slapping his round belly and laughing. "As you can see, I'm not late for many meals. It'll keep just fine. Lenor told me if I hurried home she'd make sausage and potatoes and green beans. Where she gets her ideas for seasoning things just right, I'll never know. Lenor might be the best cook in Galium, I'd wager. If you didn't already have plans with your friends, I'd invite you to join us."

Felton smiled. He believed Tobin meant it. The dwarf internally scolded himself for lying about his plans. He wasn't going to meet anyone. Likely as not, he'd run into a familiar face and be able to join them for a pint, but that would be entirely coincidental. And anyway, he would not have accepted the invitation, feeling as though he would not make very good company. Plus, he wouldn't want to burst the jovial halfling's bubble by telling him that his Aunt Cleary would probably give Tobin's wife a run for her coin.

"... but keeping your obligations to your friends is a good thing. When things get tough, friends are the ones that are always there for us. You never know when you're going to need one," Tobin finished.

Felton grunted his agreement, having missed most of what the halfling had said.

Tobin chuckled, puffing out a white cloud. "You know, I wagon with an old dwarf who grunts like that. I've gotten pretty good at knowing his meaning, even though he doesn't use many words. Lenor says I use enough words for the both of us." He laughed, returning his pipe between his teeth. "You don't seem old enough to grunt like that ..."

Felton shook his head in amusement, believing the halfling's wife might be right about his words.

As the pair rolled up to *The Hungry Hog*, Tobin pulled on the reins to slow the wagon. The lamplighters were out and about, lighting the lamps around the city. The designated trainees from the warhog station muttered to themselves as they completed the task, lighting the lamps near the gate. *The Hungry Hog* had been built just outside the station as a respite where the warhog riders could grab a drink and let off some steam.

Felton had visited the place many times over his years as a warhog rider. He and his compatriots had frequented the establishment. The dwarf would almost go so far as to say they had brought the fun with them, starting up boisterous chants and songs and riling up competitive tavern games. Though, over the years, he'd seen younger dwarves think the same thing as they took up the mantle of starting the tavern songs and buying rounds.

He recalled one night when he and a couple of his mates from the 7th Cavalry had gotten into a tussle with a few dwarves from the 3rd. Felton had been coaxing folks into arm wrestles with his old sergeant, who was unbeatable—at least, Felton had never seen the old dwarf lose. When the dwarves from the 3rd realized they were getting hustled, a brawl erupted.

Dwarves usually work things out quickly, and after everyone had gotten a few licks in, Felton offered to buy a round for everyone. A few drinks later, they were all singing arm in arm. Felton snickered, remembering he'd paid for the drinks with the coin he'd hustled from them.

The distant memories warmed Felton's belly. Maybe this was exactly what he needed, even if he hadn't planned on the outing. Seeing his former haunt and surrounding himself with old friends would certainly lift his spirits. Enjoying a pint or two and joining in on the songs—a little merriment was overdue.

"... and anyway, if you ever need a ride again, you just let me know, now. I'd get you where you need to go quicker and more comfortably than any other wagoner in Galium, I'd wager. You just ask for me at the wagon depot, and Shem will set it up. Don't you hesitate, at all."

"Thank you," Felton said, appreciating the halfling's offer, even if the dwarf never expected to take him up on it. "You've been most kind."

"Ah, well," Tobin said bashfully. "You know, I can't help it. I've got an awful lot to be thankful for. Everyone has loads to be thankful for if they have the eyes to see it. And, when we're filled up with gratitude, it often overflows as kindness."

Felton's brow furrowed as he nodded, taking in the halfling's words. He'd have to remember that. For a moment, Felton wondered what other pearls of wisdom he might have missed while he was lost in his own thoughts.

"Can I help you down, Mr. Felton?" Tobin asked.

The dwarf shook his head. "No," he said. He did not know whether it was his time with the wagoner or the sight of his old stomping grounds, but Felton had a renewed fervor. He hooked the knobbled top of his cane on the edge of the driver's box and slowly worked his way to the ground. He pressed against the cane and stood straight, looking up to the halfling above.

Tobin gave him an encouraging nod and puffed his pipe.

"Thanks again," Felton said.

"Any time," Tobin said, and the halfling snapped the reins. The horses pulled the wagon, and off the wagoner went.

Felton watched for a long time until Tobin's wagon rounded a building and rolled out of sight. The dwarf turned to face *The Hungry Hog*.

He stood there as the evening grew darker, watching and listening. Several dwarven warhog riders made their way into the place. As the door swung open, the boisterous noise from inside spilled into the quiet night.

Felton smirked and hobbled toward the entrance.

L aughter rang out from a table in the center of the tavern as dwarven warriors arm wrestled for their week's wages. Others, gathered round to bet on the outcome, tossed small sacks of coin to one another after each bout. Felton laughed at the younger dwarves, lining up for a match.

Sergeant Grisham held the table down as he emptied another mug of ale. He flopped his head from side to side, popping his neck and rolling his shoulders as a new challenger sat across from him. He looked up and caught Felton watching as he hobbled by. The old sergeant's eyes widened, and he gave Felton a nod that said he needed a minute.

Felton chuckled, amused that the foolish young warriors hadn't learned their lesson yet. The warhog sergeant had been hustling youngsters at this game for years. Yet, each year, a new batch of recruits would try their luck.

Grisham dropped his elbow on the table and stretched his thick hand over the middle. His bald head glinted in the lantern light.

Is he sweating? Felton wondered. He didn't remember the old sergeant perspiring. Maybe the next young dwarf stood a chance.

The next challenger sat in the chair across from the sergeant while others patted him on the back and shook him encouragingly. As the young warrior grasped Grisham's hand, the others began to place their personal bets with each other.

"For glory and honor!" one of the standing dwarves said and slapped a hand on the table.

The younger dwarf tensed immediately, throwing his weight and effort into his arm. Grisham's arm flexed with stout banded muscles. An ominous smile crept across the bald dwarf's face. With his other hand he picked up another mug of ale and began to drink. The onlookers laughed. The younger dwarf, embarrassed by the move, grunted as he pressed even harder, trying to pin the old dwarf's arm to the table.

Grisham's arm didn't budge.

When the sergeant finished his mug, he placed it on the table calmly. He looked the younger dwarf directly in the eye and said, "Next round's on you, lad." His muscular arm bulged, and he pressed the younger dwarf's hand into the table.

Cheers erupted. Several groans also resounded, for some foolish warriors had made bets against the old sergeant.

Grisham slid out of his seat and patted the young warrior on the shoulder. "Keep at it," he encouraged. "One day."

When another dwarf took the challenger seat, Grisham told the gathering they'd have to continue without him. Several bemoaned grunts echoed, but the sergeant's seat was quickly filled by a cocky dwarf who thought himself the next to dominate the table.

Grisham greeted Felton with a grip of the shoulder. "Felton, come to have a drink with your old sergeant?"

"Aye," he said. "Just the dwarf I was hoping to see."

"So, you got a taste for the mead while you were with the garvawk warriors, eh?" Grisham asked, as he shimmied into the booth across from Felton. He slid a mug over, and Felton pulled it in gratefully.

"It's not bad," he said. "You should try it."

"Bah," Grisham said, waving his hand as if to ward the stuff away from him. "Ale suits me just fine. That sweet stuff is dangerous. Too easy to drink. Before you know it, you're out cold."

"Maybe," Felton said, taking a swig.

"You were only with the garvawk warriors for a couple weeks before the battle?" Grisham tried to remember.

"Aye," Felton said sullenly.

"That's muck luck, there," Grisham grumbled. Felton took another swig, not needing a reminder of how unlucky he'd been that the Battle of Galium occurred so soon after the *glendon* that led to the capture of his garvawk. "Don't suppose you even had time to move into Bannett Hall."

"I hadn't," he admitted. "We were going to contract some engineers to build stairs and bore rooms on another level in the hall, but they hadn't gotten to it. And now ..."

His words faded at the thought of all the empty rooms that once housed some of Galium's most honorable warriors.

Grisham mumbled a practiced prayer and nodded knowingly. "Well, I'm sure they'll find another garvawk soon, and you'll be back in the saddle in no time. You were always skilled, but more importantly, you worked harder than any other warhog warrior I led," he said with a lift of his mug toward Felton. "It's the whole reason I recommended you for the garvawk warriors."

Felton lifted his mug in response. Joining the garvawk warriors of Galium was one of the greatest honors a dwarven warrior could achieve. It came with great risk, of course. Flying on the back of a great cat against winged foes was a far different task than riding warhogs on patrol in the Drelek Mountains surrounding their home. Warhog patrols had often fought trolls and bands of goblins, but the garvawk warriors protected the city against major threats.

"I spoke to Foredwarf Lotmeag, and he is ... less certain," Felton said quietly.

"Bah! The miners are always digging. It's only a matter of time."

"But ..." Felton said. He pulled his cane up so Grisham could see the knobbled head of it over the table. He tapped it gently against the table's edge.

"Hey now," the barkeep said as he passed by, "don't be dinging my table now."

"Sorry, Tullen," Felton said sheepishly.

He and Tullen had a somewhat checkered past. Felton had been involved in several rambunctious songs and rollicks that may or may not have resulted in broken chairs. Of course, he and his compatriots had doled out plenty of coin to make up for damages, but Tullen never seemed overly pleased to see him or any of the others involved. He was cordial and served them hospitably enough, but he never got too friendly with any of them.

"How you doing on coin?" Grisham asked, concern edged the old dwarf's face.

"Alright," Felton said with a shrug. "I wasn't spending any coin while I was in the healing ward. So, I've got a little saved."

"And the healers said nothing of fixing up that leg?"

"They don't know why it's not better. It *will* get better ... I think." It was the first time Felton admitted he wasn't sure. He wanted his leg to get better. He wanted to get back to normal. How long could he go on hoping before he had to accept this as his new normal?

"Well, what are you going to do for coin in the meantime?" Grisham asked, finishing his ale.

"I'm not sure," Felton admitted. "I thought I'd go by the commander's office tomorrow and have a chat with her. Maybe I can get assigned a new warhog and get back on patrol."

Grisham's eyes narrowed, and he seemed to be chewing on something as his lips pressed together and moved from side to side. After a long while, he said, "I'm going to get us another round."

He slipped from the booth before Felton could get a word out. He watched the bald dwarf maneuver between full tables and saunter up to the bar. Felton swirled the remnants of his mead and downed it. His old sergeant's sudden discomfort left Felton uneasy. Grisham had always believed in him. He'd always encouraged him and shown nothing but the utmost faith in him. If the old sergeant had reservations about Felton's future ...

Nearby, a boisterous young dwarf hopped onto one of Tullen's tables as his companions urged him on. He swayed slightly as he stood and lifted his mug high. He cleared his throat and started singing a well-known ballad that was quickly joined by most of the patrons in *The Hungry Hog*.

There once was a land
With a glorious plan
For every dwarf and halfer and man.

They went on to name it Galium.

But once it was found
Trumps of war did sound.
Protecting their home and solemn ground
Became the need in Galium.

Rise up every dwarf.
Stand as warrior.
Mount up with your kin on hogs of war.
Protect your home of Galium.

They sang every verse of "Ride for Galium." Many around the tavern locked arms and raised mugs high. Felton slid out of the booth and held onto one of the young warriors at the table. Grisham made his way back, handing Felton a refilled tankard of mead and joining the song.

The song spurred others, and several ballads had been sung before Felton and Grisham made it back to their booth.

Felton slid his cane under the table next to him as one of the barmaids, a lovely human woman, brought them another pair of mugs, courtesy of the young warriors they'd been singing with.

"This is why I have to go see the commander tomorrow," Felton said, though his words came out slurred.

"I don't begrudge your situation," Grisham said. "I'm just not sure what you should be expecting."

"You think I can't do it. You think I'm not fit to ride a warhog anymore," Felton said, bemused.

"I didn't say that," the old sergeant said. "You just don't know how long you're going to be dealing with that leg of yours."

Felton's nose prickled, and his eyes glossed. He blinked several times, angrier at his old sergeant. "What can it hurt?" he asked with more venom than he intended.

"I suppose nothing," Grisham said, eyeing him cautiously. "I suppose the worst thing the commander can do is say 'no.' But wouldn't it be better to talk to her when you're healed up and—"

"And when is that going to be?" Felton growled.

"I don't know …"

"What if it's forever? What then?"

Grisham gave Felton a hard look. "If it's forever, then I have no doubt you will find something to put your efforts toward. You are still a young dwarf, and in all my years as a sergeant of the warhogs, I have rarely seen a dwarf that works as hard as you. Your effort knows no bounds."

"What if effort isn't enough this time?" Felton asked quietly, his mood swayed by his drink.

"I don't think there has ever been a time in the history of Finlestia when effort was not of value. Though results vary, effort, when rightly placed, is always worthwhile."

Grisham slid out of the booth and walked around to Felton's side. He stood at the end of the bench and looked him over. After a long while, he smiled compassionately at the younger dwarf. "Regardless of your vocation, I will always call you friend."

"Where are you going?" Felton asked, feeling more friendly, though his head grew heavy.

"I have to go back to the barracks. I've got to get the unit up early for drill tomorrow."

"Bah," Felton groaned with a wave of his hand. "Go on then. I'll come see you tomorrow after I speak with the commander."

"Get some rest," Grisham said. "Maybe think on it for a few days, and I'll see you when you do come to the station."

Felton only heard the first part of Grisham's words, but he didn't want to rest. He hated sleep. When he slept, he had no control. His dreams took him to places he didn't want to go.

No, he would just have another drink, then when morning came, he could go see the commander. That's what he'd do.

Felton looked toward the bar; it appeared far away. While some of the tables were beginning to empty, it still seemed a maze to his impaired vision. Hobbling through and navigating the place promised to be a rather daunting task. He reached across the table and grabbed Grisham's mug. It was almost full.

Why would he leave such a full mug? Felton wondered. *He must have left it for me.*

Felton downed the ale, not caring it wasn't the mead he'd enjoyed all evening. He'd spent years drinking Tullen's ale, and it tasted just right. He mumbled a "Thank you" to Tullen and then another to Grisham for being so kind as to leave it for him.

What had Grisham said? Get some rest?

Felton's head grew heavier, and he laid his forehead on the table. *Just going to close my eyes for a minute and ...*

CHAPTER 6
BREAKFAST WITH THE BARKEEP

A loud banging sent waves thrumming inside Felton's skull. He grimaced at the painful intrusion upon his ears. More banging rang out, and he groaned.

"Mmmm," he moaned and grumbled, "Aunt Cleary, what are you doing in that kitchen?"

"Aunt Cleary's not here, Master Felton," an old voice said. Felton knew the voice, though it rang like a distant memory as he heard it.

He realized the pain in his head throbbed toward his forehead which rested awkwardly on a hard surface. He wasn't lying on a couch in his aunts' apartment after all.

Slowly he reached up, placing his hands on the table, and lifted his head. He blinked and squinted. The sunlight that poured through the windows seared his eyes.

"Oooh," he groaned again.

"Welcome back to the land of the living," Tullen said as he took another chair off a table nearby and dropped it on the ground. A loud bang reverberated as the chair's feet hit the hard floor.

Felton gripped his head, feeling it might explode. "Do you have to do that so loud?" he asked.

"No," Tullen said, a smirk spreading across the old dwarf's face. He stroked his long white beard for a moment then pulled another chair down with an intentional thud and a chuckle. Felton winced.

Tullen said, "Last one—at least, last one for me. You can get the rest while I whip us up some breakfast."

Felton squinted at the old tavern owner through bleary eyes. Tullen stood there awaiting his answer. "Really?" Felton moaned.

"Really," Tullen said, indicating the whole room. He spun toward the bar and called over his shoulder. "I've got just the thing."

Setting the chairs around the tavern was long and arduous work for Felton as he maneuvered with his cane from table to table. As he did, he tried to remember his conversation with Grisham the night before. Much of the evening was a blur, but he had the sneaking suspicion that he hadn't been entirely kind and needed to apologize to the sergeant for something—though it might take time to remember exactly what he should apologize for.

By the time Felton finished setting up all the chairs, Tullen was placing plates on a small table near the bar. Felton had never sat at that table. Usually, the two-seaters were taken up by some warhog rider with a date. Felton had tried to woo a couple of dwarven women but had never given it as much effort as he had his training. Becoming the best warrior he could for Galium had always taken precedence.

"Come. Sit," Tullen said kindly. "It won't make you right as rain, but it'll definitely help. I've made some tea, too."

Felton sat and scooped the tea mug into his hands. He breathed in the warm steam rolling off the hot tea. He took a tentative sip, and the drink gave him a boost. He set the mug to the side and inspected the breakfast before him. The plate was piled high with scrambled eggs topped with sliced green onions. Next to the pile was a stack of flapjacks, thick and fluffy.

Tullen finished a quiet prayer to the Maker and eagerly grabbed his fork. He shoveled a bite into his mouth and sighed happily.

Felton cut a bite from one of the flapjacks and placed it in his mouth. The warm bite immediately drew moisture back into his dry mouth. "Tullen!" he exclaimed through the bite. "What in Finlestia did you do to these flapjacks?"

"A dash of cinnamon." The barkeep winked. "Don't go telling everyone my secret now."

Felton grunted his agreement through another bite, shaking his head to assure the old dwarf that his secret was safe with him.

"Don't forget your eggs, too. They'll really help with the headache," Tullen said.

"Thank you," Felton said sheepishly. "Not sure what came over me."

Tullen chuckled. "You think you're the first warhog veteran to sleep one off in *The Hungry Hog?*"

Felton huffed a small laugh but winced at the pain in his head. "I suppose not."

In truth, Felton had nearly slept in the tavern on a number of occasions. In the past, he'd always been with his compatriots, and they'd shouldered him back to the barracks. He'd done the same for many of them. But this time, he'd not had anyone to bring him back, nor did he have a bed at the barracks.

"Thanks anyway," he said.

"No thanks necessary." Tullen waved the gratitude off. "It's difficult to find a new path when the one you've been following all your life is no longer before you."

"What?" Felton asked quietly.

Tullen smiled and took a sip of his tea. "It happens to all of us, young Master Felton."

"What do you mean?" he asked, slowly taking another bite of eggs.

"It's hard for all warriors to leave the brotherhood and figure out who they are without it."

"I haven't left the brotherhood," Felton said plainly.

"Of course," Tullen said with a nod of agreement. "But when it does happen, it's difficult. When one has trained their whole life to be a warrior—a defender and champion of their people—it can be hard to find peace afterward. It takes time and new seasons in life to figure out who you are away from war."

Felton chewed quietly, watching Tullen's eyes glaze over as if seeing some far-off realm. The younger dwarf noted the tattoo on the barkeep's arm. He'd seen it many times. The tattoo of the emblem designated for the 3rd Warhog Cavalry contrasted against the older dwarf's light skin. The design was simple: three tusks crossing a double-bladed axe. Felton considered the old tavern owner's words with great weight.

"Well, I'm going to see Commander Qwen today," Felton said between bites. "I'm sure she'll reassign me with a new warhog until Foredwarf Lotmeag hears tell of a new garvawk."

"Aye. Perhaps," the old dwarf said with a shrug as he took another bite of flapjacks.

Felton was grateful for Tullen's kindness, especially since it would have been much easier for the barkeep to toss him out in the middle of the night. However, he wasn't particularly keen on the way the barkeep associated him with other veterans.

Felton wasn't like them. He was still young and strong. He had plenty left to give. He just needed a chance to somehow prove it.

CHAPTER 7
A GOOD COMMANDER

The summer sun warmed the warhog station, forcing many of the hogs to sweat and produce a particularly pungent smell. Felton, however, was not disgusted by the stench. He'd spent years at the station, living among the warhog riders and their beasts. It smelled like home.

A trainee unit rode past him as he hobbled along the road. The unit sergeant called out a cadence as the trainees attempted to keep their hogs in formation. Halflings made up a small minority of the warhog riders, but Felton had known several during his years with his unit. As he glanced over the rest of the unit, he noticed quite a few halflings. He wouldn't have expected such a high ratio in a single training unit.

Three of the warhogs snorted and swerved away from the others to inspect a patch of delicious-looking flowers. The rider of the lead dissenter pulled on his reins and whispered hurriedly to the hog, trying desperately to return to the trotting unit. The other two riders, whose hogs had curiously followed, did the same.

The sergeant hurled insults and bellowed commands. The dwarf on the lead rogue hog turned bright red, almost matching his beard. The halfling on the warhog next to him convinced his hog that getting back in formation was better than whatever flowers the other two were munching.

Felton chuckled as the training sergeant circled the rank breakers, a stream of swears and insults pouring from his mouth. Once the hogs had gobbled some flowers, they were more amenable to rejoin the group, which nervously attempted to keep its warhogs in line.

Of course, the damage had already been done. Felton knew the trainees would be doing push-ups and running. Having been in their position himself when he was a trainee, he pitied them—but not too much. In the end, the extra discipline would make them tougher warriors.

Felton continued his determined walk, his cane hitting the dirt road with muted thuds. The bottom of the cane was collecting dust. He should probably clean it when he got the chance. He wouldn't want to track a mess into buildings.

He strode toward the command building, catching a glimpse of a unit in the midst of physical training. They did so with uniformed precision and effort. Felton paused to watch them.

They ran over an obstacle course, lifting and hoisting one another into flips and barrel rolls over short walls. They crawled under ropes and balanced across beams. The unit, to Felton's eyes, looked to be in good shape.

He breathed in the summer air and listened to the noises all around him. For the first time in months, a sense of calm washed over him.

"Felton Holdum," someone said behind him, sounding surprised. "What in Finlestia are you doing on my training ground?"

Felton's smirk broadened into a smile. He turned to greet his old commander. "Commander Qwen," he said, "I don't suppose you'd be willing to have a chat with me?"

"I've always got time for a chat with the first rider under my command to be selected for the garvawk warriors," the dwarven commander said. Her freckled face split into a grin of her own, revealing brilliant teeth. She eyed Felton with pride.

Becoming a garvawk warrior was a great honor for any dwarven warrior, but it also reflected greatly on the dwarf's former unit. The whole of the 7th Cavalry would have shared in the honor, even if they weren't the ones selected. In truth, the whole unit would have had a hand in helping to shape and form the warrior into a worthy selection.

Felton took a couple of steps closer to the commander, cursing the cane that helped him cross the distance. "Perhaps we can take this inside?"

"Can I pour you a drink?" Commander Qwen asked as she picked up a glass decanter from a side table. Above the table was the emblem for the 7th Cavalry: a warhog's head on a shield, its mighty tusks bared and a 7 on its forehead.

"No," Felton said a little too quickly. Tullen's breakfast had done wonders for him, but his head and stomach were still not quite right. "I mean, no thank you, ma'am."

"Rough night?" the commander asked him with an amused chuckle. She poured herself a glass of the amber liquid, and Felton wondered if it was the same brandy she'd shared with him the day she told him he'd been selected for the *glendon* team. She moved to a chair and waved him toward another. "So, what can I do for my favorite garvawk warrior?"

As much as Felton appreciated the comment, it made him wince. His gut clenched as he wondered if he was letting down his entire unit. Was their honor diminished by him no longer being able to serve with the garvawks?

"Well, you see," he hemmed, trying to formulate his words through the sudden onslaught of doubt. "That's why I'm here, Commander."

"Call me Qwen, Felton," she said kindly.

"I'll try, Commander."

"Qwen," she said again.

"Qwen," Felton agreed, though the name emerged awkwardly from his mouth. "It's just that Foredwarf Lotmeag doesn't have a garvawk lined up for me. As you know, it could take months or even a few years before the miners find garvawk sign again. Then we'd be able to form another *glendon* team, of course, and attempt a catch."

"Of course," she said, sipping her brandy and nodding thoughtfully.

"And see, Comman—" Felton stopped himself and tried again. "Qwen." She smiled at his discomfort, but he pressed onward. "I was thinking: it would do no good for me to sit around and do nothing while I wait for a new garvawk. So, I thought I'd come and ask you for a new assignment with the 7th Cavalry."

Qwen expelled a deep sigh and narrowed her eyes as she nodded her understanding.

"And," Felton quickly added. "I know my leg is hurt right now, but I'm sure it'll get better in no time." A pang of guilt ran through Felton at the lie. He wasn't sure at all. "And even if it doesn't, I'll be mounted on a warhog, and the hog will do the running for me."

Qwen raised a hand, halting a continuation of the warrior's stream of selling points. "Felton," she started gently, "you and I both know you can't perform the duties of a warhog rider while you're recovering from an injury. Especially one so grievous as you've experienced."

"I've been working at healing and I—"

"You fell from the sky and crashed into the side of a mountain," she said frankly, cutting him off. "Felton, you've performed your duty. You've displayed great honor, and the glory of your name is greater than you know. The tale of the garvawk warrior that survived falling from the sky has filled the 7th Cavalry with pride. We've had riders ask for transfers weekly. You're a hero."

The word stung like a barb.

A hero? Felton thought. *What kind of hero can barely get himself across the city? What kind of hero is afraid to go to sleep at night, for fear of what he might see? What kind of hero sleeps on his aunts' couch?*

He was no hero. He just happened to survive. If Commander Qwen would only give him a chance to get back into the cavalry, maybe he could prove himself a hero again.

"Commander," Felton said. He didn't correct himself, even under Qwen's disappointed glare. "You have to help me get back to the unit. I know, if you just assign me a new warhog, I can prove my mettle again. I can—"

"Felton," she said with a commanding tone that quieted him, "you have done your duty. As I've said, the 7th looks on you with pride. Your story inspires them. Would you change that by walking around the training ground with a cane? Would you dampen their spirits on physical training days as they watch you struggle to walk or balance or jump or run?"

"I ..." Felton started to reply, but he couldn't argue her point. A flash memory of the day he'd visited Bannett Hall and his garvawk warrior brothers fluttered in his mind. They had been full of life and excitement when he'd entered, but by the time he left ...

He remembered the somber silence. He didn't want to be the cause of fallen morale on his old warhog unit, too.

But if he didn't belong here either, where did he belong?

"Felton," Qwen's voice softened again, and she leaned forward in her chair, "even if you were further along on your recovery, I have no hogs to assign. Between all the transfer requests and new recruits, the station is bursting at the seams. After the battle, every young dwarf and halfling in the city wanted to join our ranks."

"That's ... that's good," Felton said slowly.

"It is," Qwen said with another thoughtful nod. She licked her teeth and pressed her lips together, eyeing him as he mulled everything over.

"Listen," she said at long last. "This is a long shot, and—I'm serious—you shouldn't get your hopes up. In your condition it may not be feasible, but I am good friends with Captain Bradnir of the Galium city guard. I know it's not the same, but he's mentioned to me a few times recently how dire their recruitment has been. Apparently, the warhog tales of glory during the Battle of Galium have excited the minds of the people, and everyone wants to serve with the riders, leaving few to serve in the city guard."

Qwen stood and walked to a table strewn with parchments and ledgers of all kinds. She picked up one of the scrolls that held her seal and handed it to Felton. He took it, confusion etched on his face. "What's this?" he asked.

"It's a letter of reference I've written to Captain Bradnir. In it, I speak of your impeccable character and heart to serve. Take it with you when you go to see him."

"What?" Felton asked quietly. "How did you ...?"

"Sergeant Grisham visited me this morning before he took the unit out for drill. Good friends are hard to come by. So when you find them, you should treat them well. And," she said slowly, "I know you, Felton. Even before Grisham told me what you were coming to see me about, I knew what you'd want to say. You've got a noble heart, and you've dedicated your life to service. How could I expect anything else? Knowing that and knowing I couldn't give you what you wanted, I pondered a great deal this morning. This is the solution I came up with. I wouldn't be a very good commander if I didn't know my riders. Even if you were with the garvawk warriors, you will always be one of mine."

Felton sniffed and blinked, trying to ward off the welling tears that caused prickling on the bridge of his nose. "Comm—" He stopped himself again. She gave him an approving nod as he corrected himself. "Qwen ... I don't know what to say."

"Well, don't get your hopes up," she said to him. "Even if Captain Bradnir is desperate for recruits at the moment, I don't know if he'll be able to take you under your circumstances."

"I understand," Felton said. "Thank you, ma'am."

Commander Qwen showed Felton to the door and watched him limp away. Before he was out of earshot, she called out, "Oh, and Felton!"

"Yes, ma'am?" He turned back.

"Promise me you'll never give up—no matter what the answer is. Promise me you'll never give up, even if life takes you in a wholly unexpected direction."

"Yes, ma'am," he said determinedly.

She smiled at him, revealing her brilliant teeth, and gave him a nod of approval.

Felton moved slowly through the station, keenly aware that warhog riders might be looking at him in a completely different light.

CHAPTER 8
THE CITY GUARD

As Felton approached the headquarters for the city guard, he pondered how small the place was compared to the warhog station. The station was on the edge of the city of Galium, requiring a vast swath of land to accommodate enough space for warhog training fields, barracks, and the like. In many ways, the station was like a miniature city of its own. The city guard headquarters, however, was an entirely different story.

The building was large, to be sure, but a singular building nonetheless. It had been erected near the city's castle, likely so the king had easy access to the captain of the guard. Felton remembered Lotmeag and his former foredwarf, Bendur Clagstack, answering King Thygram Markensteel's call on a few occasions during his limited stint with the garvawk warriors. He assumed the captain of the guard would be similarly called upon by the king regarding safety reports within the city.

Being so near the castle, the building had been constructed with the same mountainous stone early settlers had carved away from the front range. While it was a large building, it did not have any particular architectural beauty—a fact that didn't bother Felton in the least. The warhog station buildings might have been the ugliest buildings in the city, constructed entirely with utility in mind and no thought of aesthetic, and those buildings had always felt like home to him.

Several guards exited the headquarters on their way to somewhere Felton could only guess. He worked his way up the stairs and entered the main hall of the building. A halfling sat behind a table strewn with parchments. As Felton neared, the clicking of his cane on the hard stone floor caught the halfling's attention.

"Good afternoon, sir," he said, though his tone wasn't entirely cheerful.

Halflings were smaller than dwarves, but this one seemed downright tiny. His hair was trimmed tight, and his mousy features highlighted the annoyed look on his face. His eyes returned to whatever notes he was writing on three different pieces of parchment. Felton wondered for a moment whether there was a method to the halfling's messy desk.

"Something I can help you with today?" the halfling offered bemusedly.

Felton cleared his throat and stood taller. "I'm here to see Captain Bradnir," he said.

The halfling's face scrunched, and he flipped over another set of parchments, riffling through them until he found the one he sought. "I don't see the captain having any appointments today. Perhaps you've got it for another day?"

"I don't have an appointment with the captain. I've just come from—"

"No. No. That won't do," the halfling said, shaking his head. "I can set you up an appointment with the captain."

"That would be swell," Felton agreed.

"Can you do Thrensday?"

"Thrensday?" Felton repeated in shock. "You just said the captain doesn't have any appointments today. Can't I see him today?"

"Oh no. That won't do."

"Why not?"

"I don't put any appointments on the captain's schedule day of. What if he were called by the king? Then I'd put a conflicting appointment on the schedule for him when he thought he was to be available to the king all day."

"Wouldn't the king's beckon take precedence even if the captain had an appointment?" Felton asked, scrunching his face and rubbing the scar over his brow.

The halfling stared at the dwarf as if he had said something entirely stupid or brilliant. "Right, you are," the halfling muttered. "I hadn't considered that."

"Might be something to consider for the future," Felton encouraged.

"Definitely should," the halfling said and turned back to the parchments he'd been writing on earlier.

Felton stood for a long time, waiting for the halfling to acknowledge him again. After a while, he decided the clerk may never speak, so he cleared his throat.

The halfling looked up to him again. "Good afternoon, sir," he said, though again his words contained no warmth.

"Good afternoon," Felton said, but before he lost the halfling's attention again, he continued, "I'm here to see Captain Bradnir."

"I'm confused, sir," the halfling said, looking at the dwarf as if he was crazy. "I thought you didn't have an appointment."

Felton smacked his forehead and gritted his teeth. "I don't have an appointment, and neither does the captain. I was hoping to talk to him, if he's not too busy."

"I think he's got availability on Thrensday, if you like."

"Threns—" Felton stopped himself. He was about to lose his mind. "I'll tell you what, can you pass a message to the captain for me?"

"Of course, sir," the halfling said, twirling in his seat and pulling a small piece of parchment toward himself. "What shall it say?"

"Let him know that Felton Holdum, garvawk warrior and former warhog rider with the 7th Cavalry, is here to see him—sent by Commander Qwen."

"Wonderful, sir. I'll get this message to him right away," the halfling said as he turned back to the parchments he'd been working on.

Felton brought his cane up and pinned the sheets to the desk. The halfling blinked at him, completely affronted. "Right away would be now, laddie," Felton growled.

The halfling stood, picking up the note, and scuttled down a hallway.

Felton shook his head. If potential recruits received a similar greeting, it might explain the city guard's low numbers. He found himself a seat on a chair in the waiting area and made himself comfortable. He had no idea how long he'd have to wait. If the clerk communicated with his captain as poorly as he did with visitors, Felton might be there a while.

A short time later, the halfling reemerged at the end of the hall, a tall man with a dark beard in tow. The halfling was whispering and pointing at Felton, and the dwarf got the distinct impression that the clerk was tattling on him.

Felton stood from the chair and maneuvered himself to greet the man. He reached a thick hand out to the captain and asked, "Captain Bradnir?"

"That's me," the man said, taking his outstretched arm. "You must be Felton Holdum?"

"Aye, that I am. I was sent by Commander Qwen to speak with you." Felton pulled the scroll from his cloak and made to hand it over. "She thought I might be able to help you."

"Help me?" the man asked quizzically.

He took the scroll and broke the wax seal, unrolling it and reading it quickly. He muttered something under his breath and turned back to the dwarf, who was patiently waiting for his attention. "Felton, this seems a letter of reference ..." He paused for a long moment, inspecting the dwarf.

Felton did his best not to flinch under the captain's scrutinous gaze. The halfling clerk stood nearby, eyeing the dwarf with his arms crossed over his thin frame. Captain Bradnir did not miss the awkward tension. "Let's retreat to my office. We can discuss the matter privately there."

"Aye, sir. A discussion is all I ask for."

They walked down the hallway, Captain Bradnir's long human strides difficult for Felton to match. The captain began to speak before realizing the dwarf had fallen behind. Felton winced when the captain returned to his side with a soft sigh.

"I'm sorry," the man said. "I didn't mean to leave you behind."

"It's nothing, sir," Felton said. "This leg will be better in no time."

"I see," Bradnir said appraisingly.

They entered the man's sparsely decorated office. A potted plant that looked like it had seen better days sat in the corner by a window. A side table that Felton assumed was designed for drinks was instead covered with parchments and ledgers. The captain's desk was orderly and well kept. He didn't sit behind the desk but instead chose a chair beside the one he offered Felton.

"Felton, I don't know if you know this, but I take Commander Qwen's words very seriously," the captain said. "She is a good friend of mine, and I trust her judgment."

"Aye, sir," Felton agreed. "She's one of the finest commanders in all the cavalry."

"Agreed," the man said, sitting back in his chair and stroking his thick black beard. Felton watched him. Though the beard was thick, it was trimmed, keeping it neat and tidy. The dwarf imagined it wasn't easy for a man to be in such a position in a dwarf-run city, but that beard certainly didn't hurt. "Why don't you tell me why you're here?"

Felton shifted in his seat. That was a loaded question. Admittedly, he wasn't even completely sure why he was sitting in the office of the captain of Galium's city guard. In truth, he wouldn't be there if Commander Qwen had been able to assign him a new warhog. When he realized he hadn't answered the captain's question, he said, "Commander Qwen said you might be able to use my help. Said you've been having troubles with recruitment."

Captain Bradnir laughed. "She did, did she?" He stroked his neat beard as he mused over that bit of information. "You're rather blunt, you know?"

"Aye," Felton said sheepishly. "I get it from my Aunt Gael."

"I appreciate the honesty. Commander Qwen wrote very highly of you in this letter," he said, waving it nonchalantly. "Do you know what it says?"

"No, sir," Felton said.

"Would you like to?"

Felton hesitated for a long moment. He wasn't sure he wanted to read it. Seeing the pity in people's eyes was one thing.

He wasn't convinced his heart could take reading it in a letter from the commander he respected so much.

When Felton didn't answer right away, Captain Bradnir's eyes narrowed on him, and the man's chin jutted thoughtfully. "I'll tell you what," he said, standing and circling the desk. He warmed a wax stick with the lit candle on his desk and poured the melting wax on the scroll. He pressed it with his own seal and smiled when he was done. "I want you to take this."

He walked back around and handed it to the dwarf.

"I don't understand," Felton said quietly.

"Life as a city guardsman isn't always easy. Sometimes it can be difficult, and we face tough things. Having something that reminds us of who we are, even when times are tough, would be nice. You've already faced some of the most difficult things in this life. I have a feeling you'll need what's inside that scroll someday."

"But, sir," the dwarf said, "the letter was for you."

"I got what I needed from it," Captain Bradnir said with a smirk. "Now it's for you. Or at least, it will be when you need it."

"I see," Felton whispered, thinking the gift a consolation. "Well, I thank you for your time, Captain. I didn't mean to intrude."

"Nonsense!" The captain waved him off. He stood and crossed to the side table with the piles of parchment. "I'm glad you came. Commander Qwen wasn't wrong. I could use all the help I can get."

The man sorted through the parchments, looking for one in particular. Felton sat dumbstruck, not sure he'd heard the man correctly. "Are you saying you've got an assignment for me?"

Captain Bradnir chuckled. "Well, it may not be as glorious as riding into battle on garvawk. You have to understand, I won't be able to put you on assignment in any of the inner-city districts, but there are many districts that are shorthanded."

Felton stood, hardly believing the captain was giving him a chance. "Wherever you need me, Captain."

"I appreciate that," Bradnir said, finding the sheet he was looking for and turning back to the dwarf. "Now, you have to understand, being part of the city guard isn't the same as being a warhog rider or a garvawk warrior. You can't just intimidate people to keep the peace. Besides, not everyone is so squeamish as my clerk."

Felton released an awkward chuckle. "Sorry about that."

"It's good for him," the captain said with a smirk. "The city guard was created to protect and serve the peoples of the districts. If that letter is any indication, I think you'll be able to do the latter with great efficiency."

"And the protect part?" Felton asked tentatively, wondering what the captain had in mind.

"Where I'm assigning you, there shouldn't be too much of that. Every district in the city has at least one guard on daily patrol, except one. It's a quiet place. Should be the perfect assignment for you."

"And where's that?" Felton asked nervously.

Captain Bradnir smiled at the dwarf and said, "The Garome District."

CHAPTER 9
BASKET OF GOLD

As Felton walked through the door to *Bend's Bakery*, the warm scent of freshly baked bread enveloped him in its welcoming embrace. His cane plunked on the wooden floor as he strode to the counter where a human woman was placing a new basket of long baguettes.

"Well, hello there," she said cheerily. "You must be Felton."

"Aye," he said, stunned. He hadn't met the woman before.

Since Felton had been back in the Garome District, he'd made himself scarce while he awaited the delivery of his city guard uniform. His purpose was two-fold: he hoped he could recover as much as possible before he started patrols, and he wanted the people of the district to look at him not as a cripple but rather as a guardsman. However, word traveled fast in the district, and he was recognized yet again.

She smiled at his surprise. "I'm Lana Smith," she said with a nod toward the door. "My husband Warner and my son Waen run the smithy across the street."

"Oh, I see …," Felton said, though he still didn't know how she knew him. "It's nice to meet you, ma'am. I saw your son and husband sometime back while I was passing by. Haven't had the pleasure of meeting them yet."

"Not to worry, Master Felton. I also heard you had an encounter with my other son, Laen. He's been helping Roey as a caller for the tavern."

"Ah, yes." Felton nodded, recalling the boy. "Enthusiastic lad."

Lana laughed. "He is, at that. Always been loud, that one. Between you and me, Warner couldn't take it. Said the smithy is a place for focus and precision. Laen was just too loud."

"Sounds fair for a smith," Felton said, shifting his weight to lean more on his cane. "I imagine he feels as though he has to work extra hard being a human smith in a dwarven city."

"That he does," Lana said whimsically. "He can be a stubborn man, but the way he works metal ... there's an elegance to it. An art, you know?"

"Aye," Felton agreed. "I know the type. Just like the cavalry. You can train and train and follow every tactic and rule in the book, but some warriors simply fight with the grace of a dancer. An art, like you said."

"Sometimes the art gets lost in the business, though. Having to make things others want just to afford food takes some of the joy out of it. That's why he's so hard on Waen all the time."

"I saw the lad a while back," Felton said. "Couldn't quite make out what he was working on."

Lana laughed again as she pinned a note to a basket of bread and swung it up into her arms. She moved around the counter and waded to one of the tables that lined each side of the bakery. She placed the basket in an empty spot, next to several others, similarly marked.

"Waen is a tinkerer," she mused. "He's always getting distracted with ideas. Loves to make things better. Warner doesn't always like it, but sometimes Waen's ideas make the metalworks even better. It's a tough balance between a father and a son. Boys in their teens have a hard time hearing their father's words, and their fathers have a hard time remembering with compassion what it was like to be that age."

Felton smirked, remembering a similar time in his life. If human men were stubborn, dwarven men were even more so.

"I'm sorry," she said. "I'm sure you didn't come here to visit with me. What can I do for you?"

Felton had stopped by the bakery on errand for Aunt Cleary. She'd sent him to get Bend's special of the day. He, of course, had not been keen on leaving the apartment, but the threat of not being allowed to partake in the dinner she was making spurred him out the door.

His walk to the bakery had been slow. He hadn't been thrilled about the prospect of having to talk with anyone, but standing in the middle of the bakery, breathing in the delicious smells and soaking in the warm sunlight that poured through the windows, he found himself quite content to speak with the woman.

He stammered out, "Ah, yes. My Aunt Cleary asked me to get some of Bend's special of the day?"

"Of course," she said. "Bend is just wrapping up another batch."

As if on cue, Bend exited the back door. His eyes lit up at the sight of the dwarf. "Mister Felton! It's good to see you on this fine day," the baker said. Bend was no less covered in flour than the last time Felton saw him. He assumed it was a badge of honor for bakers to be coated in the stuff.

Bend carried a large basket filled with what looked like yellow biscuits. They had a sweet scent to them, and even from where Felton stood on the other side of the counter, he thought the basket brightened the room even more.

"Just finished this batch of corn bread," Bend said with an excited chuckle. "A little something new I'm trying."

"Corn bread?" Felton asked.

"Aye. Sweet and fluffy. Here," Bend said, taking one out of the basket and handing it to Felton.

The dwarf tossed it from hand to hand, trying to escape the heat. His hands had not been forged in a baker's oven, and the steaming bread was too hot to hold. Not wanting to fall over but unable to hold his cane and continue bouncing the bread, Felton set it on the counter. "That's hot!" he said.

"Oops. Sorry about that," Bend said sheepishly. He abruptly whirled through the door to the back room, saying, "I almost forgot."

Lana shrugged. "He's as much a tinker in the kitchen as Waen is in the smithy."

Felton snorted a chuckle.

Bend returned, a jar of honey in one hand and a knife with a glob of butter in the other. Felton cautiously eyed the baker who pulled the corn bread in two pieces and wiped the knife across the steaming face of the bread. Butter smeared and melted into it.

"Try it now," Bend said excitedly.

Felton hesitated, already having burned his fingers once. He took it anyway and bit into the warm bread. It melted in his mouth the way the butter had melted on the bread.

"Mmmm," was all he could say. He breathed in deeply, relishing the flavor. Finally, he added, "Bend, this is amazing."

"Wait until you try it with honey," the baker urged, as he spread honey on the other half of the corn bread. "Try this."

Felton didn't hesitate. He took the bread and popped it in his mouth. The sweetness of the honey raised a whole new flavor palette and earned a euphoric moan from the dwarf.

"Shave me," he muttered.

"So, you like it?" Bend asked, a wide grin forming above his tidily braided beard.

"I love it," Felton said. "Please tell me that's the special of the day."

"It is," Lana confirmed. "Let me fill you a small basket. Your Aunt Cleary usually only wants a few."

"Go ahead and double it," Felton said quickly but then added, "Please."

He left *Bend's Bakery* with a basket full of a dozen golden corn breads, not entirely sure they would all make it back to the apartment.

Felton avoided eye contact with any passersby, electing instead to glance up at the buildings around the district. The miller's storefront looked far better than it had a couple of weeks prior, much of the reconstruction having been completed. The old tackle shop next to it had been boarded up—likely to keep others out until someone was willing to repair and reopen it.

The scent of the corn bread was less intoxicating in the evening air than it had been in the bakery where Felton had been surrounded by the aroma, though he still caught whiffs of the bread as he walked slowly back to the apartment. He overheard Laen hollering to some folks that *Roey's Tavern* was hosting Castle Brick matches that evening. Felton had to hand it to the boy, he was loud.

He walked down the street toward the back end of the tavern and his aunts' apartment. Felton looked the place over. It could use a fresh coat of paint. Since his aunts had kindly allowed him to stay with them, Felton thought he should take care of some of those needs for them.

When Felton opened the door, he was blasted by an entirely new aroma.

"Aunt Cleary," he called through the apartment, "I've got your bread. I think you're going to like it.

"Got here just in time," Aunt Gael called out. "She's been stirring that forever, waiting for you to get here. I just convinced her we might have to eat without you so we're not late for Castle Brick at *Roey's*."

"You wouldn't want to miss this," Felton said, waving the small basket high.

"What kind is it?" Aunt Cleary asked, bringing bowls to the table.

"Corn bread."

"Corn bread?" Aunt Gael asked, pulling away the cloth that covered them as though it protected a basket of gold.

"Aye, it's really good. What'd you make for us tonight, Aunt Cleary?" Felton asked.

"Gumbo, deary," she said in her singsong voice. "Grandma Ley's recipe from when she lived in Tarn in the far south."

Felton poked at it with his spoon, inspecting it as the steam bathed his face. There were vegetables and rice and some kind of sausage in the gumbo. He spooned a bite into his mouth at the same time Aunt Gael bit into one of the corn breads. The two dwarves nodded to each other with astonished looks on their faces.

After several bites of gumbo, Felton's tongue started to feel warm. He wiped away the sweat that beaded on his forehead and took several gulps of water.

"Got a little kick to it," Aunt Cleary said with a chuckle.

"Aye, it does," Felton said. "Though it's delicious," he added as he took another bite, unable to help himself.

"You think this is spicy, you should have tried Grandma Ley's," Aunt Gael said, laughing. "I'm not sure that woman's tongue could taste spice in her old age."

They ate quickly, his twin aunts in a hurry to get to *Roey's* and not miss the opening matches of Castle Brick. Felton shook his head, wondering how many construction workers his aunts would relieve of their coin by evening's end. As they finished, Felton offered to clean up so Aunt Cleary and Aunt Gael could get a move on.

Just before they left the apartment, Aunt Gael popped her head back in the doorway. "I forgot to mention, a courier came by while you were out. Delivery from a tailor in the Castle District."

The door slammed, and Felton set the bowl on the counter. He grabbed his cane and rounded into the sitting room. A twine-bound bundle rested on the couch where he slept. He eyed the package for a long time, working up his courage to open it. Why was he nervous?

Eventually, he worked his way around the couch and sat, pulling the bundle into his lap. Felton tugged at the twine; its easy knots unfurled as he did so. The contents were wrapped in unmarked canvas. He pulled the canvas away, revealing the guardsman tunic inside. A handwritten note read, "Welcome to the city guard," signed by Captain Bradnir. Felton silently thanked the man.

The tunic was of a fine weave, sewn with great skill. The blue that dyed the shirt echoed the deep blue of the sea. The emblem of the guard, a silver mountain below a rising axe, was stitched onto the piece over the left breast.

Gazing upon the fine cloth elicited deep emotions within Felton. A tear rolled from his eye, disappearing into his great brown beard. More tears soon followed as he held the tunic closer and sobbed. It was not the exquisite craftsmanship of the piece that summoned his emotions but rather what the uniform stood for.

Captain Bradnir had given him a chance. Donning the garb of the city guard would be a new season—the chance to prove to everyone he could return to the garvawk warriors.

Felton sat on the couch for a long time, composing himself and wiping the tears from his face. He'd glanced numerous times at the other couch cushion, under which he'd hidden the letter from Commander Qwen. With all the roiling emotions within him, he debated opening it. He forced those notions away, however, feeling as though he weren't worthy to open it.

After a while, he decided it was time to get back to work. As much as the tunic had moved him, he had promised to take care of dinner cleanup, and he was a dwarf of his word.

As he rose from the couch, he heard an awkward rattling. He grabbed his cane and tapped at the floor, thinking a board might be loose. When he heard it again, he realized it was coming from the front door. His aunts weren't due to return until late. A wave of worry washed over him as the door handle shimmied again.

Someone was attempting to get in.

Felton had only just opened his guardsman's tunic and feared he'd have to stop his first crime before he even donned the uniform.

The door creaked as it opened.

CHAPTER 10
INTRUDER

When the intruder pushed through the door, Felton lunged forward the best he could and swung his cane in a vicious arc. The cane connected with something soft, and a human woman let out a startled yelp. The cloth bags she had been carrying flew to the floor, scattering their contents. Fruits of different shapes and sizes rolled across the floor. Berries of all colors trickled away. Even a few small jars tumbled from the bags.

"What in Finlestia are you doing?" the woman demanded, kneeling quickly to recover the jars so the contents didn't spill any further.

Felton stared, dumbstruck. The woman was tall and lean. She wasn't tall by human standards but taller than him and most dwarves he knew. She pulled back long blond strands of hair that had escaped the bun on the back of her head as she checked over the jars, ensuring that none had broken.

She turned on the stunned dwarf with her wide blue eyes. "Well, are you going to help me or just stand there gawking at the mess you've made?"

Her question shook Felton back to reality. He knelt to the floor and quickly gathered berries that had rolled nearby.

"I—I'm sorry," he stammered. "I thought you were a burglar or a thief trying to sneak into my aunts' apartment."

She laughed, a short burst of amusement. "Who says I'm not?"

Felton paused and eyed her for a moment.

The woman caught him staring. "Really?" she asked incredulously. "I mean, I love Aunt Cleary and Aunt Gael, but have you seen this place? Not much to strike a master burglar's fancy, I'd say. Unless they were really into knitting. Or cooking."

That made Felton chuckle. "There's always Aunt Gael's secret button collection. She's got it stashed under her armchair."

The woman laughed again. "I'll keep that in mind the next time I go on a thieving spree in the middle of the night."

"Just let me know ahead of time. I can catch you and become renowned in my first week on the job, capturing such a notorious criminal as yourself."

"Now where's the fun in that," she teased, looking over her shoulder at him. "The chase is part of the fun."

Felton smirked at her, a little rose coloring his cheeks above his big brown beard. He gathered the berries he'd collected and placed them in a small basket.

"Sorry about this," he said again. "You startled me."

"I startled you?"

"Well ..." he said bashfully, "I was just looking over my new guardsman uniform, and I wasn't expecting anyone to come into the apartment."

"Fair enough," the woman said, gathering some fruit and taking them into the kitchen.

Felton watched her as she maneuvered the kitchen with ease, placing jars and fruits and berries in the places Aunt Cleary liked to keep them. She'd obviously been there before.

Who is this woman? Felton asked himself.

He gripped his cane and hoisted himself from the floor, balancing the small basket of berries in his other hand. He moved carefully. It was hard enough to get on the floor to gather them once. He didn't want to do it again.

"So …" he said, long and slow, as he joined her in the kitchen. "If you're not an infamous thief here for Aunt Gael's precious buttons, who are you?"

She chuckled softly. "Tillinda Marigold," she said. "My friends call me Tilli."

"Tilli," Felton repeated.

"Oh, are we friends now?"

"Oh, sorry," Felton retracted.

She narrowed her eyes and placed a finger to her pursed lips as though she were working a puzzle. "Last I recall, you tried to bludgeon me with a stick."

"It's my cane," Felton said, holding it up apologetically. "I didn't mean to …"

One of Tillinda's eyebrows popped up as though she expected some great explanation. When Felton couldn't come up with anything, he sighed and shrugged helplessly. Tillinda's face shifted and split into a wide grin. "Tilli's fine."

Felton relaxed.

She turned again and started replacing some of Aunt Cleary's jars of herbs.

Felton tensed again. *He* wasn't even allowed to touch his aunt's herbs. Who was this woman?

"So, Tilli," he said tentatively. "Do you come into my aunt's kitchen often?"

She shot him an amused glance. "Yes. Aunt Cleary is well aware that I replace her herbs. I was here a few weeks ago, but Aunt Gael said you'd gone into the inner city. Said you were going for a long walk."

"Aye," Felton said with a nod.

"That's a pretty far walk, but I suppose you'll be doing a lot of that as the Garome District's new guardsman."

"How'd you know I was assigned to this district?" Felton asked, eyeing her back.

"How were you going to catch me in my criminal escapades if you weren't in my district?" she said with a wink. "Besides, Aunt Cleary mentioned it to me when she came by to tell me what she was running low on."

"Oh," Felton said. He was starting to get the picture. "So, you have an herb shop somewhere?"

"No," she said quickly. "I wish. Maybe someday. That would be a dream come true. *Tilli's Herbs & Tea,*" she added with a far-off look. "Or something like that. That, of course, will have to wait until I retire from my extravagant life of crime."

Felton snorted but stared at her, no less confused.

"She came to my home," Tilli explained. "My house is the one in the garden. I'm the garden keeper. Among other things." She added the last part with a shrug and a roll of her hand.

"I passed the garden when I went on my long walk."

"You should have stopped in. The garden is beautiful right now. Well, some of it—the parts that weren't burned by the dragon fire." She paused, as if remembering the night of the battle, then shook her head. "Fall is coming soon, so you should soak in as much of the green as you can before the seasons change."

"I thought about stopping by, but there was a giant tortoise guarding the entrance."

"Guarding it?" Tilli asked with a laugh. "Templeton is as sweet as they come."

Felton recalled his interaction with the tortoise. It certainly seemed like the creature was guarding the garden. Then again,

Felton was going through a lot. Maybe he'd read too much into the tortoise's stance. But the way the creature eyed him …

"I don't know," he said slowly.

"Either way, you should stop by the garden soon," Tilli said sweetly.

"I'll try," Felton said, not sure if he meant it. Though he had to admit, he was rather enjoying his interaction with the woman.

"Fair enough," she said, running a hand along his shoulder as she passed him on her way to the door. "I'm sure you're going to be mighty busy rounding up the Garome District's expansive criminal element."

Felton shot her a bemused look. She returned it with a charming smile.

"You're welcome at the garden any time," she said, stepping through the doorway. She turned back and narrowed her eyes at him. "Though I may have to hit you with a stick."

"Fair enough," Felton said, borrowing her phrase.

She smirked and bid him goodnight before closing the door as she left.

Felton rubbed his scarred brow, trying not to smile, but for some reason, he couldn't stop. He picked up the bowls he'd promised to clean for Aunt Cleary and started to wash up.

Felton hit the wooden floor hard as he tumbled off the couch. He dove in front of the wicked orc's throwing axe to save Tilli. He pressed himself up from the floor, desperately ripping at the blankets that twisted around him. When he realized it wasn't ropes that bound him, he blinked furiously to get his bearings.

The side of his face hurt from taking the brunt of the fall. The couch sat next to him, empty. His body heaved as his breath tried to catch up with his racing heart. Tears streaked Felton's face as he realized it had been a dream.

It had seemed so real. Logic, of course, proved it to be a figment. He had never once been in a battle scenario with Tilli. He'd never even met the woman until that night. It made no sense, and yet ...

So real ...

"Felton, deary?" Aunt Cleary whispered as she emerged from her room in the darkness.

Felton wiped his face hurriedly. Even if the moonlight weren't peering through the windows, dwarves saw well in the dark. It was a brilliant skill; for many of their kin lived in marvelous caverns under distant mountains. Felton cursed the gift, knowing Aunt Cleary would see his emotions.

He pulled himself up onto the couch as she rounded it. "Are you alright, deary?"

"Fine, Aunt Cleary. Sorry for waking you," he said, trying to force down the shaking in his body. An earthquake rumbled within him.

"Night terrors again?"

"Aye."

Aunt Cleary stared at him for a long moment, neither of them saying a word. She stepped around the backside of the couch and reached over it to hug him in her comforting arms. She kissed the top of his head and strode away.

Felton assumed she had gone back to bed, but clinking from the kitchen told him she was rooting around for something.

"Aunt Cleary," he whispered, sorry to have woken her, "I'm fine. Please don't let me keep you up."

"Just making some tea, deary," she called back in a whisper.

Shortly, she returned to the sitting room with two steaming mugs. Felton graciously took the mug and held it in both hands under his face. The hot steam wafted into his nose and moistened his cheeks.

"Chamomile," Aunt Cleary said. "With a little honey," she added with a wink.

"Thank you," he whispered.

"Should help calm you. Calms the mind and the body."

"Really?" he asked, taking a sip.

"Won't put you out like ale or mead or brandy, but it's better for your heart."

Felton thought one of those beverages might be a better option for him, but his aunts didn't have much of anything. Aunt Cleary had a nearly empty bottle of wine that she used for cooking, and he wasn't keen on taking her wrath for finishing it off.

He wondered briefly if *Roey's* were still open but remembered the last time he'd gone to a tavern. Waking up, facedown on one of *Roey's* tables, was not the impression he'd like to make on the people of the Garome District. That wouldn't instill much confidence in their new guardsman. He decided Aunt Cleary was probably right.

Felton sipped the tea quietly. His aunt sat next to him in silence, not forcing him to talk, and drank her own tea. He wasn't sure if it was her nearness or the mere fact that she cared enough to sit with him in the middle of the night or the magical workings of the tea, but—whatever it was—relief washed over him. His heart slowed. His lungs were bringing in enough air. The night fell calm, and he recognized the safety surrounding him in the cozy apartment.

When they'd finished their tea, Aunt Cleary took Felton's mug and went into the kitchen. He heard the clinks as she placed them on the counter and turned to meet her gaze before she slipped back into her room.

"I'll let you wash those up tomorrow morning," she said. And with a wink to her nephew, she said, "Get some rest, deary."

Felton laid back on the couch once more. His eyes remained open for a long time. If he were honest, he was afraid of what he'd see when he closed them. As the night wore on, exhaustion eventually won, and Felton fell asleep.

FALL

CHAPTER 11
LADY LILI

F elton's cane clicked beside him as he walked down the street. Over the past few weeks, his maneuverability had increased, but he remained glued to the cane. He couldn't figure out why his bum leg still pained him and wasn't improving.

Despite his leg, the Garome District's guard had spent his first few weeks on the job moseying around the area, exploring every square inch. He inspected alleys and shops. He stopped to meet some of the locals. He'd watched folks from out of district, like construction workers and various visitors, to understand their travel patterns.

He still hadn't entered *Roey's Tavern,* opting to take his meals at the apartment on the backside of the building. He wasn't too keen on subjecting himself to conversations with locals outside of official business. He made an exception for Bend, the baker, and his assistant. The two had won him over with the incredible breads produced in the bakery.

A pang of guilt shot through Felton as he turned the corner onto the street where the garden's entrance lay. In all this time, he'd avoided the garden even more than the tavern. Fall was upon them, and he hadn't taken Tilli up on her offer to see the garden while it was still lush and green. Many of the trees sported orange and red leaves, drooping heavily over the garden walls.

He slowed as he approached the entry arch and glanced about warily. Felton reached the open gate and peered in. He scanned the inside and saw more of the garden. It was larger than it appeared from this side of the wall, stretching deep through thick swaths of trees. To Felton's untrained eye, it looked like a mysterious forest.

As he scouted the scene, he spotted Templeton farther in. The tortoise wasn't facing him and stood rigid. The creature stood so statuesque, Felton almost missed him.

The dwarf spotted a group of pumpkins, large and round, looking ready to harvest. When he glanced back to the tortoise, the creature had moved to another spot in the garden but remained as unmoving as a statue. Felton shook his head.

He leaned heavier on the wall, hoping to spot Tilli somewhere in the garden. He inclined his ear, trying to hear her humming a tune like he had the day he went into the city. He heard nothing but a rustling of vines above.

"What are you doing?" A sweet voice drifted down from above.

Felton took a step back and peered to the top of the stone wall. A human girl sat atop the wall, her legs dangling. Her wide blue eyes watched him curiously, and the light fall breeze rustled her strawberry blond hair. "What are *you* doing up there?"

"I climb the wall all the time," she said, picking at a vine that had browned much quicker than the others.

"Don't suppose your mom likes that too much," he said softly.

"It's okay," the little girl said. "Mama says I'm like a lizard. I can climb almost all the trees in the garden."

"Almost?" Felton asked with an appraising smile.

"Big Barth is the only one I haven't been able to climb," she said, pointing high toward the center of the garden. "Mama says he's so big because he was the first tree planted in our garden."

"Is that so?" Felton asked, as he tried to see the tree from his vantage. He couldn't make out which one she spoke of with the foliage colors creating a glorious living painting. He glanced at the charred area of the garden, wondering how many trees and other plants had been destroyed in the dragon's fire. "Were you here when the dragon came?"

"No," she said, tossing another brown leaf and watching it flutter to the ground. "I went with Aunt Gael and Aunt Cleary when everyone was evac ... evac ..." Her face scrunched as though she were thinking hard.

"Evacuated," Felton offered. Many of the citizens had been evacuated prior to the Battle of Galium. The wagoners of the city had loaded their wagons with as many passengers as they could and headed for Crossdin until the battle was over. Felton hadn't realized his aunts might know this little girl. He realized she must be Tilli's daughter. He wasn't sure why he hadn't put it together. "You didn't go with your mom and dad?"

"No," the girl said. "Mama wanted to stay behind and protect the garden. Said if the battle was won, people would need a beautiful garden to lift their spirits in the after ... the after ..."

"The aftermath," Felton finished quietly.

"Yes!" she shouted victoriously.

Felton winced at the loud outburst. He looked into the garden, and his eyes landed on Templeton staring his way. Felton turned back toward the girl and asked her, "Where was your dad?"

"Papa died when I was really little," she said.

"I'm sorry to hear that," Felton said.

"I was little, so I don't remember."

"You're still little," the dwarf said, smiling at her upbeat attitude.

"But I was *really* little," she said, squinting and squeezing her fingers together to show him how small.

Felton chuckled. He chanced a glance back into the garden and yelped, nearly jumping out of his skin. Templeton was only a few feet away, glaring at him, unmoving.

How'd he do that?

The girl atop the wall chuckled. "Are you afraid of Tem?"

"Tem?"

"He's just a tortoise," she said, laughing uncontrollably.

"I'm not afraid of him," Felton said, as he jumped again. Tem was almost close enough to reach out his long neck and bite the dwarf.

The girl laughed so hard, Felton worried she'd topple right off the high wall. "Easy now," he said, backing away slowly, not looking away from the tortoise's unwavering stare. "Don't want you to fall."

"I never fall," she said, wiping the jovial tears from her eyes. "Why are you afraid of a tortoise?"

"I'm not afraid," Felton lied as he slowly moved away.

"Where are you going?" she asked, still giddy.

"I've got important guard work to do."

"I thought you came to see my mama," she said, stepping along the wall to match his pace.

"I was ... I mean, I wasn't." Felton took a breath as he hurried away from the entrance. "I've been meaning to come see the garden. I have to inspect the whole district—part of my duties."

"Oh!" she said excitedly. "I can help you. I know every spot in the garden."

"Soon," he said, glancing back at the entrance. Tem stood motionless, staring at the dwarf disconcertingly.

"Okay!" the girl said. "Bye, Mister Guard."

"Felton," he said, realizing he hadn't told her his name. "My name's Felton. What's yours?"

"Lili," she said.

"Nice to meet you, Lady Lili," he said with a slight bow and a smile.

Lili giggled at the display. "Come back soon?"

"Soon," Felton promised before he turned and strode away. Though he wasn't enthusiastic about running into Templeton again, he meant it.

CHAPTER 12
SLEEPY DISTRICT

The tapping of metal rang rhythmically down the street. Since he'd donned the garb of the city guard, Felton had found little in the way of real work to be done. Most of the citizens of the Garome District lived mild lives, opting to live peaceably with others. Even the construction workers that came through the district daily matched the calm demeanor of the area.

Felton still hadn't gone to *Roey's Tavern*, not trusting himself or inclined to get into too many conversations with folk. It had been easier to avoid than he'd expected, since he'd heard no tell of trouble from Roey whatsoever—not even a single tale of a disruptive patron who had one drink too many. The district had been so calm over the previous weeks, Felton wondered if *anything* happened there.

He did not know what drew him to the ringing down the street—boredom or curiosity—but he moseyed toward the smithy nonetheless.

Waen sat near the open entrance, bending some metal with his tongs. He hammered and twisted the metal piece, inspecting it with a shrewd eye. Felton noted the lad had several similarly worked pieces lying nearby. Waen tossed the one he'd been working on into the pile and stood. He stopped short as he noticed the dwarf approaching.

"Good afternoon, Mister Felton," he said politely.

"Hello there, Waen," Felton returned the greeting. He huffed his amusement and nodded toward the pile of metal items. "What are you working on there? Not going the way you planned?"

"Oh, these?" the gangly teenager asked as he picked one up. "These are going to work perfectly."

Felton moved closer, his cane tapping softly on the road. Waen extended the piece of metal for the dwarf to inspect. It was as long as the boy's forearm and worked into an angle on one end. It looked to be shaped into some sort of hook on the other.

"What is it?" Felton asked.

"It's a bracket," the young man said.

Felton scratched his beard thoughtfully. "A bracket?"

"Yes," Waen said excitedly. "Here."

He pushed the piece of metal into Felton's hand and spun away into the smithy. Felton watched the lad grab another piece from a pile and hurry back.

"I'm going to attach this underneath," Waen said with some awe. "Hold that up right here ..."

Felton did as instructed, and Waen held up the new piece, indicating where they'd be attached. The new piece was rather ornate and consisted of swirling rods that made it look like metal vines looping around each other. Felton was impressed by the craftsmanship, but he still wasn't quite sure what the bracket's purpose was.

"Aye. Lovely," he said.

Waen laughed. "They're for flowers."

Felton was really confused. "Flowers?"

"Yes!" The boy laughed again. "I came up with the idea while talking with Pa. He said he and Ma spoke with Tilli at the tavern the other night. Tilli was saying it would be nice if we could make the district as beautiful as it was before the dragon fire. Well, we didn't move here until after that, but Ma agreed and asked Pa if there was any way we could help. He mentioned it to me, and I came up with this."

"And what will these brackets do?" Felton asked.

"Well, you know the lanterns that hang from the buildings on brackets?"

"Oh," Felton hummed, starting to understand where the boy was going. "You want to hang flowers from the brackets?"

"Yes!" Waen exclaimed. "Well, baskets of flowers from them. It will be so beautiful. Think what it will look like in the spring."

Felton smiled at the boy's far-off optimism, though he couldn't quite see it in his mind. He'd never found much purpose for flowers. Sure, they were pretty as they clothed a hillside with a rainbow of colors, but Felton had always been a dwarf with purpose. The notion pricked at him like a barb. He'd found his own duties of late to seem ... unneeded.

What purpose do I serve ...?

"Mister Felton?" Waen asked, his head leaning to the side as if he were wondering where the guard had gone.

"Ah ... well," he said, straightening. "Very interesting idea."

"Thank you," Waen said. The hammering from the back of the smithy paused, forcing the young man to shoot a glance over his shoulder. When the hammering continued, he turned back toward the guard. "Pa doesn't always like my ideas. Says a blacksmith needs to stay focused—that's how you craft with beauty. And he's right, of course. Look at these." Waen lifted the ornate piece that looked like metal vines.

"Your father does fine work," Felton agreed.

"Truly," the teen said. "He's good at making things. I like to figure out how things work."

"Seems to me that would make you a good team," the dwarf reasoned.

"I think so. Pa liked this idea because it helps our district and shows our abilities. Says it's good for our neighbors and good for business."

Felton wasn't really sure how flowers would help their neighbors, but he didn't want to dash the boy's enthusiasm. He didn't plan on being there long enough to see the hanging flower baskets in all their splendor anyway. The cool of fall was setting in, and the dwarf imagined he would be healed and back with the garvawk warriors—or at least the cavalry—by spring. If his blasted leg would just get better already.

Admittedly, the blacksmith's work was done with elegant precision. If the brackets worked the way Waen explained, they would certainly display the blacksmith's skill to anyone moving through the district.

Waen watched the dwarven guard for a long moment, as though he were waiting for something. Felton straightened himself and said, "Seems a clever idea, lad."

"Thank you!" The boy brightened. "I've got loads more. And not just for metal. I could show you some of my sketches," he said, tossing the metal pieces into the pile at his feet and hurrying toward another table strewn with parchments.

"Oh, lad," Felton called after him. "I really need to be going. Wouldn't be a very good guard if I didn't complete my patrol."

"Of course," Waen said, a mite disappointed. "Very important work, Mister Felton."

"Aye," the dwarf said, but he lingered for a moment longer. "I'd love to see some of your ideas soon, though."

"Yes, sir!" Waen said, regaining his full level of enthusiasm.

Felton chuckled as he walked away. Waen was a good lad. He thought the teen was probably too smart for his own good, a problem Felton thought he'd never struggled with himself. Sure, he had a propensity and savvy for tactics and being a warrior, but that was the only thing he'd ever been any good at.

Though he would never admit it to anyone, as he walked the street, his cane clicking along next to him, he wondered if he would ever be good at anything again.

Aunt Cleary piled a heaping mound from the casserole dish onto Felton's plate. By the way she scooped it onto Aunt Gael's and her own, Felton wondered if she thought he was still a growing dwarf.

A hint of spice wafted into his nostrils as the noodle mound steamed. He poked at it with his fork, finding diced tomatoes and ground meat inside. His mouth began to water, so he dug in. When he did, his eyes widened, and he no longer cared if Aunt Cleary had a misinformed notion of his growing status.

Pile it on!

Aunt Gael slurped a long noodle that she was struggling to control with her fork. She chewed it quickly and turned on Felton. "Did you get to do anything on your patrol today?"

Felton sighed. He loved his Aunt Gael, but she could be blunt sometimes. "Not much. I stopped by the smithy and spoke with young Waen."

"He's a good lad," Aunt Cleary said between bites.

"He is," Felton agreed. "Smart lad, too."

"Well, at least you did *something*," Aunt Gael said.

Felton sniffed. "Not much else happening around this sleepy district."

"That's not true, deary," Aunt Cleary said.

"Not at all," Aunt Gael added. "You just aren't looking in the right places."

Felton eyed her suspiciously. "What do you know ...?"

"Seems like common sense to me." Aunt Gael shrugged. "Can't find what you're looking for when you're looking in all the wrong places."

"After supper, we're going to *Roey's,*" Aunt Cleary said. "Most of the district will be there. We're planning the Fall Festival."

"The Fall Festival?" Felton asked. How had he not heard of it before?

"Yes, deary. It's always a good time. We do one every year."

"Yeah, and we're not going to let a little dragon fire ruin it," Aunt Gael added.

"There'll be plenty 'happening,'" Aunt Cleary said, emphasizing Felton's own word against him. "And it will be a good way to get to know some of the folks in the Garome District better. Then, you'll know what's happening better than we do."

"I doubt that," Aunt Gael muttered. She leaned toward Felton conspiratorially and motioned her head toward her sister. "How she finds the scuttlebutt in this district is a true gift. She has no equal."

"Either way ..." Aunt Cleary shot her a scolding look, "you should come with us."

Felton couldn't argue with her logic. Though he'd been avoiding it for a long time, he couldn't become a better guard without getting to know the people of the Garome District. The Fall Festival seemed like an event he should know about as the city guardsman of the district.

He released a resigned sigh and said, "Fine."

"Well, hurry up then, deary. We'll have to clean up after supper before we go."

Felton responded to his Aunt Cleary's encouragement by shoveling the noodle dinner into his mouth, savoring the brilliant combination of subtle spicy flavors.

CHAPTER 13
ROEY'S TAVERN

F elton hesitated as he strode around the corner of *Roey's Tavern*. The evening was cool, and the stars lit the night with a billion pinpricks of light. A warm glow poured out of the windows of the tavern, curtains masking the inside from view. Music and merriment emanated from the place, indicating it was busy.

The guard had heard the noises many times before. His aunts' apartment was shielded from much of the noise of the tavern, but he'd stepped outside to breathe in the night air many times. Often, he'd pull at his pipe, puffing away while listening to the rambunctious lot.

He was nervous for some reason. His Aunt Cleary tugged at him, not letting him fall into his usual habit of not participating. While he'd met many of the district's folk with a nod, he still tried to keep his distance. He felt like a wee dwarfling whose aunt was about to throw him into the deep water of a river. Would he sink or swim?

Felton stepped quickly, leaning into his cane for the extra speed to grab the door for his aunts. While he tried to remain chivalrous as much as he could, the guard held the door more in an effort to steal one last moment before entering the place. He breathed deeply, and Aunt Cleary patted his shoulder as she followed Aunt Gael into the tavern.

Several excited cheers rang out from one side of the room as Felton entered. He quickly realized the ruckus was for his aunts. They walked in like they owned the place and headed straight for a table where a game of Castle Brick was in full swing. The patrons at the table shifted their seats, making space for his aunts. Felton shook his head in amusement as Aunt Gael settled in. A pile of tiles was quickly slid in front of her. She flipped and organized the tiles with dexterous ease. Felton smirked, knowing she was about to run the table.

"Felton," Lana, the baker's assistant, called from a table nearby. "How do you do this evening?"

"Oh, hello, Missus Lana," he greeted her. He nodded in the direction of his aunts, fully engrossed in their game. "My aunts convinced me to come out tonight."

"I see that," she said. A man and an old dwarf sat with her, Warner Smith and Kinson the glasswright. Lana indicated an empty chair at their table. "Grab yourself a drink and join us?"

"Aye," Felton said with a slow nod.

He looked over the tavern. Lanterns hung around the room, and a pair of iron chandeliers bathed the place in amber light. There was nothing particularly fancy about them when compared to the chandeliers Felton had seen in Galium's castle. They reminded him of the utilitarian ones of *The Hungry Hog*, though devoid of leather straps—a hazing ritual of the cavalry. They teased newcomers in their units by tossing one of their tack straps onto the chandeliers. They'd pour the new rider ale until they could hardly see straight before telling them where their tack had been tossed. Some clever riders—and those who had a particularly strong proclivity for holding their ale—managed to retrieve their straps. But still, many hung from the chandeliers to this day.

Felton glanced toward the bar at the back of the tavern, realizing he'd have to maneuver around tables filled with patrons. An eerie sensation washed over him. Was everyone staring at him? The raucous laughter and merriment faded in his ears as all eyes turned toward him. His heart beat hard in his chest, thrumming in his ears. Darkness at the edges of his eyes crept over his vision.

A sudden pat on his shoulder jarred him back to reality. The general noise of the place resumed, and his vision cleared. It seemed that no one was actually looking at him. Instead, the patrons enjoyed the company of their tablemates, not noticing him in the least. Felton blinked a couple of times, trying to make sense of the scene. He could have sworn they were all looking at him ...

Only one pair of eyes rested on him. The man standing next to him was tall and spoke kindly to him. "Felton?"

"Aye ... what?" He managed to say.

"I was just saying, I'd be glad to buy your first drink," Warner Smith said.

"Oh ... right. Lead on," he said gratefully to the man.

Warner eyed him for a moment with a kind smile. "You alright?"

"Fine. Just fine. Just thirsty is all," Felton said with a forced smile, trying to lighten the tension and divert the man's focus.

"Of course," the blacksmith said, patting Felton on the shoulder and stepping through the room.

Felton followed quickly, hoisting his bum leg with great effort, so as not to get left behind. Several folk raised mugs to him from tables they passed and called out greetings. Felton nodded awkwardly.

"Seems I'm not the only one keen on buying you a round tonight." Warner grinned.

The guard followed the blacksmith to the bar. The man stood high above it while Roey's halfling height barely placed her chin above the bar.

"Hi, Roey," Warner said cheerily. "Another round of ale for my table. And an ... ale for our guardsman?" he added, shooting a questioning glance toward Felton.

"Aye, that'd be—"

"Oh, no," Roey said to the blacksmith. "The first guard that Garome District has had in years is going to get his first drink on the house."

She twirled and grabbed several mugs to fill.

"Quite the popular fellow," Warner said with an impressed nod to Felton.

The guard flushed. He didn't know why so many folk were eager to buy him a round. "Can't say why," he mumbled.

Warner scrunched his nose and smiled. "Folks are just excited. They've seen you on patrol and, likely as not, just want to get to know you. You'll find the Garome District to be much warmer than others around Galium."

Felton's lips pressed together, and his eyes narrowed thoughtfully as he glanced around the bustling tavern. He expected to see more than one person turn away awkwardly when he caught them staring, but none did. Everyone seemed to be enjoying their evening, not worried in the least about him or his blasted leg.

"Here you go, loves," Roey said as she placed the four mugs before them. She turned on Felton. "Been waiting a while to see you come through my doors. I think our ideas of 'soon' might be different."

Her smirk told him she was teasing, though his cheeks burned nonetheless. "I ... I'm sorry about that," he said sheepishly. "I've been busy."

"Surely," Roey said, not losing her sweetness. "Big job being the first guard in Garome in years."

Her placing so much worth on his position made his excuse feel that much more hollow. One edge of his mouth popped as he pressed together an uncomfortable smile.

"Anyway, let's make the next 'soon' happen a little quicker," she said with a wink. "Folks will love to see you around here. Makes them feel like you're here to stay."

A flash of guilt flowed through Felton, warming his veins. He didn't have any plans to stay long-term in the Garome District. If he could get his leg working again and Foredwarf Lotmeag should call on him with a new garvawk opportunity, Felton would be gone in a heartbeat.

Roey was called away to refill mugs down the bar. "Come on, mate," Warner said to him. "You got your mug, or shall I carry it for you?"

"I've got it," Felton grumbled.

They strode through the tavern, Felton attempting to avoid eye contact with folks at the tables they passed. One ale wouldn't hurt, but he didn't want to overindulge. It would be easy to do with so many people looking to treat him. A band of musicians played from the corner, the bard singing a song Felton had never heard before. Patrons closer to the band sang along, knowing all the words.

As Felton trudged, his face downcast, he ran into a woman, nearly knocking her over. He tossed his cane to the floor and reached out to steady her. Pulling her in was an impressive maneuver, displayed all the more by the ale in his hand that had not spilled a drop, eliciting cheers from those gathered at nearby tables. He held the woman close, not daring to move, for fear of dropping her or losing his own balance. He stood unsteadily with his cane tossed aside.

"There are easier ways to ask a lady to dance, Mister Felton," the woman said.

Felton scrunched his face in embarrassment. Of all the women he could have run into, it had to be this one? "Aye," he said, and without missing a beat, he said in the smoothest tone he could muster, "but it's hard to convince a lovely lady to dance with you when you've got a bum leg."

Where did that come from? he wondered.

Tilli laughed. Her wide blue eyes sparkled as she grinned. "You may have more charm than you give yourself credit for. Shall we dance?" she asked, placing the tray she'd been carrying on the nearest table.

"I ... well," Felton stammered. All his cavalier talk fell away. "I can't," he said softly. "My leg ..."

"Oh, sure," Tilli said, straightening herself awkwardly. "Of course. I didn't mean to ... well ..."

"No. Of course," Felton grumbled, letting her go. "My apologies."

"Very good," Tilli said, brushing the wrinkles out of her apron. She smiled at him and said, "We can have that dance another time."

Felton's face flushed, and he hoped she couldn't see his cheeks rose in the warm lantern light of the tavern. "Aye. I'd like that," he said, bending down to pick up his cane.

"Though you still haven't come by the garden," she added playfully, picking up the empty tray again and twirling it.

"I tried to stop by the other day ...," he said slowly.

"Yes," she said, eyeing him. "Lili mentioned you stopped by. Said you were afraid of Tem."

A vision of the tortoise's leering gaze flashed through Felton's mind. "I'm not afraid of him," the guard said. "He just ... the way he stares ... it's just—"

"Tilli," someone called from a nearby table.

"Oh," she said. "Duty calls."

Felton finally put all the pieces of the puzzle together as he realized she was working the tavern as a barmaid. "Oh, you work here."

"A girl's got to earn coin to feed her family. It's either a respectable job like this, or I can go on another crime spree," she said a with a wink. She hurried to the table, and Felton overheard her ask, "Alright, what can I get for you lot?"

Despite himself, Felton smirked.

"Waen wouldn't stop talking about how you visited him today," Lana said, chuckling. "He was beside himself. Told us you were interested in the brackets he was working on."

"A fine idea," Felton said with a nod, though in truth he didn't get the point of brackets that would hold baskets of flowers. With more honesty, he said, "The design is quite beautiful—marvelous metal work."

Warner raised his mug and nodded toward the dwarf. "Much appreciated, Felton."

"That boy o' yers is sharp as an axe," Kinson said in his gravelly voice before taking a swig of his ale. The elder dwarf still showed great strength in his sturdy arms, though the hair on his balding head was wispy and white to match his beard. "Ye know what he says to me?"

Warner groaned, obviously concerned what his son might have said.

"He says to me, he has an idea to form a window railing and a rod arm to prop it up. That way, folks can open their windows even when it's raining. Says it'd be like an awning."

"That's interesting," Felton said, musing over it. The window in his aunts' kitchen swung out sideways. He'd attempted to open it one evening as Aunt Cleary was getting creative in the kitchen and filling the apartment with smoke. He had to close it shortly afterward because the rain soaked the counter.

"No shortage of ideas, that lad," Warner said, shaking his head.

"I don't know," Felton remarked with a tip of his head. "That one seems like it could work. Just the other day, I—"

The musicians stopped mid-song, and Roey stepped up onto the bar and shouted over the gathering. "Oy!" She waited a moment while the whispers dissolved. One dwarf continued to chatter. "Darbin Toller, don't make me come over there and pluck your beard."

"Sorry, Miss Roey," the young dwarven man called back.

Snickers ran through the tavern as a bemused Roey shook her head. She continued, "Alright then, we're all here to discuss plans for the Fall Festival. So, let's get discussing."

Felton watched in awe as Roey controlled the room, speaking of each task and to each responsible party in turn. They discussed topic after topic, making Felton's head spin. He couldn't keep track of who was taking care of which job.

A sense of foolishness gripped the guard for not realizing how large the event was going to be. As he sat and listened, he tried to focus on learning people's names as Roey spoke to them, though he had a hard time keeping up.

Everything went quiet, and Felton got the strange feeling that everyone was looking at him again. This time when someone nudged him, however, he blinked and realized that everyone was, indeed, staring at him.

"Felton," Lana whispered to him.

"Aye ... what?" he stammered.

Chuckles rippled at tables nearby. Roey composed herself and repeated, "Mister Felton, as the city guardsman for our district, we were hoping you would be one of the judges for our pie contest."

"Pie contest?" he muttered. "I ..."

"What was that?" Roey asked, leaning forward and cupping a hand around her ear as though she couldn't hear him.

"He said, 'Aye,'" Darbin Toller relayed.

Several enthusiastic claps erupted from tables around the place. An approving pat on the back from Kinson shook Felton before he could correct the error.

"Lucky dwarf," Kinson said to him. "I'll be making my famous meat pie."

"Meat pie? I didn't realize you baked," the guard said.

"A glasswright has to eat, too," Kinson said, chuckling into his mug.

When the formal proceedings finished, some folk turned back to their conversations with renewed fervor, while others took it as their cue to disperse. Lana and Warner Smith bid Felton good evening, since Lana needed to be up early the next morning to help at *Bend's Bakery*.

Felton tidied their table and worked his way out of his seat. He stole a glance over at his aunts who'd resumed their game of Castle Brick. He wondered how much coin Aunt Gael would coax out of her opponents. They'd likely want to stay a while longer, so he decided to head out.

He bid Kinson goodnight, and the glasswright raised his mug to the guard before heading to the bar for a refill.

Felton made for the door but was intercepted by Tilli, who swiftly stepped before him.

"Headed home, are we?" she asked.

"Aye. I've got to get an early start," he said.

"To protect and serve," she chimed, standing straighter and prouder.

Felton chuckled. "Hasn't been much need for protection around here."

Tilli's sweet face shone brighter than the lantern light. "Well, if you need to do any serving, I could use some help at the garden. Lots to do before the festival. I'll be working on some things tomorrow."

"I can't tomorrow," Felton said, genuinely regretful. "I have … other business to attend."

"Of course," Tilli said, embarrassed.

"But perhaps the day after that or the day after that?" Felton added, wanting to relieve her discomfort.

"I won't be getting it all done tomorrow," she said. "I'll certainly still need help then."

"Good," Felton said. "It's a date."

Tilli huffed a suppressed laugh.

"I mean … it's a date … I mean, like I'll make sure to be there this time …" His words fell away as her smirk evolved into a wide grin.

"I look forward to it," Tilli said. And with that, she strode toward a table in desperate need of cleaning.

Felton stood by the door, stunned. He looked over at the woman, the blond bun of her hair wobbling as she leaned over and rubbed a cloth atop the table. She glanced back at him, and he dumbly raised a hand. She smiled at him and gave him a short wave before returning to her task.

He shook his head and blinked as he strode out the door of *Roey's Tavern* into the crisp night that covered the Garome District.

CHAPTER 14
WHAT'S BEST

Foredwarf Lotmeag eyed Felton as he slowly approached. The foredwarf was giving instruction to one of his garvawk warriors, Kel. As Felton neared, Lotmeag dismissed Kel to run the drills the warriors had planned for the day. Kel gave Felton a friendly nod before he turned back into the training area of Bannett Hall and barked orders to the others.

Lotmeag didn't wait for Felton to reach him, instead opting to meet him halfway and redirect him into the adjoining hallway.

"Felton," he said with a nod.

Felton had never thought Lotmeag unkind. He still didn't, but the guard could tell he'd frustrated him. "Foredwarf Lotmeag. I—"

"What are ye doing here?" Lotmeag asked as gently as he could muster through his chagrin.

"Just thought I would stop by and check in. See if there had been any garvawk sign."

"No," the foredwarf said quickly. "Well, there was some sign, but—"

"Really?" Felton gasped, letting his excitement slip.

"But," Lotmeag said, elongating the word for emphasis, "it was old sign. Whatever garvawk had been there has been gone for a long time."

"Oh," Felton breathed. "So ... no new prospects."

"None."

"I see."

"How's yer leg doing?" Lotmeag shifted the conversation.

"Better," Felton lied.

One of Lotmeag's eyebrows shot up as he inspected the cane in Felton's hand.

This wretched cane, the guard cursed his support.

For a while, the foredwarf appraised him, not saying a word. The only sound in the hallway was the echo of training weapons and grunts from Bannett Hall. Lotmeag let a deep sigh exit his nose as he scratched at his thick beard. "I heard ye were patrolling the Garome District with the city guard," he finally said, breaking the silence between them.

"Aye," Felton said slowly.

"That is a good thing ye do."

"Aye. But it's not the garvawk warriors."

Lotmeag nodded, and his eyes narrowed on Felton. "Ye do know there are other honorable ways to serve Galium. The cavalry is no less honorable than the garvawk warriors and—"

"But Commander Qwen wouldn't take me," Felton blurted, interrupting his foredwarf for the second time. He winced at his own bullishness. Felton had never disrespected one of his superiors in all his years of service. On the other hand, no one seemed to be listening to him.

"Aye. She and I have talked about that," Lotmeag said patiently. "We met with Captain Bradnir at the city guard to discuss yer situation."

"Oh, I see," Felton growled. His frustration boiled into anger.

Lotmeag cast the discerning look of a good leader recognizing something out of place. "Felton, we only want what's best for ye. We think—"

"What's best for me is getting me back in a saddle with a battle axe in my hand. It's the only thing I've ever known. It's the only thing I've ever been any good at," he seethed. "Why does everyone think they can discuss what's best for me without hearing what I have to say?"

Lotmeag straightened in a clear attempt to keep himself composed before the fuming Felton. "Yer skill as a warrior was never in question. We would not have chosen ye for the garvawk warriors if it had ever been in doubt."

"Bah," Felton said, waving his hand and leaning into his cane as he swiveled away.

"Felton," Lotmeag's commanding voice echoed off the stone walls of the hallway, stopping the guard mid-stride. Felton turned to meet the foredwarf's gaze. "Yer skill as a warrior wasn't what made us choose ye. Ye're not defined by the position ye hold but by the qualities that well within ye—yer tenacity and yer work ethic. Yer effort to always do yer best. Yer genuine care for the dwarves beside ye. Those are the things that make ye great."

Lotmeag paused for a moment, sadness edging his face. "I know ye've forgotten those things in light of yer grief and anger. For my part, I'll keep looking for garvawk sign while ye try to heal. But I hope that ye'll take this time to remember what makes ye the dwarf we all believe in."

Felton huffed a laugh. "I don't even know who I am if I'm not a warrior ..." he grumbled as he turned away again. He gripped his cane and, even quieter, said, "I don't even know if *I* believe in myself."

The disheartened dwarf wandered around the Castle District of Galium for a time. He didn't try to process his thoughts or his conversation with his former foredwarf. He didn't attempt to navigate his ocean of feelings to find some definable substance in the torrent. He merely walked in silence, save for the soft clicking of his cane.

Felton felt numb.

After he'd meandered long enough to break his brooding rage, he headed toward the city guard headquarters—his real purpose for entering the inner city. He was due to report to Captain Bradnir about his district. In truth, he had been far more intent on checking in with the garvawk warriors. As he hobbled up the steps to the headquarters, though, he wished he'd never gone to Bannett Hall.

The halfling clerk at the desk began his greeting, not looking up right away. "Good evening, s—" He stopped when he noticed it was Felton, shooting a bemused glare at the dwarf.

"Hey, Thrensday," Felton said as he walked past the desk.

The halfling blinked at him in confusion, not understanding the joke at his expense.

Felton strode through the hallway toward Captain Bradnir's office. Lead guards had standing invitations to report to the captain any time without an appointment. As Felton was the only guard in his district, he had become the lead guard by default. The captain's door was closed, indicating he was in another meeting. Felton sat in one of the upholstered wingback chairs that stood on either side of a small side table.

As he sat, he realized how tired he truly was. He couldn't say whether it was the extensive hobbling he'd done or the pure rage that had circulated through his system. Whatever it was, sitting down came as a welcome relief. He sank into the chair and leaned into the high wingback. He closed his eyes for a moment, going over the report he'd prepared for Captain Bradnir. There wasn't much to report, so he ran through it quickly. Soon enough, exhaustion took over, and Felton drifted off.

When Felton awoke, Captain Bradnir was sitting in the wingback chair opposite him, sipping a steaming cup of tea. Realizing what had happened, Felton bolted upright, flushed with embarrassment.

"Captain," he said quickly, wiping at his dry mouth. "I was just waiting and ... and ..."

Captain Bradnir chuckled. "It's alright. These chairs are comfortable. Slept in this one a few times myself." The captain stroked his black beard, fondly remembering some distant instance. "I had Clarenze make us some tea."

The man indicated another steaming mug on the side table between them. Felton nodded his thanks and took a long sip. It was a dark tea and had a nice bite to it, giving him a small jolt of energy.

"Who's Clarenze?" Felton asked.

"My clerk," Captain Bradnir said as though it were obvious.

"Oh, Thrensday?" Felton said with a chuckle.

The man smirked. "He does like to fill up my Thrensday appointments."

Captain Bradnir was gracious enough to sit in companionable silence for a long time while the tea worked its way into Felton's system, rejuvenating him. Eventually, the guard presented his meager report, explaining how little had happened in his district.

"You know," Bradnir said, setting his empty teacup on the table. "I've found that sometimes the little happenings can be the most important."

"I don't know ..." Felton said softly. "It feels like nothing is happening. How can I protect people if there's nothing to protect them from?"

"Hmm," the man mused. "You have a rare opportunity."

"And what's that?" Felton asked curiously.

"Well, in many of the districts, protection takes precedence out of necessity. But you have the opportunity to show the other side of the city guard. We're here to protect *and* serve. You have the opportunity to show the serve side of the guard in a way most don't."

Felton pondered those words for a long while. He thought of Tilli and how she'd asked him to help her at the garden. He supposed that would be considered an act of service, though it seemed trivial by comparison to his service in the cavalry.

As if the captain could read his thoughts, Bradnir said, "Some days, it'll be hard to remember that just because you don't think something is important, doesn't mean it's not important to someone else."

Felton's mouth fell open slightly, and he was unsure how to respond.

Bradnir smirked and continued, "You've been so used to discipline and dedication and honor and service, taking pride in everything you do. It's a hard transition to work with people who don't know that life. They have different priorities and hold different tasks dear. Not everyone is on the same mission with you all the time. It's tough to grasp that."

"How do you know all this?" Felton asked, holding his new captain in higher esteem in light of his words.

"You're not the first warrior to join the city guard. As much as you might think you're alone, you're not."

Felton's chin quivered under his thick brown beard. His eyes glassed, and he turned away down the hallway as though he heard something. He didn't want Bradnir to see the tears welling in his eyes.

"Thank you, Captain," he croaked out. "I'll do my best."

Chapter 15
Glass Bubble

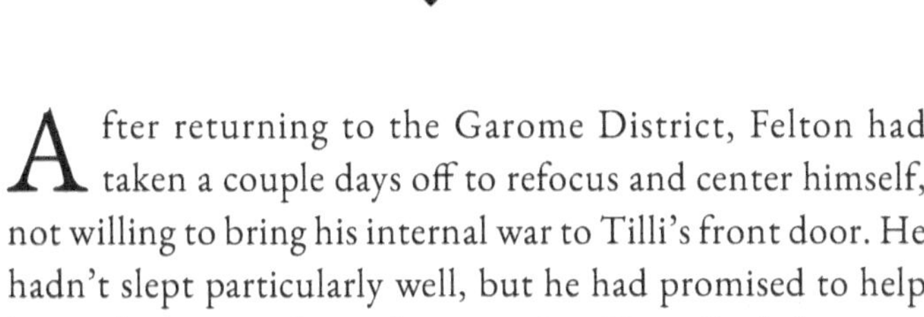

After returning to the Garome District, Felton had taken a couple days off to refocus and center himself, not willing to bring his internal war to Tilli's front door. He hadn't slept particularly well, but he had promised to help her and meant to keep that promise. He walked the street toward the garden, trying to keep his mind open.

When he arrived at the stone arched entrance to the garden, he peered in cautiously, scanning for the tortoise. He saw nothing and took a tentative step through the entryway. He tested the dirt path as though he were dipping his toe into a stream to determine its temperature. For some reason, he expected the tortoise would know the second he entered. Once he fully stepped through and Templeton did not reveal himself from some hidden position, Felton heaved a relieved sigh.

"What are you doing?"

Felton nearly jumped out of his skin at the curious voice behind him. He held a hand to his heart, feeling the rapid thrum through his chest.

"Lass, you just about slew me," he said, eyeing Lady Lili who kicked her legs from atop the wall.

She giggled. "Why were you walking so funny?"

"I have a cane," he said, raising it.

"Not that," she said. "It looked like you were sneaking. That's how I do it, too, when I surprise Mama from the trees."

"I wasn't sneaking," Felton denied the accusation.

"Of course he wasn't," Tilli called from nearby as she strode toward him. "Mister Felton is the guard of our district, lovey. He's the one that *catches* the sneaking criminals. He doesn't do the sneaking."

Tilli pulled gloves from her hands and smiled at the dwarf. Her trousers and apron were covered in dirt, though the soil did not diminish her brightness. She'd gotten an early start on the work she'd planned for the day. Her wide blue eyes took him in as she pulled several rogue strands of her long blond hair behind her ear. The rogues had escaped the bun that held their kin captive.

"How many times have I told you not to climb on that wall?" Tilli asked.

"Mama, it's the best way to see the garden," Lili moaned.

"And the best way to get hurt. Why don't you come down and give Mister Felton a tour of the garden so *he* can see it?"

"Oh, alright." Lili groaned as she climbed into the branches of a tree and shimmied her way to the ground. She hurried to the dwarf and excitedly asked, "Do you hit the criminals with your cane?"

"Only when they surprise me," Felton said. Tilli's lips pursed as he smirked at her. "Though it gets more use when I loan it to mothers whose children don't listen."

"Good to know," Tilli teased.

"That won't be necess ... necess ... necessary?" Lili said, not entirely sure of the word. "I'm Mama's best helper."

"That you are," Tilli agreed.

"It's good she's got a wonderful helper like yourself. I wanted to be more like you, so I thought I'd come and help a bit," Felton said to Lili.

"Actually, I'm almost done gathering the apples. Why don't you show Mister Felton the garden, and I'll join you when I'm finished."

"Okay!" Lili grabbed Felton's hand.

"Whoa, not so fast there, Lady Lili." Felton laughed as he struggled to keep up with the energetic girl. He smiled back to Tilli, who smirked as she watched them go.

Lili led Felton through the garden, stopping along the many paths to point out her favorite things. There wasn't much she didn't point out, Felton noted, save for the scorched sections of the forest—a scarred reminder of the Battle of Galium.

She identified withered plants and explained how they would flower in various colors in the spring. She showed him which bushes produced which kind of berries. Lili even told him her favorite ones: blackberries, blueberries, strawberries, raspberries, huckleberries, griffinberries, and even a couple Felton had never tried. He was pretty sure she liked all berries.

The garden was larger than he'd realized, expanding far beyond what he'd seen from the entrance. As they explored the garden, he spotted the house along the wall. It was a small dwelling, covered in brown vines. He imagined it quite cozy in the spring when the vines were green and lively. It had a few windows overlooking the garden. A single door sat square in the middle. The house was built between two parts of the wall. Felton guessed there was a door on the outside as well.

Lili showed him an area of the garden near a great wide patch of blackened earth. Next to it were plants and bushes of all shapes and sizes.

"These are all the plants to make tea with," Lili said, no less enthusiastic than at the start of the tour. She listed off a dozen different teas, counting them on her fingers as she went.

She walked him to some of the taller trees in the middle of the vast garden. "This is where all the big trees are."

"I can see that," Felton said, scanning the large trees before him. "What are these ones for?"

"They're just really great for climbing," Lili said. "Except for Big Barth," she added, pointing at the largest one. Big Barth stood with a thick trunk and high branches, coated in brilliant red leaves. Felton could see it would be difficult to reach the bottom branches.

They soon reached a swath of trees that had already lost their leaves. Fallen leaves had been raked into heaping mounds, and Lili pulled the guard toward them. "This is the most fun," she said. "Watch this."

Lili jumped up and grabbed a branch above her. She swung her leg up and looped it over the branch before hoisting herself on top.

"Stand back," she called and then hollered, "Onward!"

Lili leapt from the branch. Experiencing a moment of panic, Felton's stomach leapt into his throat. Lili plunged into one of the heaping piles. Leaves exploded outward and fluttered away. Felton drew closer, scanning the pile for the girl.

"Woo!" she called as she jumped up, hands raised high, scattering more leaves. "You want to try?" she asked Felton, her blue eyes wide.

The dwarf roared a mighty laugh. He thought his outburst was more from relief that the girl was fine than her humorous offer. "I think I'll save that for another visit," he said.

Felton maneuvered to another of the piles and started swishing his cane through it. A *thunk* stopped him, and Felton curiously prodded the hard pile a couple of times.

"Oh, you found Tem," Lili laughed. "He loves sleeping under the leaves. He's the one that moves all the piles around."

Felton recoiled, taking several steps backward. "Let's go find your mama, yeah?"

They found Tilli stacking the last of the apple baskets into the cart she'd been preparing.

"I would have helped you with those," Felton offered as they came down the path.

"It's alright," she said with a bright smile. Sunbeams lit her hair like glinting gold. "Did you have a good tour?"

"Aye. We did."

"Yeah, Mama. I showed him everything!" Lili added.

"Oh, everything?" Tilli asked, looking to Felton, impressed.

The dwarf chuckled and shrugged.

"Did you show him the glass bubble?"

"Oh, no!" Lili cried. "I forgot."

"The glass bubble?" Felton asked.

"I'm so sorry, Mister Felton. I completely forgot."

"It's alright," he said.

"Yeah," Tilli said. "I'll take him over there now that I'm finished. Have you seen Tem?"

"Yeah," Lili said, giggling as she looked at Felton. The dwarf flushed. "We found him napping in the leaves again."

"He does love those leaves," Tilli said, tucking her gardening gloves into a pocket in her trousers. She caught Felton glancing over his shoulder to see if the tortoise was tracking him. "Come on." She chuckled. "I'll keep you safe from the big bad tortoise."

Lili giggled, and Felton squinted at her with faux disdain, which only made her giggle more. The little girl looked over the apples and grinned at him when she found one that looked particularly tasty to her. He couldn't help but smile back as he caught up to Tilli.

The woman guided him to an area of the garden that had been badly burned in the dragon fires. In the corner, he saw what looked like a glass bubble. As they drew nearer, he saw droplets of water gathered on the inside of the glass, making it shimmer with a billion refractions of light. Inside, a green plant grew. He thought he saw some yellow, too.

"What is this?" the dwarf asked, almost reverently.

"It's our glass bubble," Tilli said quietly, matching his tone. "When the dragon came, the fires spilled into the garden and melted a window we had next to the shed."

Felton hadn't seen a shed on his tour. He glanced about.

"Oh, the shed is gone," Tilli said. "I couldn't save it."

"So, you saved the garden from the fires all by yourself?" the dwarf asked.

"Well, as much as I could," she said, lifting a hand to indicate the charred area around them. "I couldn't save everything."

"That's mighty brave of you," Felton acknowledged. He thought about how scary that night must have been for her.

"I couldn't just let it burn," she said.

"Why would you risk your life for a garden?" he asked.

A sudden haunt of sorrow shaded her countenance. "It was a gift ...." Her words fell away, and her blue eyes seemed distant for a moment. She shook it off. "Anyway, when I found this old window while I was cleaning up after the fires, I didn't think much of it. Truth be told, I worked around it for a while, until I noticed something growing underneath."

Tilli slid her fingers under one edge of the glass dome and lifted it, so Felton could see beneath it. A bright yellow flower in full bloom stood as strong as if it were the end of spring.

"What in Finlestia ...?" Felton murmured.

"My thoughts exactly," Tilli said. "I've been thinking about it a lot. I think the glass warms in the sun and turns the dew inside to rain." She wiped a finger along the inside of the dome and held it up. "I think it could possibly keep the plants warm and happy in all conditions. During some of the summer thunderstorms, this little guy was safe while other plants were battered."

"Very interesting," Felton said, genuinely intrigued.

"I was thinking. What if you could build a bigger one and cover even more plants? They could grow in the dead of winter—or at least that's my guess."

"Not a bad idea," Felton said. "Do you really think it could work?"

"Plants are resilient," Tilli said, lowering the glass. Her words came out with more excitement. "Many of them look dead through winter but come back full and healthy in the spring. But what if we could keep them warm and happy in the winter, too?"

Felton smiled at her enthusiasm, realizing where Lili had gotten hers.

She grinned back at him awkwardly. "Sorry. I get a little carried away."

"No. No," he said. "It's a great idea. I would be very curious to see how it works."

"Me too."

"If I can help somehow, I'd be glad to."

She smirked. "You going to be busy during the Fall Festival?"

Felton shrugged. "Apparently, I'll be judging pies. Something I can help you with?"

Tilli's blue eyes landed on him. "Oh, I can think of a few things."

CHAPTER 16
GLAD TO BE OF SERVICE

Felton gripped the ladder as it wobbled underneath him. "Steady now. Steady ..." he said nervously.

"Do you want to trade places, Mister Felton?" Waen called up to him.

It took everything in Felton to decline the teen's offer. If the elderly glasswright, Kinson, could get to the top of his ladder, shuffling up a wrapped pane of glass, then Felton could certainly do it. "No, lad. Just hold the ladder steady."

"I am," Waen replied, but the way the teen gawked at the inner workings of the mill with utter fascination didn't instill great confidence.

"Almost there," Kinson encouraged from above. He leaned on his ladder, propped next to Felton's—both tools leaning against the wall next to a high cutout.

The twirling gears and wooden machinery of the mill were louder than Felton had expected. He'd never actually been inside a windmill before and, like Waen, had been completely fascinated by the inner workings at first. By then, the noise of the milling stones and spinning parts gave him the sense that the world was abuzz around him, making him feel even less stable high atop the ladder.

"There you are, lad," old Kinson said, patting Felton on the shoulder.

Outside the rectangular cutout Warner Smith and Arth, the miller, were atop another pair of ladders, fastening some metal rails into place. Arth nodded to Felton with a kind smile, his long red beard blowing sideways in the wind. A large sail whooshed behind them, and Felton's heart dropped. A moment later another sail whooshed by. If he thought the movement inside the windmill was nerve-wracking, he couldn't imagine having the great sails whipping behind him.

"Thanks again, fellows," Arth said. "This is going to make clearing snow from the sails much easier. Your boy is a clever lad."

"Too clever sometimes," Warner joked. He finished mounting a long piece of iron and said, "Alright then. Let's place it."

"You ready, Felton?" Kinson asked, unwrapping the canvas that covered the windowpane.

Felton said nothing but nodded. He held tightly to his ladder with one hand and reached over to help Kinson with the heavy glass.

"Careful now," Enny Miller called from below.

"They've got it, love," Arth said.

"Only encouraging," she retorted. "I'll have some refreshments for you all after it's done."

"Not now, love," Arth called down inside the mill. He gave the others an embarrassed grin.

As the pair on the ladders got the glass pane through, the second duo helped with the weight from the other side. They maneuvered the pane into place, the designed notches slipping into their spots with an automatic ease. They swung the window inward, high above their heads, and Felton and Kinson held it there while Warner quickly inserted some metal pins.

"Go ahead and try the rod now," he said with a nod.

Felton gingerly released the window, leaving it to Kinson, hoping it wouldn't be too heavy for the glasswright. He grabbed the rod attached to the wall next to the window and slid the end of it into a designated notch on the metal frame around the window. Kinson slowly let go of the window. Everyone held their breaths.

When the rod held the window open, they all laughed.

"It works?" Waen called up to them.

"Aye," Felton called back, laughing. "It works, lad. Just like you drew it up. Well done!"

They enjoyed a celebratory lunch prepared by Enny Miller and their oldest son Dennez. The Millers were an odd dwarven family. It was not uncommon to see human families with half a dozen children running around, but the longer-lived dwarves tended to have fewer children, usually spread out over a greater span of years.

The fact that Enny had birthed six children in the span of ten years made them quite the oddity among their kin. Moreover, every single one of her children was a boy. So unordinary was their family dynamic, that it elicited good-natured jokes around the Garome District about "something powerful in the grain."

Felton was rather tickled by the mayhem. His father's family had been an example that pairs of twins were not unheard of among dwarven households.

Waen chased some of the little dwarven children, who scrambled away with playful squeals, giggling so hard they could barely breathe. Enny Miller talked feverishly with Warner about how his wife was doing and what they planned to do at the Fall Festival. Kinson spoke slowly with the younger dwarf, Arth, who kindly listened to the old glasswright reminisce about the days when his own family was young.

Felton sat quietly, taking it all in. On one hand, he felt like the odd dwarf out, as if he didn't belong in the company of such folk. On the other, he had a strange sense of peace sitting there with no pressing task or mission to complete. The two parts of him seemed at odds with each other, but he chose to lean into the side that allowed him to be present and enjoy the moment. As he sat there, he wondered if he could apply that mindset in all circumstances.

Enny turned to him. "Mister Felton, what kind of pie is your favorite? I know what Roey and Bend like. I'm curious to know your favorite."

Felton's features scrunched. "Oh, are Roey and Bend the other judges for the pie contest?" He had assumed they would be baking pies to compete.

"Aye," Enny said with a disbelieving chortle. "Wouldn't be much of a contest if the district baker and tavern owner were allowed to enter. The rest of us folk wouldn't stand a chance."

"I suppose not," Felton admitted.

"Don't let her fool you," Arth said humorously. "She's been trying to win that pie contest for years. Her pies are good, but they're not *that* good."

"Arth Miller!" Enny scolded him with a punch to the shoulder. Arth rolled with laughter. "See how much pie you get for a comment like that."

"Only teasing, love," he said through jovial tears. "Besides, if Mister Felton told you his favorite pie, you'd have an unfair advantage. And after all these years, is that really the way you want to win?"

Enny narrowed her eyes at her husband and scrunched her nose. "Fine." She exhaled.

"Thanks again for all the help," Arth said to them as they left to head back into the Garome District. He tapped Felton on the shoulder as the guard passed. "If you ever need anything, please stop by my shop in the district—whatever I can do. I really appreciate your help today."

"Just glad to be of service," Felton said.

He politely excused himself and caned quickly to catch up with his companions. Felton walked quietly beside them. Finally helping someone invigorated him, and he really was glad to be of service. The new window in Arth's windmill would make life much easier for the dwarf through the winter.

Winter! Felton suddenly remembered.

"Waen," he said, "I've been thinking about an idea that might help Tilli at the garden."

"Oh?" the teen replied curiously.

Kinson and Warner slowed to listen.

"Tilli showed me a glass bubble in the garden that melted during the dragon fire. The glass seemed to protect the plant underneath and even help it thrive. She was wondering what a bigger bubble could do. How would you build a small cottage of glass? Is that even possible?"

"Hmm ..." Waen thought for a moment, stroking his beardless chin. "Mister Kinson, would it be possible to make a glass bubble as big as a cottage?"

"No, lad. Tilli mentioned the glass bubble to me recently. I told her it was a wild accident in the fires, not something we can make. Not that big anyway."

"Hmm ..." Waen said thoughtfully. "Do you think we could stack windowpanes on top of each other?"

"I wouldn't advise it ..." Kinson hemmed.

"What if we made a skeletal structure of metal—something that could house all windows instead of wooden walls? Build the skeleton of the place with metal and insert grooves just like we did for Mister Miller's?"

"Could that really work?" Felton asked.

Warner clicked his tongue, his eyes far off as though he were trying to make sense of something. "Could be ..."

"The windows would be smaller, easier to work with. Easier than making a glass wall. Stronger too. Then she'd also be able to open them to let the fresh air in," Kinson reasoned.

"Aye, during the summer. She'll want to keep them closed in the winter," Felton said.

"Will have to keep the snow off in the winter, too," Waen added. "If the skeleton wall works, couldn't we do the same thing for the roof?"

"Perhaps," Warner said quietly.

"Do you think this is something you three can help me with? Maybe keep it a secret—a surprise even?" Felton shrugged.

"For Miss Tilli? Anything." Kinson said.

The old glasswright's eagerness surprised Felton.

"Yeah," Waen said warmly. "Miss Tilli may be the nicest woman in town."

"I've noticed that," Felton said quietly.

"Always brings me tea when I'm not feeling well," Kinson said.

"Ma says Miss Tilli brings new herbs for Bend to test at the bakery all the time as well."

"Right shame. A lovely lady like that out in the garden alone ..." Kinson said with a soft whistle and a shake of his head.

"What happened to her husband?" Felton asked.

"Got sick and died some years back. Bought her that garden cottage before he died. Sad thing, really."

"That is sad," Felton said, a pressure squeezing his heart.

"Should have seen it when she and Lili moved in. The whole garden has flourished with them there. Tilli brightens up the place."

"I'd say she brightens the whole district," Waen said whimsically.

Felton smirked at the smitten teen. He couldn't begrudge the young man; Tilli was a lovely woman. The dwarf glanced over at Warner who'd been rather quiet. "What are you thinking, Mister Smith? Can it be done?"

"Perhaps ..." he said slowly. "Waen, let's build a test model and see if it can work."

The teen's step stuttered, and he looked at his father in surprise. "Of course, Pa."

Warner's face betrayed a slight smirk as he turned back to Felton. "When do you want to get this done?"

"We have to get it set up soon." Felton breathed through his teeth. "Needs to be in place before winter."

"We'll have to work fast," Warner said to Kinson.

The old dwarf bobbed his head toward Waen. "Let the boy figure it out, and you two get me the measurements. I'll worry about the glass."

"How are you going to keep her away from the garden long enough for us to build it and surprise her?" Waen asked.

Felton chuckled and said, "I've got an idea."

CHAPTER 17
FALL FESTIVAL

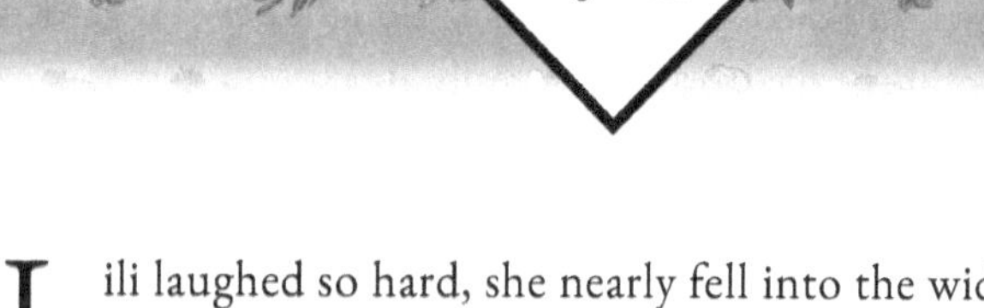

Lili laughed so hard, she nearly fell into the wide barrel they gathered around. Felton huffed and puffed, trying to catch his breath. Water poured from his beard like a great waterfall.

"It's not as easy as it looks, lass," he spluttered to the hysterical little girl.

"You can do it!" she cheered him on.

He shook his head and stared over the wobbling surface of water. Crisp red apples floated along, eluding his greatest efforts. An apple bobbed below him, taunting him. He plunged, face-first, after the piece of fruit. The apple dipped under the water, rolling away from him. He chased it with his nose, attempting to nudge it toward his mouth.

Lili burst into another cackling fit as he reemerged, sopping wet.

"You think it's so easy, you try it," Felton poked back.

Lili pressed herself against the edge of the wide barrel. She leaned over the apple she'd pinpointed as her target. Felton watched, expecting her to plunge into the water and surface as wet as he had. Instead, she bent low toward the apple and opened her mouth wide, revealing her smile with four missing teeth.

She'd made a point to tell the dwarf four were missing since she'd lost another one a few days prior. "Mama said it's a sign I'm growing up to be a lady," she'd told him.

The focused child leaned down slowly and plucked the apple up from the surface, not even dipping her nose.

"Tada!" she mumbled.

"Shave me," Felton exclaimed. "You've practiced that in the garden!"

Lili exploded into maniacal laughter.

Felton closed in on her and squeezed the remaining water out of his big brown beard, splashing her. She squealed and ran, not losing her gap-toothed grin.

Tilli appeared behind Felton and asked, "She beat you again?"

"She beats me at all the games," Felton grumbled.

Tilli chuckled. "Just got all the pumpkins set, now I can spend the rest of the festival with you two."

"Sounds good to me," Felton said. "Hey, Sprout, why don't you give me a little bite of that apple, since I didn't win one?"

Lili approached cautiously, eyeing the guard's thick beard, trying to discern if it were dry or if he could use it against her again. "Okay ... but just a little bite."

She extended it to him, and Felton took the biggest bite he could muster from the apple, reducing it by a huge chunk.

"That was a huge bite!" she accused.

Felton laughed. "You want to see a huge bite?" he asked, faking as though he were going to take another.

"No!" Lili said, swiping at it.

"I thought we were sharing it," he teased.

"No, you have to win your own apple."

Felton gave it back to her, and they all laughed as Lili inspected the bite with awe.

The Fall Festival had come together over the past week. Folk from all over the Garome District had helped with the festivities. There were games and contests set up for the more playful types. Lili convinced Felton to try many of them. After losing most of them to her, he was pretty sure she'd played them all before. For Felton, many of the sights and events at the festival were brand-new experiences.

People from nearby districts also joined the fun. Vendors sold all sorts of sweet treats. Tilli convinced Felton to try roasted pecans that were candied in some sort of sweetness.

"How do they do that?" he asked in amazement, his eyes widening as he grabbed a handful and shoved them in his mouth.

"Wait until you try the candied apples," Tilli told him.

"Well, I better be careful," Felton balked. "I still have to judge the pies."

They approached the area designated for dancing to listen to the local band play folk ballads.

A wagon rolled by, and Tilli spotted Warner, Waen, and Kinson guiding it. "Where are you three off to?" she asked.

Waen's eyes bugged, and he shifted uncomfortably. He stammered but no words of the common tongue—or any known language—could be discerned.

"We're making a quick delivery before we join the festivities," Kinson said in his gravelly voice.

"Oh, on the day of the festival?" she asked disapprovingly.

She rose to her tiptoes, trying to see what they carried in the wagon. Warner ruffled the burlap sacks they'd used to conceal all the parts.

"We'll be back soon," Warner said with a nod. "You all have fun."

"Well, that's too bad," Tilli said as they rolled away.

Felton caught the wink and gesture Warner shot his way. Tilli started turning back to see the wagon, but Felton grabbed her hand and said, "Wouldn't you know it, I love that song!"

"You do?" Tilli asked, squinting at him.

"Aye," Felton said, lingering to hear the song. He didn't recognize it, but the slow melodic song seemed good enough to his untrained ear. "I do owe you a dance, after all."

"I thought you couldn't with your ..." She hesitated, letting her eyes fall to his cane.

"Oh ... aye," he said sadly.

"Though I'm sure we could manage," Tilli said cheerily, grabbing his hand and dragging him into the dance area.

Felton realized all the dancers were holding each other close and swaying to the slow ballad. He flushed and hoped the bare patch of skin above his beard hadn't turned as red as Lili's apple.

Tilli smiled at him, her golden blond hair twisted up in her usual bun. She placed one hand on his shoulder and then grabbed his cane-less hand and placed it on her side. She rested her other hand on his other shoulder and swayed slightly with the rhythm of the music.

"See," she said. "Not so bad."

"Aye ..." Felton said quietly. His heart thudded in his chest as though it might pound right through his ribs. "Not so bad."

"I always thought this song was a little too ... romantic," she said.

"What?" Felton tensed.

"The Ballad of Lornawel and Verith?" she said with a chuckle. "Definitely. It's all about Verith pining for the love of his life for hundreds of years before finding a flower that opened his eyes. The flower just so happens to be braided into the hair of an elven princess. All very dramatic ... and romantic," she said, smirking at Felton.

Felton was pretty sure his eyes betrayed his horror. He had no idea what the song was. He was merely keeping her distracted while his companions conducted their secret mission.

Tilli continued to watch him as they swayed, her smirk cracking and growing into a wide grin. It took Felton a while to realize she might be messing with him. He cocked his head to the side, hoping to hear the lyrics better.

The bard sang:

The stars over Elderwood Forest
Shine like the rivers floweth,
Endlessly bright
Like the golden night.

Where would I choose if the choice were to
Find a new home without you?
Carry me home.
I'm never alone.

When the words registered in his mind, Felton was certain she was messing with him. "Shave me," he grumbled. "I thought you were serious."

Tilli barked a laugh. The mirth on her face brightened the world around them. She held him closer as they swayed. "Still a good song to dance to."

"Aye," Felton said softly. "That it is."

A warmth welled within him and rolled down his arms and into his thick fingertips resting on the side of the woman who made him feel … made him feel … well, he wasn't really sure how she made him feel.

The song ended, and an upbeat tune rang out as the band stomped on the makeshift stage the district had erected.

"Well," Tilli said quietly, taking a step back. "Thank you for the dance."

"Any time," Felton said.

Lili flew in from out of nowhere. "My turn!" she said, grabbing Felton's hand and dancing around him. He laughed and led her into twirls as she giggled and bounced. The guard glanced at Tilli who watched them with a pure joy Felton had rarely seen on anyone's face. He liked that look.

Wait until you see the surprise, he thought.

By the time the pie contest came about, Felton's co-conspirators had reemerged at the Fall Festival, mingling with family and friends as if they'd been there the whole time. Warner had given him an inconspicuous thumbs-up. When Waen made eye contact with him, the teen's face lit up with excitement.

Good, Felton thought. *Everything must have worked as planned.*

Tilli and Lili needed little convincing to stay at the festival for the duration of the pie contest. It was, after all, one of the most anticipated events of the year. The winner was granted a lovely blue ribbon rimmed with gold cording, artfully crafted by the local elven seamstress, Melwin. Aside from that, the winner would be the talk of the district for the rest of the year.

Felton had not realized how great an honor it was to be a judge for the contest until he saw the gathered crowd of people. He hadn't even realized there were so many people in the Garome District. Of course, many were probably from the neighboring districts. The mass crowd initiated a nervous thumping in his chest. He could stand before warriors and deliver a valiant and inspiring speech before they rode into battle, but this …

Thankfully, Roey took the lead, speaking over the gathered crowd. She explained there were dozens of pies entered into the contest they'd be judging. She introduced Bend the baker, who waved to the crowd's cheers before taking his seat at the table on the stage. When she introduced Felton, panic struck him, and his mouth dried.

Tilli's eyes locked with his, and she motioned as though he should wave to the roaring crowd. Lili quickly joined her mother's efforts, waving at him. Felton raised a tentative hand, and the crowd got even louder. His nerves had clogged his ears, making him feel as though he had water in them. Felton heard nothing Roey was saying. Soon Tilli discretely motioned her head toward the table as though he should sit, Lili pushing her hand out to indicate the same.

His body started working again, and he sat down sheepishly, leaving the center seat at the table for Roey.

The contest was quite the affair. Lana Smith was asked to facilitate the contest, another person deemed too skilled at baking craft to compete. She lifted the first pie for the crowd to see. Oohs and aahs rippled across the gathering before excited whispers rolled out.

"This is a blueberry pie," she announced before setting it on the table for the judges to see.

Felton thought it a lovely looking pie. The crust had been cleverly cut into strips and crisscrossed over the top. Roey and Bend immediately started scribbling notes on the parchment before them. Noticing that, Felton wrote on his own.

Blueberry pie number one. Pretty.

Lana cut slices for each of them, placing a small triangle of pie before them. It smelled good, too. Felton thought back to what

Aunt Cleary had said—something about half the taste is smell. That boded well for this pie. He scribbled another note.

Smells good, too.

When he took his first bite, a burst of flavors enveloped his tongue. The juicy blueberries were sweet with a hint of tang. The buttery pie crust brought moisture back to his mouth like a breaking dam. Felton gobbled the slice down and scribbled another note.

Delicious.

Lana displayed and announced the next pie and placed it before the judges. Felton realized his notes might need to be more detailed. That pie was also pretty. It also smelled good. And as he tasted it, the pie was also delicious. Halfway through that triangle, he realized the other judges had only taken a bite of theirs.

Roey leaned over to him and whispered, "You're going to want to slow down—lots of pies to try. If you eat every piece, you'll be sick by the fourth slice."

"Oh," Felton whispered, glancing over to the side table where Lana was grabbing the next pie. He hadn't considered what eating dozens of slices of pie would feel like, but he could imagine. "Thanks," he said.

"You'll get the hang of it," she added with a wink.

The pies continued across the judges' table with no end in sight. They tried huckleberry and blueberry and strawberry and griffinberry pies. There was even one called a razzleberry pie, which, Roey explained, had raspberries and blackberries and blueberries all in one pie. Finally, Lana announced the last berry pie, and Felton glanced over to the pie table, still half-full. His eyes widened, and he adjusted in his seat, puffing his cheeks and blowing out air.

"Might want to loosen your belt." Roey chuckled.

On to the fruit pies they went. They tried cherry and apple and peach and pear and mince pies. One surprising flavor for Felton was pumpkin pie. It didn't look much like the others. It appeared orange and mushy, with no top crust. The guard found it surprisingly delicious, though. The bite was creamy and rich, sweet with a little spice, the crust crumbling perfectly. He made a note.

Really like this one.

When three more pumpkin pies found their way in front of him, he cursed himself for not being more specific with his notes.

After they completed the fruit pies, Felton was glad to see they were in the final stretch.

A surprise meat pie came next—its savory flavor a welcome relief from all the sweetness they'd had. A sweet potato pie came after that, followed by a tart rhubarb pie that made his mouth pucker. When the next rhubarb came, he was hesitant to try it, though his obligation and duty as a judge won out. He found that one to have a much better balance between the sweet and sour.

The final pie was a curious one. It was brown and covered in nuts. Lana Smith had announced it as a pecan pie. After trying the roasted pecans earlier, Felton was intrigued by the last entry. Though he was certain even one more bite of pie would make his belly burst.

His bite of the slice was thick and buttery with a soft crunch. His eyes lit up as though he'd never known such wonder existed in all of Finlestia. Despite his bursting seams, he shoveled another quick bite into his mouth—just to make sure. To his surprise, his fellow judges also moaned with delight, each taking second bites themselves.

"Have you ever tasted anything like this?" Felton asked Roey.

"No," she said softly, turning to ask Bend the same.

The baker shook his head in response, licking his lips with utter happiness.

Their whispered deliberations were short-lived. Roey did a good job giving every pie its due discussion, but ultimately, they came back to the pecan pie, something Bend hailed as new and inspired.

"While there were many great entries in the pie contest this year," Roey announced to the rambunctious and waiting crowd, "we believe that one of the pies has distinguished itself above the rest." Lana handed Roey a note that told the halfling who the baker of the pecan pie was. Roey chuckled before continuing. "The winner of this year's pie contest is none other than the pecan pie made by our very own Missus Enny Miller!"

The crowd erupted into raucous cheers. Enny had a baby dwarf strapped to her with a sling and stood in shock. Arth patted her on the shoulder, exclaiming that she'd actually won. It took some coaxing, but eventually, the folks around her convinced her to move up to the stage to accept her award. She stood stunned before the crowd as Roey gave her the huge blue ribbon. Arth and their kids hooted and hollered loudest of all.

Felton congratulated her. "Your pie was *that* good!" he said with a chuckle.

"Thank you," she breathed, barely able to get the words out. "Don't suppose Arth will be able to tease me about my pies anymore!"

Felton laughed. "Go easy on him. He's cheering louder than the whole crowd."

Enny looked out and saw her husband, a little dwarf on his shoulders. The miller was patting others around and pointing up at her, exclaiming, "That's my wife!"

The champion baker shook her head and grumbled, "I do love that man."

As the festivities wound down, Felton offered to walk the Marigold ladies back to the garden. They happily accepted the invitation, glad to stroll home together in the cool evening.

Lili opted to hold Felton's thick hand, hers tiny in his. The sweetness of the act made his heart feel as though it were melting. As much fun as the little girl had at the celebration, he'd had just as much with her. There had been many weeks where Felton had wondered if he would ever have fun again. Being dragged around the Fall Festival by the little lady had proved he could.

Then there was the dance with Tilli. The nearness with which they swayed. Her lack of discomfort or awkwardness with his bum knee holding him back. The way she joked and smiled with him. He would not soon forget those moments.

The soft tapping of his cane on cobble was rhythmic, the only sound in the darkness as they walked back to the garden, exhausted. Eventually, Lili let out a big yawn, and Felton hoisted her into his arms to carry her. Her little human frame was heavier than he'd expected, but he simply leaned into his cane for more support as they walked.

Tilli pressed together an amused smile as quiet snoring soon seeped from the little girl's mouth. Drool also trickled out, wetting Felton's shoulder. Tilli offered to take the snoozing girl, but Felton shooed her away, a sweetness welling in him that he'd never experienced. He wouldn't trade the cuddle away for anything.

When Tilli started down the street on the outside part of the garden wall toward the house door, Felton whispered after her. "Let's go through the garden."

"Are you sure?" she asked, nodding toward the girl, whose sleeping form had become entirely dead weight at that point. "It's quicker to the cottage this way."

"Aye," Felton replied. "But this way I get to see the garden under moonlight."

"Alright," she said, giving in.

"Plus," the guard added with a chuckle, "I get extra cuddles."

"Yeah, but your cloak may feel like you've been out in the rain," she teased.

They stifled their laughs, not wanting to wake Lili. As deeply as she was snoring, Felton was pretty sure nothing would wake her.

"Besides," he said. "I've got a surprise for you."

"A surprise?" Tilli asked, her face scrunching. "What are you up to?"

"You'll see," Felton whispered.

"You know, I'm not really a notorious criminal, right? You don't have to set some elaborate trap to capture me."

Felton chuckled and insisted, "You'll see."

On they walked through the garden, Felton's heart thumping in his chest. He wasn't sure if he was excited or nervous.

CHAPTER 18
HOUSE OF GLASS

Tilli gasped, dropping the sack of leftover apples she'd been carrying. Several of the apples escaped the hold of the sack, rolling along the dirt path.

Felton marveled at the house of glass as well. It wasn't as big as the cozy cottage nearby—more the size of a large shed. The glass glinted like silver in the moonlight. The structure's black iron skeleton gave it an elegant look. The dwarf's shoulders dropped back, and he nodded, his mouth agape. His co-conspirators had outdone themselves.

"How in Finlestia ...?" were all the words Tilli could string together.

"Do you like it?" Felton asked, sidling up beside her.

"I love it ..." Lili mumbled, rousing from her nap and lifting her head. "What is it?" she asked, rubbing her eyes.

"It's a glass house," Felton said to her, pointing with his cane.

"Pretty," she said through a yawn and laid back on Felton's shoulder. Her soft snores continued as though she had never said anything.

"Come on," Felton whispered excitedly to Tilli. "Don't you want to see the inside?"

He paused and looked back to the woman. Her eyes were glossed, and she stood still, as though she were unable to move.

"Tilli?" Felton asked softly, taking a couple of steps back toward her.

"You did this?" she asked, a quaver in her voice.

"Well ..." Felton hemmed. "Waen came up with the idea of the metal framing. And of course Kinson and Warner helped make all the materials. The three of them assembled it while we were at the festival today."

Tilli shook her head.

Felton smiled at her. "Come on," he prompted gently.

The woman nodded and managed a slow pace toward the glass house. Felton noticed a parchment pinched in the door. He chuckled and said, "Mind getting that?" He shrugged helplessly under the weight of the snoring Lili.

Tilli pulled the door open, snagging the parchment before it fell. She unrolled it and read aloud. "Dear Miss Tilli. Thank you for your kindness. You make our district brighter by your mere presence. We hope you love your new glass house. Fill it with all your wonderful plants and make it green. Maybe we can call it a greenhouse." She paused to chuckle. "With much affection, Kinson, Warner, and Waen. P.S. This was all Felton's idea."

Felton sensed the blush rising in his cheeks.

Tilli's eyebrows danced, and she bit at her lip as if she weren't sure how to feel.

"I ... I may have come up with the idea but ..." Felton started to explain.

Tilli huffed a laugh and said, "Thank you. This is ... thank you."

They lingered around the beautiful greenhouse—as they called it, liking the name the others had come up with. Eventually, Tilli led Felton into her cottage. He was grateful. As much as he enjoyed Lili's sweet cuddles, she was getting heavy in his arm.

As they entered, Felton glanced about in awe. The cottage was full of potted plants, many of them atop miscellaneous furniture or tables. Tilli weaved between potted plants on the floor with a natural ease, knowing the route intimately. Felton followed carefully, doing his best to avoid the plants. She led him to a small room with a tiny bed, covered in richly colored quilts and knitted blankets—one of which looked oddly familiar to Felton, though he couldn't quite put his finger on why.

Felton tucked Lili in nice and tight, brushing her strawberry blond hair out of her face. Her snoring quieted, though she let out long, slow breaths, a sign she was peacefully asleep.

He crept out of the room and swung the door closed as quietly as he could, finding Tilli pacing the living area. As if the woman had suddenly remembered something, she stopped and quickly gathered bottles and jars from the low table in the center of the room. She hurried them over to a shelf filled with a myriad of similar jars that stood almost to the ceiling. Felton stepped closer and noticed they were all marked with different names. Many he didn't recognize, while others he knew to be herbs and spices his Aunt Cleary used for cooking.

"I'm sorry about the mess," she said, quickly turning and gathering more jars. "We don't often have visitors."

"It's alright," Felton said, honestly not concerned. "Though it seems to me you may need some help moving plants to the greenhouse," he mused, his eyes scanning the many plants which covered almost every flat surface.

She stopped tidying. She hadn't met his eyes since they'd come into the cottage, and he wondered if he had overstepped with the greenhouse.

"What you did ..." she whispered. "That's the nicest thing anyone has done for me in a very long time."

"Glad to be of service," Felton said humorously.

"No," she said, stepping closer to him and letting her eyes finally meet his. Her blue eyes seemed even bluer, glossed over as they were. "You ... thank you."

Felton pressed his cane into the floor and stepped closer to her, hating to see the tears. He reached out his hand toward her arm, and she leaned into his touch. "Ah, well ... you're very welcome."

Her body jittered as she inhaled.

"I didn't mean to make you upset," he said, taking one more step toward her. An odd heat rose between them—something he had never felt before.

She enveloped him in a hug and allowed her tears to flow. She did not sob or cry out. She merely held him close for a long time. Felton breathed in her lavender scent, glad to accept her affection. After they'd embraced for a long while, she pulled away slightly and leaned in to plant a quick kiss on his cheek.

If it weren't so dark, Felton was sure she'd see his cheeks as red as the fieriest tomato.

"Thank you," she whispered.

"Of course," he stammered.

"Suppose you might know someone who could help me move some plants into the greenhouse tomorrow?"

Felton chuckled. "I just might."

WINTER

CHAPTER 19
HEAVY SNOW

The first snowstorm of winter descended upon the city of Galium like an avalanche. Thick ominous clouds gathered over the peaks of the Drelek Mountains to their north and dumped mounds of snow on the city for several days straight.

When the sun eventually broke through the clouds again, the children of the Garome District relished in the thick fluffy powder, playing and tossing snow with excitement. The adults were less enthused. Several banded together with shovels, clearing paths down the main street and toward the entrances of shops, apartments, and homes. Others worked with the woodsman from the next district over to carry bundles of firewood to Garome homes in need. Felton found himself among the second group of helpers.

The week following the storm had seen little activity from the people and more snow piling on in spurts. Once again, Felton found his guard duty to be lacking any particular opportunity to protect or serve, save for the limited wood bundles he delivered.

One morning he was walking along his patrol route, gingerly planting his cane and stepping with caution to avoid slipping, when he heard a scream. He hurried around a corner to find a lovesick young couple. The man threw a playful snowball at the young woman, who called him "a brute" through her wide grin. He flashed her a roguish smile of his own before sweeping her into a kiss. Felton shook his head and continued his patrol.

He'd seen Tilli a few times at *Roey's Tavern* and made a special point to visit Lili in the cottage at the garden every couple of days. He'd even made a special delivery from Aunt Gael. The strange orange and purple knitted cap was not the most attractive thing he'd ever seen, and to his estimation, it appeared far too small for even Lili to wear. But he would take any excuse to visit the Marigold ladies.

When he delivered the handmade item, Felton learned it was intended for Templeton. The tortoise had greatly appreciated the moving of most of the house plants into the greenhouse. He had much more room to lounge inside the cozy cottage and spent the majority of his time burrowing beneath blankets next to the hearth and taking long naps.

The cottage was also much warmer and more inviting. With most of the plants moved to the greenhouse, the dwelling looked less like a jungle and more like a well-loved home.

Felton had spent many days there playing games with Lili or reading stories to her, even telling her some of his own. He chatted on the couch with Tilli, enjoying her presence.

Every time he visited, he inspected the bottles and jars, noting that Tilli had reorganized them in some fashion or another. There was a warmth about the place that made him miss it when he wasn't there. Thinking of the ladies as he patrolled, Felton thought it might be time to stop by the tavern for lunch—and maybe to see Tilli.

He turned and ambled toward *Roey's,* waving to Enny Miller who was rotating a sack of flour in the Millers' storefront. The window next to theirs still looked disheveled. The slanted roof kept the snow on the outside, but the place seemed a sad sight since it had not been taken over by a new store owner.

A sudden creaking and a loud snap diverted Felton's attention down the street. Others in the street looked toward the tavern curiously and murmured. With a sickening crack, half the tavern's roof collapsed in on itself beneath the growing weight of the piling snow.

Felton rushed toward the tavern, somewhat galloping in the closest thing he'd come to a run since his injury. Several others arrived at the tavern entrance before him, pulling the doors open and pouring inside. Felton glanced about the interior. Sunlight spilled into the tavern through a wide opening in the ceiling. Snow powdered everything. A large bank sloped on one side.

"Tilli!" Felton called. "Where are you?"

"Urfff ..." he and the others heard near the bar.

They rushed over to find a beam had fallen and crashed atop the end of the bar. A slight hand pushed at the snow on the bar as Roey pulled herself upright, her other hand pressed to her head.

"Are you alright?" Felton asked her quickly.

"Fine, fine," Roey moaned. "Just got a knock to the head is all."

"Where's Tilli?" Felton asked frantically.

"I ... I don't know," Roey said slowly.

"I'm here," Tilli called from behind a huge pile of debris and snow.

Felton hobbled toward her, gathering a couple others to help him shift some broken parts of the roof. He found Tilli sitting near the wall, examining herself. He knelt beside her, pawing at her shoulders and conducting his own inspection.

"Are you alright?" Felton asked, worried.

"Yeah. I'm alright," she said with a weak smile. "No major injuries."

Felton squeezed her into a hug.

She chuckled under his embrace but melted into him.

"You okay, Roey?" Tilli called out.

"I'll live," the halfling called back. "You?"

"Alive as well."

"Good. Guess I should have gotten the roof fixed after the fires."

"Looks that way."

Felton shook his head at their nonchalant interaction. "Was the tavern affected by the dragon fire?" he asked.

"This whole wall had to get repaired," Tilli explained. "Thought the roof seemed alright, but the smoke must have done more damage than we realized."

Felton helped her to her feet, and Tilli called over to Roey again. "Might have to close the tavern for a bit."

Roey barked a laugh. "I think you might be right."

Others in the place chuckled along, though out of humor or relief that no one had been seriously hurt ... who could say?

CHAPTER 20
GRATITUDE

Felton spent a couple days doting on and ensuring that Tilli was, indeed, fine. He'd been so worried that she might have suffered some unseen injury that he visited the garden cottage every day.

Tilli assured him she was alright, though she didn't mind if Aunt Cleary wanted to keep sending delicious meals. He'd brought the Marigold ladies something Aunt Cleary called jambalaya—a dish she said would warm them up. He'd stayed and shared supper with them that night.

Finally convinced Tilli was going to survive, Felton trudged into the city headquarters to report on the Garome District to Captain Bradnir. He discovered similar incidents had happened in other districts around Galium—another side effect of their encounter with the dragon.

By the time he was done at headquarters, it was far too late and cold for Felton to return to the Garome District. He decided to get a room at *The Hungry Hog*. He hadn't visited since his unfortunate incident during the summer, when he'd slept facedown on a table. He hoped to display a more respectable side for Tullen.

To Felton's great excitement, Sergeant Grisham was there, relieving more unwary warhog riders of their coin. To the chagrin of naive riders awaiting their chances to take on the old dwarf, the sergeant removed himself from the champion's seat and joined Felton at an empty table. Tullen swung by with an ale for Grisham and eyed Felton pleasantly.

"Nice to see you, Felton," the barkeep said. "A mead for you?"

"Maybe an ale this time." Felton chuckled.

Tullen winked at him. "That I can do."

"Oh, and Tullen?"

"Aye?"

"I'd like a bed this time if you have any open."

"I think we can do that, too."

Grisham took a swig of ale and slammed it on the table. "Felton! How are you, my friend?" He clapped a hand on the guard's shoulder.

"I've had a strange time since last we sat in this place together," Felton said honestly.

"Been strange times all over," Grisham grumbled.

"How do you mean?"

"With the garvawk warriors training and readying for deployment."

"What?" Felton's brows furrowed.

"Oh, ye haven't heard," Grisham said, glancing to either side to make sure no one could hear him.

Tullen popped up out of nowhere and slid an ale across the table to Felton before slipping away to another patron.

"Haven't heard what?" Felton pressed, gripping the mug in his hand.

"I don't know if I should rightly be telling ye this," the sergeant murmured.

"Grisham," Felton said, "I'll be back with the garvawk warriors as soon as my leg heals and they find a new garvawk. You're not telling me anything out of place."

"Well ..." Grisham said slowly. Felton's determined glare gave the sergeant no space to back out. The older man leaned over the table to keep his voice low. "Remember hearing about the attack on the orc city of Calrok?"

"No," Felton said, narrowing his eyes in disbelief. Last he heard, the men of Whitestone and the orcs of Calrok had formed an alliance.

"Where have you been?"

"I ..." Felton thought for a moment, but he didn't know how to respond. Instead, he said, "Keep going."

"Well, the men of Whitestone went to aid the orcs of Calrok against an attack from Kelvur."

"Kelvur?" Felton asked incredulously, thinking of the mysterious land beyond the Gant Sea.

"Aye. The king of Whitestone led the Griffin Guard into the battle himself. Meanwhile, some of the king's friends, including the orc gar of Calrok, were kidnapped and taken across the sea to Kelvur!"

"Shave me ..." Felton uttered, struggling to believe such a wild tale.

"Yes," Grisham pressed. "What's worse, apparently, they sent a Griffin Guard squadron across the sea to save them. They fought in some battles, and now the king of Whitestone has asked King Thygram if he'd send the garvawk warriors out to Whitestone. Our good king said, 'yes.' Apparently, they're assembling the largest allied force ever to sail across the sea and battle a wicked sorcerer and his minions."

"That can't be," Felton said, unable to pry his contorted gaze from the sergeant.

"Aye, it is, my friend. Captain Qwen relayed it to me herself."

Felton sat across the table from his old friend, stunned. A myriad of emotions bubbled within him, and he couldn't seem to sort them. This would be the first time his old unit went to battle without him. He should be there. He should be going with them. He should be …

He was acutely aware of the weight of the cane leaning against his leg.

Flames raged across the sky, spouting like fire from the depths of Malkra. Felton patted Honor on the shoulder, and they dove away from the dragon that chased them.

"Mud and shale!" Felton swore as they dipped under the dragon's reaching claw.

The dragon roared and swerved after another garvawk warrior. Felton and Honor turned and gave chase. They flew with great effort and speed, swerving to evade the spouts of flame erupting around them.

They couldn't catch the dragon. The beast was impossibly fast.

Dread filled Felton—a warm tingling running up from his legs and a sourness churning his gut. He could not save his friend … his friend … who was it?

His vision zoomed and focused on the garvawk rider desperately fleeing the deadly dragon. Grisham screamed as the great beast opened its maw and clamped down, devouring the sergeant.

"No!" Felton roared, reaching as far as he could in a desperate act to save his friend. His garvawk disappeared, and he plummeted toward a spraying fountain of fire.

Felton hit the wooden floor hard, landing on his shoulder and the side of his head. It took him a long while to realize he was in the room Tullen had rented him. Felton panted and cursed under his breath as he wiped the sweat from his face.

A knock at the door jarred him. His whole body tensed, and his heart pounded. Another knock resounded, and a voice spoke through the door.

"Felton, are you alright in there?" a groggy sounding Tullen asked.

"I'm ... I'm fine ..." Felton managed.

There was a long pause before Tullen spoke again. "I'm going to come in, alright?"

"No. It's alright," Felton croaked, trying to release himself from the net of blankets that tangled him on the floor.

Tullen opened the door anyway, a candle in his hand. He held the flickering flame away from his braided white beard. His eyes fell upon Felton, who had given up the fight against the blankets.

To Felton's surprise, the old dwarf's eyes didn't seem judgmental or laced with pity. Instead, they were soft and kind.

Tullen slowly moved across the floor and knelt next to him. "It's okay to not be alright sometimes," he said softly, looking into the guard's eyes.

"I think I need some help," Felton choked out. He could no longer hold in the flood of tears that flowed down his face.

"We all need a little help sometimes," Tullen said, pulling at the tangled mess of blankets to release Felton. "Come. Let's make some tea."

Felton watched silently as Tullen poured steaming liquid from the kettle into a pair of mugs behind the bar. The old dwarf twirled, placing the kettle on the stovetop before grabbing the mugs and returning to Felton. He set one of the steaming mugs before the guard and sat in the chair across from him, groaning as he settled. "There we go," the old dwarf said.

"I was hoping to not find myself in this position again," Felton said, a tone of apology in his voice. "Not that I dislike your company. I just wanted to present a more respectable bearing this time."

Tullen chuckled, carefully sipping from his steaming mug. "Aye. It's hard to keep up a pleasant demeanor while a war rages within."

Felton gulped quietly. The steam from the mug wafted into his face as he slowly inhaled its warmth. His heart had returned to its normal cadence. "I just don't know why I keep having these night terrors," he finally relinquished.

Tullen nodded thoughtfully, as if he knew what the younger dwarf were experiencing. "Dreams are difficult to control. And when you've seen the ravages of war ... your imagination runs wild."

"Are you saying my mind is broken? Will this never go away?"

The barkeep smiled patiently at Felton. "I wouldn't say broken. Broken things require repairs. This is something that requires tending."

"You mean like a garden ..." Felton said, thinking of Tilli and the garden in Garome.

"Aye. Like that—or like nurturing a child," Tullen said with a smirk and a glance toward some distant memories. "The more love you pour into them, the stronger they grow and the farther they steer from the wicked. It's kind of like oil and water. They don't mix. Pour enough of one in the cup and it pushes out all of the other. You've got to fill your cup with the right stuff."

Felton picked at the mug handle with his thumb. "So, you're saying if I can somehow fill my days with good, I can get rid of these night terrors once and for all?"

Tullen breathed deeply, smiled, and slowly released the air. "I would be lying if I told you they go away completely. I still have bad nights on occasion."

"You?" Felton asked. He'd never considered that the barkeep may have personal experience with the matter.

"Aye," Tullen said, lifting his arm to show Felton his tattoo. "You think I have this 3rd Cavalry tattoo for no reason?"

Felton huffed a laugh. "I suppose not."

"I earned it, just like you earned yours," the barkeep continued. "And just like you, I saw horrible things that are hard to unsee. Even more difficult than that is wading through the mire of your mind when you feel you're all alone."

Felton's eyes fell away from the barkeep's compassionate gaze. *Alone.*

No word had ever rung more true for the dwarf. He'd always known a certain brotherhood and comradery. Warriors who experience great hardship through training and battle together are forged in a mold that bonds them in a way that is, by its very nature, hard to describe. It's something to be known, not explained.

Recently, Felton found himself unable to be in the presence of his fellow warriors any longer. Tullen was right: the guard had never felt more alone.

"You don't have to wade through this alone," the barkeep said quietly.

"How have you done it?" Felton asked, gulping the lump that rose in his throat, hoping to also bury his rising tears.

"For one thing," the barkeep said, placing his mug on the table, "never believe that your best days are behind you. It's easy to feel buried under the burden and think you'll never be able to crawl your way out of the hole. Don't believe it for a second. I can sit here and tell you, it's just not true. There will be brighter days to come."

Felton shifted uneasily, adjusting the cane that leaned against his leg. "When?" he asked softly.

Tullen chuckled. "I asked that same question many times," he said. "The good news is, you don't need to know when—only that they will come."

"How can you be so sure?"

"I wasn't always," the barkeep said honestly with a shrug. "I've learned over time to focus on the little things I am thankful for. Small things like the sun on my face. Or flapjacks hot off the pan. Or the smile of my daughter. Or the way she hugs me. If you are willing to let gratitude for the small things well within, you'll be surprised at the magic it can produce in your life."

Felton allowed a weak smile to cross his face as he thought about the things for which he was grateful: Aunt Cleary watching him with anticipation as he tasted something she'd made with love. The way Aunt Gael made him laugh when she leaned in to fill him in on her wily ways. How Lili jumped around, throwing her fists into the air, when she beat him at a game. The way Tilli looked at him ...

"I imagine you can think of a few things," Tullen said, watching the younger dwarf process his thoughts.

"Aye," Felton whispered.

"And I imagine many of those have to do with folks who love you. You're not as alone as you might think, but you have to let them in so they can tend to you. You don't always have to present the respectable bearing. It's alright to need help sometimes."

"Thank you, Tullen," Felton said.

"Aye, lad. There is hope. I want you to know that," the old dwarf said. He stood and gathered their mugs into his hands, preparing to take them behind the bar. The barkeep's grin shifted, and his countenance morphed to a controlled sorrow. "Just promise me you'll never give up. I've seen and known too many who have. You've got more to you than you yet know."

"I promise," Felton assured the barkeep.

"Good," he said, turning behind the bar.

Felton rose, feeling much better than he had. As he strode toward the stairs that led up to the rooms, he turned back and called quietly to the old barkeep. "Tullen?"

"Aye?"

"What about the night terrors?"

"You can't be afraid of them," the old dwarf said. "They'll get less frequent sometimes and more at others, but you can't be afraid of them. You need sleep. It's your friend."

Felton lingered at the bottom of the stairs. "So, how do I beat them?"

"What are you grateful for?"

The dwarven guard paused for a long moment, realizing what the old dwarf was getting at.

"Thanks again, Tullen."

"Aye, lad," he said. "Flapjacks in the morning?"

"I look forward to it," Felton answered.

As he lay in the remade bed, Felton cracked the curtains and gazed at the stars far above. For a long while, he recounted the things he was grateful for, picking out even the smallest of items to add to the list. Before too long, fatigue swept over him, and he slipped into the best sleep he'd had in weeks.

CHAPTER 21
FAR FROM USELESS

Repairs to *Roey's Tavern* were slow going in the winter cold. Construction workers had their work cut out for them. Many buildings around the Garome District experienced extra strain under the heavy snows, and the residences took priority. As a result, repairs for *Roey's* fell to some of the local craftsman.

Felton discovered he wasn't much help around the tavern and decided it best for him to leave the space for those who had various skills that would be useful. Returning to his patrol made him feel even more useless, since most folks were inclined to hunker indoors as much as possible in the biting winter. He was surprised to hear someone call his name as he hobbled down the main street.

"Felton!"

He turned to see Tilli hurrying to catch him.

"I was just about to come out to the garden," he said pleasantly.

Tilli smiled at him and raised her eyebrows. "Oh, is that so? Missed me while you were gone reporting, did you?"

"Aye," Felton said, and for a second, he thought the woman blushed. Though it could have been the cold rosing her cheeks. "I mean ... I was coming to talk to you about something."

"Perfect," she said. "I was looking for you to talk about something, too."

"Oh?" Felton asked.

"Yeah, though maybe we can step inside?" she asked, her teeth chattering as she nodded toward *Bend's Bakery*.

Warmth and the smell of freshly baked bread enveloped them as they entered the building. Felton couldn't be sure what warmed him more, the aroma or the heat cycling through the building from the oven.

"Hello, you two," Lana Smith greeted them. "Something I can get for you?"

"Hello, Lana," Tilli said sweetly. "We were hoping to stow away in your toasty shop for a moment to chat."

"By all means," Lana said, a wry grin crept across her face as her gaze lingered on them. "I'll just be organizing some orders if you need anything."

"So, what can I do for you?" Felton quietly asked Tilli.

"No, please," she said eagerly, "you go ahead."

Felton took a deep breath. His heart thumped inside his chest, and he couldn't say why he was so nervous. He thought of Tullen and what the old veteran had told him. Felton cleared his throat and began.

"I had a friend tell me I should do a little better at sharing some of the things I've been ... working on ..." Felton paused for a long time. Tilli watched him sincerely, waiting for him to continue. *This isn't going well,* he thought.

"You mean your patrol?" she prompted, not understanding.

"No," Felton sighed. "I mean, like the things that I've been ... I don't know ..." he said, circling his hand in front of his chest to indicate his insides.

"Oh," Tilli said, "those things."

"Aye," Felton grumbled. "I just ... well, I've felt rather useless lately."

"Felton," she said, looking into his eyes, "you are far from useless."

The way she said the words made him believe she meant them. Her hand reached out and rested on his, which gripped the top of his cane.

"Besides, if you were, I wouldn't have chased you across the district to ask for your help."

"My help?"

The door behind the counter swung open and banged against the wall, startling everyone in the room. Felton and Tilli turned at the same time Lana Smith did, pretending she had not been watching their exchange.

Bend waddled out, carrying a large tray piled high with some sort of bread. He slid the tray onto the counter and noticed the two standing in the middle of the room.

"Mister Felton! Miss Tillinda!" he said excitedly. "Not been seeing a lot of folks coming to the bakery with the weather being so bad. Most folks come to pick up their regular orders and scuttle home through the snow."

"Aye," Felton said. "It's a bit cold out. Just wanted to borrow your heat for a moment to have a quick discussion."

"Well, your timing is marvelous," Bend said, beckoning them toward the counter.

Yours less so, Felton thought with a chuckle. *What is it Tilli needs my help with?*

Despite the unspoken words hanging between them, the pair moved to the counter, eyeing the mound.

"You've got to try this," Bend said, pulling a flat round bread from the pile and placing one on a small plate for each of them.

"What is it? They almost look like flapjacks." Felton said, poking at the soft circle. It had a little give to it, but it smelled and looked like bread.

"I call it flatbread."

"Flatbread?" Tilli asked curiously, as she took a bite of hers.

"Why would anyone want their bread flat?" Felton asked, not understanding the purpose of such a creation.

Before he could inquire further, Tilli lifted his off the plate and shoved it toward his mouth. Felton took a bite through a laugh while the woman's blue eyes bugged and she nodded and moaned with delight.

The guard soon understood why. The soft and chewy texture was not like any bread he had ever eaten. The slightly nutty flavor with savory undertones surprised the dwarf.

"Well?" Bend asked, elongating the word in anticipation.

"It's amazing," Tilli said through another full bite.

"Mmhmm," was all Felton could manage as he stuffed another bite into his mouth.

"See," Bend said, clapping his hands with glee, "not flapjacks—flatbread. Though I think I have an idea for something even flatter."

"What'll you call that one? Flatterbread?" Felton teased with a chuckle.

"If you don't like it, I can take it back," Bend said, extending his hand and fixing the guard with a faux glare.

Felton pulled his plate closer and slowly took another bite. "Flatbread is fine," he said. "And I think I'll take half a dozen back to my aunts."

"I'd be happy to pack that up for you," Lana said with a laugh.

When Bend and Lana started talking work and the woman followed the dwarven baker into the back, Felton and Tilli found themselves alone in the room, with warm bellies and joyful moods.

"Ah ... well," Felton stammered. "You were saying you might need my help with something at the garden."

"Oh, at the garden? No," Tilli said tentatively. "I was actually hoping you would be willing to go somewhere with me?"

"Go somewhere with you?" Felton asked quizzically.

"Yeah," she hemmed. "Like to Crossdin."

"To Crossdin?" He repeated her words again.

"If you don't want to, I completely understand. I know it's far. It's just, I haven't had a lot of time to go there since I've been so busy at the tavern. But with it closed for repairs ..."

Her words trailed off. She eyed him shyly—a characteristic he'd not previously seen in her.

Crossdin, by the Tandal Sea, was far away. It took two days by wagon during good conditions. Felton had been there a few times. While he was with the 7th Cavalry, they'd gone to the seaside city to mount patrols in the northwest section of the Drelek Mountains. The city had easier access and mountain passes to traverse the region.

"Why ... what do you need my help with?" he managed to ask.

"Well," Tilli said, "there's a seed store in Crossdin—unlike any here in Galium. I've been meaning to go and buy seed to resow the garden, especially in some of the burned areas. Since I won't be busy with the tavern for a while, I thought I could use the time to tend some new seedlings in the greenhouse. Before you know it, spring will be here. If I can get them started before, maybe they'll flourish even more when spring arrives."

"I see," Felton said. "But what can I do for you?"

"Well," Tilli hemmed, biting her lip, "I don't like to travel alone, and I thought you might like to go with me—keep me company and maybe help me with the seed."

Felton looked at the woman standing before him. Her blue eyes scanned the floor between them. *Is she afraid?* he wondered.

"Well, I ..." Felton started to say but caught himself.

Could he really go with her all the way to Crossdin? What about his duty to the rest of the Garome District as their guard? The notion was short-lived and replaced with fear. If they traveled that distance, they'd likely have to camp for a night along the way. What if he had a night terror? How would Tilli look at him if she knew he was afraid of his own dreams?

"You don't have to answer right now," she said quickly. "I won't be ready to leave for a couple of days. I did ask Aunt Cleary and Aunt Gael if Lili can stay with them for a few days while I travel."

"Oh ... good. Good," Felton said softly.

After a long silence, Tilli finally said, "Well, I better get back to the garden. I'll see you tomorrow, maybe?"

"Aye," Felton said. A heaviness descended upon him, as though his bones were filled with lead.

Tilli nodded to him with a sweet smile and left the bakery.

Felton stood still for a long time, wondering what to do. He wasn't sure there was a way to win in the scenario. If he said no, he'd be letting the woman down. If he said yes, he could possibly change her view of him forever.

"Mister Felton?" Lana asked softly, startling him out of his thoughts. She held up a small sack for him.

He walked over to retrieve it from her. As the guard turned to walk away, the woman added, "For what it's worth, I think you should go with her."

Felton turned a wary eye on the woman as he opened the front door. He paused in the doorway, and before he left, he mumbled, "Thanks."

CHAPTER 22
FRESH STARTS

Aunt Cleary hurried to the table and placed the steaming pot in the center before turning away and coughing into her handkerchief. Her cough had worsened over the past few days, but she'd insisted on cooking. That task and her tea, she said, were the only things that made her feel better.

Aunt Gael nudged Felton to dish some of the supper into bowls for them. As he scooped, the steam erupted from hidden pockets, releasing an enticing aroma. Red beans and rice and sausage and vegetables mixed with an intricate array of seasonings harmonized like an orchestra of flavors. Even when he did make it back to the garvawk warriors, Felton wasn't sure he'd be able to stay away from Aunt Cleary's cooking. He'd been rather spoiled on it since he'd been living with his aunts.

"So, Tilli tells me you'll be watching Lili while she's out of town," he said to neither of them in particular.

"Oh, yes, deary," Aunt Cleary said excitedly. "That little doll is so sweet."

"Aye. She is," Felton agreed.

"Smart as a whip, she is," Aunt Gael said. "When she was with us during the battle, I taught her to play some games. She took to it like a trout to the stream. Almost had me a couple of times. She'll be hustling the Castle Brick tourneys in no time." She laughed wickedly.

Felton realized why the little girl always beat him at games. She'd learned from the best. "Aye," he grumbled.

"When she was here earlier, Tilli was looking for you, deary. Said she was going to ask you to go with her," Aunt Cleary said before covering another cough.

"You alright?" Felton asked her for probably the hundredth time.

"Just a cold, deary," she assured him.

He glanced quizzically at Aunt Gael who shrugged.

"Alright," he said tentatively.

"So, you'll be going with her then," Aunt Gael stated more than asked, taking another bite of the delicious meal.

"I'm not sure …" Felton hesitated.

"What do you mean, deary? I thought it would be an easy choice," Aunt Cleary said, a puzzled expression on her face.

"Well, I have a duty to protect and serve the people of the Garome District, and—"

"Which is exactly why you should be going," Aunt Gael said bluntly.

"Well," Felton continued, "if I leave, how will I be able to perform my duties in the district?"

"You've been moping around here for weeks, saying there's nothing for you to help with," she said, eyeing him. "You were all excited to serve folks, since you weren't able to protect anyone. Then the snows came, and you couldn't even do that. I'm sure Mister Jack doesn't mind the help with firewood delivery, but I don't think that's what you had in mind."

Felton grimaced at the truth in her words. *Say what you want about Aunt Gael, but she tells it like it is*, he thought.

"And Tilli—," Aunt Cleary began but suppressed a quick cough. "Is a lovely woman."

Felton leveled his gaze at his aunt, unsure what her comment had to do with anything. He wasn't blind. Tilli was quite beautiful. He'd thought it nearly every time he'd seen her. And not only was she lovely to see, she was lovely on the inside, too. Felton greatly enjoyed being around the woman. In truth, he would love to go on an adventure to Crossdin with Tilli.

"Plus, she'll need protecting," Aunt Gael added.

"From what?" Felton asked, realizing the twins were teaming up against his reservations.

"Bandits, deary," Aunt Cleary said with a shiver.

"Bandits?"

"Aye," Aunt Gael said. "When we went to Crossdin for the battle, our wagoner told us tales of bandits on the road."

"Ghost stories," Felton said. "Reports of bandit attacks on the wagon road between Crossdin and Galium are few and far between."

"But they do happen," Gael said, raising a finger to emphasize her point.

"Plus, you can get some alone time with Tilli—get to know her better," Aunt Cleary added.

Felton rolled his eyes and shook his head as he scooped another helping into his bowl. His aunts were both motivated to get him out of the apartment for a little while, each with her own reasons. Aunt Gael was tired of his moping and thought he needed fresh air, while Aunt Cleary appeared to be setting him up for some fairy tale wedding she was envisioning.

Though he wouldn't admit it, he didn't dislike the idea of either, but the problem of his night terrors persisted. He planned to practice the gratitude exercises Tullen had given him, but Felton wasn't entirely confident he'd be able to control his dreams on the road.

"So, you'll go then?" Aunt Gael asked.

"You really should, deary," Aunt Cleary added.

Felton sighed deeply. "I'll think about it."

The next day, Felton went to see Tilli. When he arrived at the garden, Lili answered the door and jumped to hug him.

"Whoa," Felton laughed and caught her, nearly dropping his cane. "Good morning to you, too. You look bright and shiny this morning."

"I am," Lili said cheerily, taking Felton's knit scarf while he closed the door and attempted to clear the snow from his boots. "Mama and I are working in the greenhouse today. She wants to make sure I know how to care for the plants before your trip."

"My trip?" Felton asked. A pang of guilt stung him. He had planned to tell Tilli he couldn't accompany her to Crossdin.

"Yeah!" Lili said excitedly. "Mama said she asked you to go with her, and I get to have a sleepover with Aunt Cleary and Aunt Gael!"

"That does sound fun," Felton mused, imagining how Aunt Cleary would dote on the girl and what game tactics Aunt Gael would teach her so the younger Marigold could hustle him even more.

As if on cue, she added, "Aunt Gael is going to teach me some new games."

"I bet she is." He chuckled. "Where's your mother?" he asked, glancing about the cozy cottage.

"She's in the greenhouse. Told me to get dressed and meet her out there."

Felton looked the girl over. She was still in her pajamas with her hair a wild tangly mess. "You best get to it then," he urged.

Lili beamed and ran to her room.

The guard cautiously stepped through the house, feeling bad about his wet boots but knowing he would need them when he exited the back door. As he strode toward the door, he found Tem, standing rigidly in the hall. Felton paused, matching the tortoise's statuesque stance. Tem looked ridiculous. His legs were wrapped with knitted sleeves, like long socks without the feet. Atop his head was the horrendous purple and orange cap Aunt Gael had knit. Tem stared, unblinking, at the dwarf.

Felton shimmied toward the wall, slowly sidling past the creature. To his surprise, he saw Tem move for the first time. The tortoise moved no muscles in his legs. Only his head swiveled, his eyes never leaving the gaze of the dwarf as he inched by. Felton turned to locate the doorknob and spun back to get his eyes on the tortoise again.

"Ah!" Felton cried, jumping.

Tem stood inches away.

Felton fumbled out the back door and closed it behind himself, hoping the door would protect him. He breathed heavily, his heart still pounding in his chest.

How does he do that? the dwarf wondered.

He crossed the several feet between the cottage and the greenhouse on the narrow path Tilli had cleared through the snow. They'd have to put down some paving stones so it didn't get muddy next winter, Felton thought.

When he entered the greenhouse, his eyes lit up. He hadn't been inside for a couple weeks and was surprised to see how much growth had happened among the plants.

"Wow," he said, unable to contain his awe.

Tilli laughed and turned to him. "I was expecting Lili," she said. "The greenhouse is working even better than I thought it would!"

"I can see that," Felton said, sliding his fingers across a wide leaf that sprang from a rather boisterous plant.

"Come look at this," she said eagerly.

Felton walked through the greenhouse, marveling at the thriving plants. He leaned heavily onto his cane as he peered past Tilli's shoulder. "What have you got here?"

Tilli tended a strange-looking plant that grew in a straight stalk, a couple feet high, before it branched into a bulb at the top.

"This guy here was one of the plants caught in the fire areas," she explained excitedly. "I noticed it sprouting before winter and wanted to bring it into the greenhouse to see how it would do. It's been growing back better than it had been before the fires. I think the fires cleared everything above the soil, giving the bulb underneath a chance at a fresh start. I never expected growth like this."

"Are you saying the fire actually helped it grow?" Felton asked curiously.

"Looks that way," she said. "I guess it's kind of like people. Sometimes a fresh start is exactly what a person needs to grow greater than they ever could have before."

"Hmmm." Felton nodded thoughtfully, brushing at his thick brown beard.

"I'm glad to see you," Tilli said, turning her blue eyes on him. "Have you given thought to my … invitation?"

"Aye. I have," he said reluctantly.

Tilli's lips twitched as she awaited his answer. Felton's heart sank. He didn't understand her hesitance. What could she be worried about? He looked at her sweet face and the hope in her eyes. How could he tell her no?

As much as he worried about her seeing his weakness when they stopped along the way, there was always the chance he didn't have any night terrors.

He gritted his teeth before grinning and asking, "When do we leave?"

"Whenever you're ready," she said, a wave of relief crossing her face. She chuckled, though it seemed more a release of nervous energy than humor. "Don't suppose you know any good wagoners?"

Felton laughed as well. "I just might."

CHAPTER 23
ON THE ROAD

"Mighty lucky the timing worked out," the halfling wagoner said over his shoulder, his smoking pipe dangling from his lips. "Just took a few days off with the heavy snows. Get too much and you can't see a blooming thing out here. Just white. The sky, the land—everything white!" He paused to chuckle at something unseen. "Gets so white, you can't tell where the sky and land meet. Like a great white canvas. You two cozy enough back there?"

Tilli suppressed a laugh as Felton replied, "Just fine, thank you."

"Oh, good," Tobin said. "Not everyone takes their first ride with me in the middle of winter. Just want to make sure the lady is warm. You know I'm all about the wonderful journey experience. Did he tell you, my lady, how we met?"

"No," Tilli replied kindly, snickering again.

Tobin was as kind a halfling as there was, though he had enough words for a dozen of his kin. Felton shook his head with an amused smile, recognizing that Tilli was enjoying the game of spurring the halfling on.

The wagon bumped along as they traveled the trade road toward Crossdin. Tobin apologized regularly, noting that the ride was usually less bumpy. Ice and snow clumped together on the road to form ruts that forced them over bumps that were usually avoidable with the wagoner's skillful driving. The bumps were not uncomfortable but rather gave the wagon a calming sway.

Tobin had created a sort of blanketed nest in the back for them, arranging barrels of goods to shield them from the brisk breeze that occasionally swept across the road. Felton and Tilli were cuddled up cozily with heavy blankets. Between the blankets and their proximity to one another, the pair kept quite toasty.

So comfortable had the halfling made the ride that, despite his efforts to stay awake, Felton dozed off several times throughout the day. Once, he awoke from a startling dream that sent his body into tremors, as though the earth quaked around him. A gentle hand rested on his chest—Tilli hoping to calm him. When his brain caught up with his eyes, Felton realized she wasn't watching him with concern as he'd expected. Instead, she was half-turned toward the driver, engaging him in what seemed to be an enjoyable conversation.

"My daughter, Button, snores like a plains bear!" Tobin said. He let out a hearty laugh. "She gets it honest, she does. Her mother, my sweet, sweet Lenor, snores even louder! I think I'm the only one in the house that's quiet at night."

Tilli laughed. "Does your daughter do that thing where she falls asleep on her face with her hind end up in the air?"

"Yes, so cute that!" Tobin agreed cheerily. "Not sure how they find that comfortable."

"Me neither," Tilli agreed. "Though my Lili has grown out of that, I'm afraid."

"Ah, well, I'd wager she does loads of other things to make you laugh. Seems to me kids have no shortage of funny to them."

"Oh, she's funny, alright," Felton said, joining the conversation. Tilli turned a grin on him, realizing he was awake. "Just the other day, she asked me how I can be so bad at games when my Aunt Gael is so clever."

"She did not," Tilli breathed, unable to contain her grin despite her embarrassment.

"Aye, she did," Felton said. "I told her it was because my Aunt Gael doesn't let anyone win—not even her own nephew. Lili asked why I didn't watch Aunt Gael's moves, and I told her I did. She proceeded to tell me I should probably watch a little closer next time."

Tilli couldn't contain her mirth. "I'm going to have to talk with that girl. Maybe she needs to spend more time with Aunt Cleary instead of Aunt Gael."

Tobin laughed from his seat above them. "Kids say some outlandish things. I'm sure every parent has a story or two where their little ones said something funny when they shouldn't have. That's what makes the saying of it funny, I'd wager." He chortled and puffed on his pipe. He started, sitting straight in his seat. "Well, would you look at that ..."

Bandits! was the first thought that entered Felton's mind as he gripped his cane in one hand and hoisted himself to see past the driver's seat.

Tilli stood next to him, gripping the driver's seat for stability as Tobin pointed. A great northern white elk moseyed alongside the road ahead. The creature moved with a majestic cadence, its head bobbing under the weight of long pointed antlers. The antlers sloped backward and toward the sky, branching into new points every once in a while. Steam blasted from the elk's nose and mouth as it grunted what resembled a greeting.

"Isn't he a right beauty," Tobin said in awe.

"Aye," Felton agreed quietly. "I thought at first you spotted some bandits."

"Bandits?" Tobin asked incredulously. "No bandits this time of year. The odd group will move into the area on occasion, but most of us wagoners are tougher than we look," the halfling said, leaning over and reaching for something under his seat. He pulled out a crossbow, a weapon Felton had only seen a couple of times before since it wasn't widely used. "Most of the time, though, they don't show up in the winter. Too cold for them to camp out in Elderwood Forest."

Felton realized that his reasoning for accompanying Tilli—to protect her—had little ground to stand on. If he weren't there to protect her on this trip, why was he there?

"Button and Lili would have loved to see that fellow," Tobin said after a long while.

"I have no doubt," Tilli agreed.

"Hey!" Tobin started. "When we get back to Galium, we should get the girls together. I'm sure they'd get along swimmingly. We could have you over for supper sometime. I'd wager you've never met a better cook than my Lenor."

"I don't know," Tilli hemmed. "I mean, the girls would most likely have a grand old time together, but Felton's Aunt Cleary is quite the cook herself."

"I don't say no to many meals." Tobin laughed and slapped his round belly. "Glad to try both! Lenor and I are always looking for new couple friends. Before the Battle of Galium, we actually had a human couple over. Well, turned out they weren't a couple, but it was fun nonetheless."

"Oh, well ..." Felton stammered. "We ... uh ... we're not ..."

Tilli smiled at his inability to speak, and to his chagrin, she made no effort to rescue him from the awkward situation.

Instead, she waited, pressing her lips together in a smirk as she appraised him.

"Well, I mean ..." Felton said, his face scrunching in confusion.

"Oh," Tobin said sheepishly. "I didn't realize. Thought you two made a lovely couple. Lenor is always saying I let my mouth run away without my brain. Never my heart, of course. That's why I thought you two were such a fine couple. Felt it right here, I did." The halfling took his pipe out of his clenched teeth and tapped the end of it on his chest.

As the halfling continued to talk—mostly to himself—Felton shook his head at Tilli with a disbelieving stare. The woman's top teeth bit hard on her bottom lip in a grin that told the dwarf she rather enjoyed his discomfort. He continued shaking his head at her disapprovingly, but the frown he attempted to hold eventually broke, transforming into his own smirk.

The wagons formed a circle in order to shield their campfire. The tall flames warmed their faces and their feet, but the gathered wagoners' fellowship and jovial spirits warmed their hearts. Tobin introduced his passengers to several of the wagoners he knew.

Tilli sat closer to Felton than he'd expected she would, her eyes watching the fire with an unrelenting wariness. It struck Felton that she had endured quite the harrowing experience during the Battle of Galium. The roaring fire might have been stirring unpleasant memories within the woman.

"Are you alright?" Felton whispered to her.

"I'm fine," she said, pressing against his side as they shared a warm blanket.

"Are you cold?" he asked, placing his hand on her back.

"No." She gave him a weak smile and leaned into his embrace. "Quite cozy, actually."

Felton smiled at her warmth.

"So, what is such a fine couple as yourselves headed to Crossdin for?" Hanla, a human woman and one of Tobin's wagoner friends, asked.

"Oh, they're not a couple," Tobin said with a chuckle. "Made the same mistake myself. They're headed to Crossdin for a seed shop."

Felton shook his head in amusement as the halfling answered for them.

"Been meaning to ask, what's so exciting about this seed shop?" Tobin continued. "There's bound to be a decent one in Galium, I'd wager."

Tilli tensed, and she sat straighter to answer the halfling's question. "Well, it's my sister's shop."

"I didn't know you had a sister," Felton said. "You only ever mentioned your two brothers."

"Oh, well," Tilli said slowly, "she's my ... well, she was my sister-in-law."

"Wonderful!" Tobin said excitedly. "Always love a good in-law. My own brother-in-law is the foredwarf of the garvawk warriors. He and I didn't always get along, but with all the training he's been doing lately and his looming deployment, we've been trying to get as much time together as we can. I'd wager, he's—"

Hanla shut the halfling up with a backhand to his shoulder as she noticed Tilli's and Felton's reactions.

"Oh ..." he whispered.

Tilli and Felton sat in silence, each lost in their own thoughts. Felton had been wondering what the woman was thinking before the halfling mentioned the foredwarf. The guard wrestled with a strange tension between his ache to be with his old unit and the newfound desire to make Tilli's sadness cease.

On one hand, his brothers were preparing for war without him. On the other, he'd been enjoying Tilli's presence in his life, even if he didn't understand the feelings welling within. He was not sure which thought fueled the rising confusion in him more.

They sat around the campfire for a long while before the conversation began anew. When it did, the wagoners kindly acted as though the awkward silence had never happened. They were a hospitable lot.

Eventually, Tobin rearranged the back of the wagon so all three of them could sleep.

Felton lay under his blankets, staring up at the night sky. Stars lit the night with an unprecedented beauty. Tobin snored nearby, the wind exiting his nose with a funny vibration. A stir from Tilli caused Felton to glance at the woman. Their eyes met, and a loud snort from the halfling made them both snicker.

"So much for not snoring," Felton whispered.

"Can't imagine the ladies in that house if he's the quiet one," Tilli teased.

The guard glanced back to the stars, soaking in the breathtaking sight. They lay quietly for a long moment before Felton faced Tilli again and said, "You know, I'm here for you."

Tilli met his gaze. "I know," she said, reaching a hand out from under her blankets. Felton took her hand. Neither of them said another word. Soon, Tilli's hand slackened, and he judged her to be asleep.

Felton watched the stars for a while longer before he started recounting the things he was grateful for, beginning with the slight hand resting in his.

CHAPTER 24
SEEDS

Tilli stood outside the seed shop for a long time, unable to cross the threshold.

"Awfully cold out here," Felton said gingerly.

"Yeah ..." she replied absently.

"Would you rather I just went in for you? Do you have a list?"

"No ..."

"Alright ..."

Felton stood patiently by her side. He wasn't exactly sure what he could do, but he knew they had to go in. Taking a wagon all the way to Crossdin and not going into the seed shop was not an option.

He glanced around them. The thatched roof buildings displayed a pleasant unity around the city. Folks moved about in the morning sun. The cold morning fog that had rolled in off the sea overnight had already dissipated while they enjoyed breakfast at the inn they stayed at the night before.

Felton knew the woman was dragging her feet, but he didn't know why. He reached out and tenderly grabbed her hand, squeezing it affectionately. The act jarred her back to reality, and Tilli shook her head and grinned.

"Alright," she said.

"Alright?" Felton asked, making sure.

She nodded, and they entered the seed shop.

The inside was much warmer, forcing Felton's body to relent an unexpected shiver at the sudden shift in temperature. Every wall of the store was covered in labeled shelves. Parchments pinned in place next to each shelf indicated what types of seed were housed there. Tables scattered the room as well, baskets and buckets strewn about with various seeds. Some of the tables were intricately carved and built with drawers. Each drawer was also labeled.

Felton almost couldn't take it all in. Seeds of every kind imaginable surrounded them. He saw flower seeds and fruit seeds and vegetables seeds and tree seeds and bush seeds and seeds he didn't even know how to categorize. The place was an extraordinary menagerie of seeds.

"Tillinda Marigold, as I live and breathe," a woman said from behind the counter.

"Harley," Tilli replied.

The woman strode around the counter, drawing near to Tilli. Harley was a couple inches taller than Tilli, and her pumpkin orange hair was tied in a long braid resting over her shoulder. She took Tilli in with an appraising look. "How long has it been?"

Tilli looked away and shifted uncomfortably. "Three years ..."

Felton started piecing together her hesitance. If this woman was the sister of Tilli's late husband and she hadn't visited in three years ... Honestly, Felton would have been hesitant to come as well.

"Has it really been that long?"

"Yeah," Tilli said awkwardly.

Harley reached out and gently grabbed Tilli's chin. She moved Tilli's gaze to match her own, and Harley's eyes narrowed as she shook her head. "And still as beautiful as ever, I see. I've missed you, sister."

A stuttered exhale came out of Tilli as she melted into Harley's open arms. The women hugged. Tilli's body heaved as she let her tears flow, and Harley wiped a few stray tears from her own face.

Felton watched the tender moment silently, letting them take all the time they needed. He knew one had lost a husband and the other a brother. More so, they seemed to have lost each other as well.

Eventually, Harley pressed Tilli back, and the two laughed at themselves.

"We're quite the mess," Tilli said, wiping at her face. "Sorry, Felton."

"No. No," Felton said, waving away her concern. He was struck by how much bluer Tilli's eyes looked when they were glossed with tears.

"Felton, huh?" Harley said.

"Felton Holdum, ma'am, at your service."

"Ma'am?" She placed a hand to her chest in mock surprise. "A true gentleman."

"That he is," Tilli said.

"Well, I ..." Felton mumbled bashfully, scuffing his boot on the floor and rubbing his scarred brow.

"Ah, the strong silent type," Harley teased. She turned to Tilli and bobbed her eyebrows. Felton wasn't sure if Tilli blushed or if her face was still flush from crying.

"Oh!" Harley said. "Where's my niece? Is Lili still outside in the cold?"

"No," Tilli laughed. "She's staying with Felton's aunts."

"Oh, Aunt Cleary and Aunt Gael?" Felton was surprised to hear the woman knew his aunts' names. Harley must have read his confused look. "Lovely dwarves. Got to meet them when the wagons brought the refugees from Galium during the battle. Been missing Aunt Cleary's cooking. She wouldn't hear of me cooking for them while they were here. Said I was giving them a roof over their heads, the least she could do was feed me well."

Felton laughed. "That sounds like her."

"Been thinking I should pay them a visit, but it's hard to get away when you run a shop in Crossdin," she said, raising her hands and indicating the store. "Especially since I'm still recouping my losses to Aunt Gael. She is a game shark, that one."

They all laughed.

"I think she's turning Lili into one as well," Felton said.

"Well, I should like to see all those ladies again. Perhaps I'll have to make the trip." She paused and turned back to Tilli. "Why didn't you come with them during the battle?"

Tilli rubbed at one of her fingers, her gaze once again falling to the floor. Her words came out quietly. "I couldn't let the garden burn."

"Tilli," Harley said, stepping toward her and grabbing the woman's elbow. "Hugh wouldn't have wanted you to save the garden at the risk of your life."

"I know," Tilli said. "I just … I couldn't let the garden burn. It's a special place."

"Aye, that it is," Felton said quietly next to them.

"Is that why you haven't visited me in three years?" Harley asked with a soft chuckle.

"No," Tilli said. Her face twisted as though she were ashamed of the real reason. "The last time I visited, I saw so much of Hugh in you. Of course, I did. You two were so alike. Hugh had died two years prior … and I felt like I was finally moving forward. Seeing you … it brought so many things crashing back.

And then, I wanted to visit last year, but it had been so long, and I was worried you'd be upset. The longer I put it off, the more it felt like I couldn't visit."

Harley pulled Tilli into another tight hug. "Tilli," she said. "Just because my brother died all those years ago doesn't mean we stopped being sisters. I'm just like you. Remember? I've got only brothers." Harley laughed. "We need each other. We're the only sisters we've got."

Tilli laughed, too. "Thank you."

Tilli selected seed after seed, packing small pouches that they stacked on the counter. While Felton was glad to help her collect the ones she looked for, he wondered why she wanted so many different flower seeds.

"Why all the flower seeds?" he asked. "I understand the fruit and vegetable seeds. Those plants will feed people, but what's the purpose of all the flowers."

Tilli chuckled and shook her head. She grabbed a handful of seeds from a drawer marked "Angelica."

"This is the Angelica. Aside from beautiful yellow flowers that grow in along wiry stems, it also has many uses."

Felton scrunched his nose and inspected the mound of tiny seeds. "Like what?"

"Well," she said with a laugh, "it's great for seasoning meat or soups or stews." Felton's eyebrow popped, unimpressed. "And," she continued before he could say anything, "it can make your stomach feel better."

The dwarf nodded warily. "Alright."

"I've also heard some herbalists think it can help with joint pain," she said, side-eying him with a smirk.

Felton started, instantly more interested in the flowers. Tapping his cane a couple of times on the floor, he asked, "We're getting some of those, right?"

"Yeah. We're getting them."

Felton was fascinated by the prospective uses of flowers that he'd never considered. Most of his life, flowers seemed fine to look at, but they never held much value to his mission-oriented mind.

After answering many more questions about flowers as they went along, Tilli said to him, "You know, even if the flower doesn't seem to have a purpose, it doesn't mean it has no value."

"What do you mean?" he asked.

"Just because something doesn't seem to have value to one person, doesn't mean it is worthless. Flowers bring joy to people. Bringing joy to people is of far greater value than many other things in this life—even if those things are held in higher esteem."

The way she said the words to him pierced the guard. Something about the sentiment resonated deep within him as though it were shining a light on some deep hidden fear. As Tilli returned to scanning the different labels, Felton caught Harley watching the pair with an approving smirk.

Tilli told him she needed to ask Harley if she had a specific type of seed. Felton asked what it was so he could search for it. Tilli winked and said, "It's a surprise."

She did, however, task him to find something called echinacea. Felton got the sense that was to keep him busy while she spoke with Harley.

He didn't hear the beginning of the conversation while he was searching for the seed, but he found it relatively quickly and tried to pretend he was still searching to give the ladies more time. Try as he might, he couldn't help but overhear their conversation.

"He's a rather handsome dwarf," Harley teased.

"Harley," Tilli scolded.

"What?" the woman said innocently. "Well-mannered, handsome, and kind. Not much more you could ask for."

"He *is* very sweet," Tilli admitted.

"I saw the two of you outside, when he took your hand, and the way you were gathering the seeds together."

Tilli said nothing, and Felton, blushing as he was, tried his best not to overhear more of their private conversation.

"Hugh's been gone a long time," Harley said. "It's hard enough to find love once in this life. If there's a seed of affection and a chance for you to tend it and let it flourish, filling your life with love again, you should take it."

Love? Felton thought.

How could anyone love him? He stared down at the cane in his hand, an ever-present reminder of his brokenness. Even if Tilli did care for him in that way ... he couldn't deny that he fancied her, and his affection could lead to a deeper love. But how could he expect her love in return? How could he put her in the position of loving a broken dwarf? That would be entirely unfair.

Tullen's words came to mind.

"I wouldn't say broken. Broken things require repairs. This is something that requires tending."

Maybe the old barkeep was right. Maybe Felton just required tending. Maybe the flowers they'd chosen would help him heal his leg.

Tilli returned to his side. "Did you find it?" she asked.

"Oh ... aye," he said slowly.

Felton realized he'd missed the rest of the ladies' conversation. What had he missed? Did Tilli have a seed of affection for him? He shook the questions away. He shouldn't have heard as much of their words as he had. It was better that way. As he helped Tilli gather the remaining seeds on her list, he caught her wide blue eyes landing on him several times. His heart began to beat faster.

Maybe ...

CHAPTER 25
THE CHASE

Little Lili stood and patted Felton on the shoulder, issuing her condolences. Felton stared at the game board before him, still unsure how she beat him.

"I'll go a little slower next time so you can learn," she said with a cheeky grin.

"Come here, you little sprout," Felton said, grabbing her and pulling her in close for tickles.

Lili squealed with delight, laughing so hard her face turned red.

"If you rile her up, you'll have to put her to bed," Tilli called from the kitchen of the cozy cottage.

Felton paused and flipped Lili over to face him. "Will you go down easy for me?"

"Uh-huh," Lili said, nodding with a mischievous glint in her eye.

Felton narrowed his eyes at the girl, unsure if she could be trusted at her word on the matter. After a short deliberation, he decided it was worth the gamble and began tickling her again. They rolled and laughed, and Lili even tickled Felton's belly, hoping to get him back. Felton feigned boisterous laughter as though he were even more ticklish than she.

Eventually, Tilli said it was time for bed and shooed the two toward Lili's room. As Felton was tucking her in, Lili asked him to tell her a story. The dwarven guard sat on the bed next to her and told her stories of the famous garvawk warriors—ones he'd known since he was a lad. He stroked Lili's strawberry blond hair as he told the tales of the most honorable warriors in Galium.

Soon enough, soft breathing told Felton the girl was asleep. Drool seeped from the side of her open mouth onto his shirt. He chuckled as he slowly slid away and tightly tucked her in.

As he closed the door behind him, he thought he could still hear her then realized the soft snores in the sitting room came from the snoozing Tem, buried under his mound of blankets beside the hearth.

Tilli sat on the couch with a mug of tea, gently blowing on it. Felton noticed the steaming tea on the side table next to the couch, an invitation for him to join her.

He sat beside Tilli, taking the mug into his hands and sipping it slowly, trying not to burn his tongue.

"I love the way you make her laugh," Tilli whispered.

"Me too." Felton huffed. "I love that girl."

"She loves you, too."

A warmth washed over him. They drank their tea in companionable silence for a long time, enjoying the dwindling embers in the hearth.

When Felton finished his tea, he stood and took Tilli's empty mug. He washed both mugs in the kitchen before returning to the sitting room. Tilli hadn't moved from her seat on the couch. Felton paused to take in the sight.

The hearth's embers bathed the woman in a warm glow. Her beautiful blond hair was up in a messy bun that had, earlier that day, been a tight bun. He smiled. No matter what she did, her fine blond hair eventually slipped from the bun she so carefully arranged each morning. He loved that.

Over the past few weeks since their return from Crossdin, Felton had spent as much time as he could with the Marigold girls. He played games with Lili and helped Tilli with the greenhouse, learning far more than he ever expected to about plants. He found more and more excuses to go to the cottage. Which reminded him …

Felton strode to the back of the couch, keeping the click of his cane on the wood floor as quiet as possible. He'd learned that Lili could sleep through just about anything, but he didn't want to wake the tortoise. Any time Tem was asleep, Felton could relax.

He placed a thick hand on Tilli's shoulder. Her own hand reached up to lay atop his, and she pressed her warm cheek against it. Felton struggled to remember the excuse he'd used to visit the cottage. He stood there, enjoying the warmth of her cheek on his hand, not saying anything for fear of ruining the moment.

After a long while, Tilli finally let out a contented sigh and said, "I suppose you'll be needing that chamomile tea for Aunt Cleary then?"

"Oh!" Felton started, remembering. "Aye. It's been doing wonders for her cough."

Tilli chuckled as she stood and walked to a tall cabinet that housed numerous jars with various dried goods. She easily plucked the jar she was looking for, knowing her organization system even if it made no sense to anyone else. Felton certainly hadn't figured it out.

She drew near to him, thumbing the jar in her hands. Felton stood absolutely still. Despite his statuesque exterior, his insides whirred. His heart thrummed, pumping blood through his body and warming his chest. He gulped nervously as she stepped close to him.

Tilli smirked. "Another flower that might seem useless at a glance. Combine chamomile with some honey and you can kick a cough in no time."

"Aye," Felton whispered, not looking at the jar but at the beautiful woman who stood before him. "I ... uh, thank you." He managed to say. "You really ought to have your own shop. Folks would pay good money for what you give away for free."

Tilli shrugged. "Maybe, but I'm simply an amateur herbalist. There are folks who know far more than I do."

"From what I've seen, you'd probably give them a run for their coin," Felton said with a chuckle. "At any rate, you're more knowledgeable than any of the rest of us in the district."

"Maybe," she said shyly. "But if I were running a shop, when would I have time to expand my criminal empire?"

"Fair point," Felton said with a nod, stroking his brown beard.

"*Then* how would I convince you to chase me?" she teased.

"I would follow you anywhere," Felton said smoothly.

Tilli looked up from the jar and directly into the guard's eyes. Everything around him slowed, as though the world turned sluggish. Did he just say that? Where did that come from? How did he let that slip out of his mouth?

Felton didn't know how long he stood frozen in horror. He was acutely aware of the cane in his hand, and the scar on his brow started to itch.

Tilli forced words through her smile. "Is that so?" she asked.

"I ... uh," Felton stammered. *You fool*, he cursed himself internally. *Think before you speak.* He took a deep breath and pieced a thought together. "I did go to Crossdin with you, after all," he said sheepishly.

"That's true," she said, eyeing him thoughtfully. "I never did properly thank you for that."

"Oh, no thanks necessary," Felton said. "Was just glad to spend more time with you."

The dwarf's eyes widened as he realized his own words. *You fool!* he cursed himself again. *I better get going before I say something really stupid.*

Tilli bit her bottom lip, seemingly amused by Felton's discomfort.

"Well," she said, handing him the jar and leaning closer to him. She whispered, "I appreciated that time as well."

She said the words so close, he could feel her breath on his lips. She tilted her head to the side and planted a kiss on his cheek. A rush of blood flooded through him, and he was certain there was no way the woman missed the rose on his cheeks this time.

Before she could pull away, Felton reached a hand up and pressed his fingers through the blond hair on the back her neck. His thumb brushed against her cheek, next to her ear.

Felton's arm rippled as he pulled her closer, pressing his lips against hers and kissing her. Tilli's hand gripped the tunic on his chest as she melted into him. After a long while, he pulled his face away from hers, still holding her and caressing her cheek. Their lips stuck for a second before peeling apart. They stood pressed to each other, breathing heavily. Tilli bit her bottom lip again and smiled at him.

"Caught you," Felton murmured, barely able to speak.

Tilli laughed and whispered back. "So you did."

Felton had no idea what had come over him. In the moment, he only knew he would kiss the woman. There was nothing else in the world.

"Suppose I'll catch you again tomorrow," he said after a long silence between them.

"I'd like that," she said.

"Goodnight, fair Tillinda Marigold."

"Goodnight, brave Felton Holdum," she replied, playing along.

Tilli saw him to the door, and as Felton walked down the street toward home, his cane swung a little lighter in his hand.

SPRING

Chapter 26
Grand Reopening

When Felton strode through the door to the newly renovated *Roey's Tavern*, he traded the sounds of springtime birds chirping and singing for the raucous laughter and songs of the tavern's patrons. It seemed as though the whole Garome District had come out for the grand reopening. Every table appeared to be full, and every stool at the bar had an occupant. Felton didn't recognize everyone. Many, he guessed, were construction workers who'd fallen in love with the place while they worked around the district.

Arth Miller beckoned the guard to join him, his wife, and Lana Smith at their table. They had the only table with an extra seat, so Felton nodded his assent. "One moment, I'll grab a drink," he said.

The dwarven miller cocked a red eyebrow and shook his head. His mouth gaped in confusion, not having heard the guard's words over the crowd's merriment.

Felton chuckled and raised a finger to indicate he would join them momentarily. He nodded toward the bar, and a light of recognition crossed the other dwarf's face. Arth grabbed the mug in front of him and pointed toward it, then himself, then held up a finger. Felton didn't know any sign language other than the tactical signs he'd used in the warhog cavalry, but he figured Arth's meaning well enough.

The guard waded through the tavern, inspecting his surroundings. The workers had repaired the establishment with great care. Many of the newly replaced timbers were stained to match the rest of the space, making *Roey's* feel whole again. Felton maneuvered around full tables overflowing with boisterous mirth. Many people hailed the guard as he passed, and Felton found it humorous how many people he recognized compared to his first visit. When he'd first stepped into the tavern, many folks knew who he was. He'd almost been a celebrity, being the first guard in the district in years. Felton was happy to know many of them now, and thankfully, most of them no longer looked at him like some sort of novelty.

He approached the bar, looking for Tilli.

"Hello, Mister Felton," Roey greeted him.

"Oh, hello, Miss Roey," he replied.

"Tilli's at the other end," she said with a wink.

"Ah," Felton said, spotting the woman at the far end of the bar serving a halfling couple.

"Something I can get for you, though?" Roey asked.

The way the halfling barkeep looked at him told Felton she knew about the kiss he and Tilli had shared that cold winter night. It had been a couple of weeks, and they'd shared several intimate moments since. The way Roey handed him a mug of ale with a smirk told him she also had a vested interest in his and Tilli's budding romance.

"Ah, I actually need two," he said.

"Oh?"

"Arth Miller asked me to grab him one as well."

"Oh, sure, sweetie," Roey said, twirling to fill another mug.

"Looks as though business is good?" Felton asked.

"More than good," Roey said. "Guess folks don't know what they'll miss until it's gone."

Felton huffed a chuckle. How many times had he had that same thought when reminiscing on his time with the cavalry and his limited time with the garvawk warriors? He gripped his cane, dangling it in his hand as he leaned on the bar.

"Soon as we reopened, everyone seemed to appreciate us more!" Roey said, sliding another mug to him. "You got both of those, sweetie?"

"Aye," Felton said with a smile and a nod. He'd gotten proficient at carrying things while holding his cane. "You don't need any help with all the extra business?"

"No," Roey said, barking a laugh. "I've had several folks ask if I was looking to hire. Something about the place feels fresh and new. If I need the help, I can always hire another barmaid."

"Fair enough. I'm going to mosey over there for a moment."

Roey looked down the bar where Felton had nodded. "Oh, of course," she said with a knowing grin.

Felton rolled his eyes as he progressed to the other end of the bar, tightly clamping both mug handles in one hand. When he reached the end, he placed the mugs on the bartop less gracefully than he'd intended.

Tilli turned, asking, "A refill for you, s—" She stopped mid-word and smiled. "Well, hello you."

"Hi," Felton said.

"I see you've already got a drink, but is there something else I can do for you, sir?"

"Well, I had thought a moment of your time would be nice."

Tilli stood tall and scanned the tavern. She placed her hands on her hips and pursed her lips. "I don't know ... I'm quite busy today. Might cost you extra."

As the guard leaned into the bar, the halfling couple watched curiously. Felton said, "A moment with you is worth whatever the price."

The halfling woman placed a hand to her mouth to muffle a snicker.

"Is that right?" Tilli asked, leaning over the bar and drawing her face close to Felton's. "What's it worth to you?"

Felton smiled, leaning even closer. He paused. Something felt odd. As though ...

He turned an eye over to the halfling couple who were watching intently. The halfling woman's brows were raised as though she were waiting for some romantic kiss. Realizing Felton had caught her staring, she flopped a limp hand against the halfling man's chest and said, "You shouldn't stare at folks."

Confusion crossed the halfling man's face, and he tried to defend himself.

Tilli chuckled. "I thought the guard of the district was supposed to keep people from making a scene, not cause one himself."

"Some scenes are worth repeating," he said slyly.

Tilli laughed and spun to fill a mug of mead. She leaned past Felton and slid the drink across the bartop toward an approaching man.

"Thanks," the man said, surprised. He swapped his empty mug for the full one.

"How are you holding up with all the extra business?" Felton asked.

"Fine," she said. She paused for a moment and turned back to him. "I hope it's not going to be like this every day. Now that spring is here, I'll be extra busy in the garden. Roey usually lets me take some time off to tend it in the spring."

"She mentioned she could always hire another barmaid if she needs the extra help."

"That's true," Tilli said, taking a rag and wiping the bar.

"She'd have to do that if you decide to open up *Tilli's Herbs & Tea,*" Felton said pointedly.

"Ha!" Tilli laughed. "You're a dreamer."

Felton snorted. If Tilli knew how terrifying his dreams were, she wouldn't say that. But dreams of a brighter future, those he could get behind. "Why not?" he asked. "I think you'd be amazing at it. And you know I'd help."

"First off," Tilli said, turning on him with an exasperated smile. "I don't have the money to start a business. And second, I told you: I'm just an amateur herbalist. There are far smarter ones out there."

"You're one of the smartest women I've ever met," Felton said. "Come to think of it, you may be *the* smartest."

She gave him a flat stare out of the corner of her eye.

"And," Felton continued. "You know more about plants than anyone else I've ever met. That I can say for certain."

"You're sweet," she said to him. "But that doesn't change the fact that I'd have to come up with the money for a shop, and that is something I can't afford right now."

"You could always start selling the jars and spices you give away for free. Folks would gladly pay you for them. I know Aunt Cleary would."

"I don't do it to get paid," Tilli said. "I do it because I love it."

"That's exactly what makes it worth paying for," Felton said, a smug smile on his face.

Tilli clicked her teeth and smiled back. "Dreamer."

The guard chuckled. "I better get this over to Arth. He's probably thirsty," Felton said, gathering the handles again. "Catch you later."

"If you can," Tilli replied with a wink.

"I've heard tell of a great parade happening on Wolsday for the garvawk warriors. Will you be there?" Arth asked Felton.

"A parade?" Felton repeated.

"Aye," Arth said, nodding into his ale. "My brother lives in the Castle District. Says they'll be honoring the garvawk warriors and seeing them off on their big mission. Says it's to be the most glorious endeavor on which the garvawk warriors have ever embarked. Some secret assignment he says the bards will sing of for ages to come. Assumed you would know that since you're one of them."

Felton winced. He hadn't known about the parade. Grisham had mentioned the mission, but Felton hadn't been back to *The Hungry Hog* in a while and hadn't been updated on events. The feeling of utter aloneness washed over him again. No one could know what he was thinking. No one could understand how it felt to be the only garvawk warrior not going across the sea on the most unprecedented mission their order had ever participated in.

"I'm sure Lili would love to see the parade," Arth continued, but got an elbow to the ribs from the more socially aware Enny. "Oh, sorry," he said. "I just thought ..."

"You're right," Felton said. "I've been telling her the bedtime stories my father told me when I was a mite. I'm sure she'd love to see them at the parade."

"Lili is the sweetest," Enny said, whimsically. "I'd love to have a girl ..."

"Aye. But you've given me a whole litter of good, strong boys," Arth said with a proud grin.

Enny rolled her eyes and turned toward Lana.

"Don't look at me," Lana said, waving her hands in front of her. "I only got boys, too. Having a little girl would be a dream."

The two women laughed, and their conversation continued around more mundane topics.

Felton faded into his own thoughts. A strange weight lingered on him as if he were wearing heavy, inflexible armor. When Sergeant Grisham had told him about the mission, he might as well have punched him in the gut. But, it had seemed far enough away that he could potentially heal and rejoin the garvawk warriors before they left. With the mission at hand, Felton would be left behind.

CHAPTER 27
THE PARADE

Banners fluttered in the wind, and people filled the streets of the Castle District. The crowds moved like waves, flowing back and forth toward one attraction or another. Lines formed around food tents. Folks gathered in bunches to watch as a street performer dazzled them with dangerous acrobatic tricks. One such performer juggled great daggers—something that mesmerized Felton and Lili. Tilli, however, suggested they move on, not wanting the two of them to get any ideas.

Felton carried Lili on his shoulders, waving away Tilli, who looked at him nervously. "I've got her," he said, holding both of the girl's legs across his chest with his free hand. "I want her to be able to see everything."

"Look at that!" Lili shouted from above, grabbing at Felton's face with both of her hands and turning his head.

A tall man strode awkwardly through the crowd; long straight legs carried him over dwarves and halflings as they milled about. He stood almost double the height of any other man.

"What in Finlestia?" Felton murmured.

The man lumbered toward them and bent down to face Lili. He pulled a flower from his pocket and handed it to her. "You're almost as tall as me," the man said.

"I wish," Lili said in awe.

As the man slowly moved away, Felton noticed that his elongated legs were wooden. "Ahhh!" Felton released a small gasp of understanding. "He's on stilts," he whispered to Tilli.

"What?" Lili asked, not having heard the dwarf.

"Nothing," he said quickly. "Want to get a beaver tail?"

"A beaver tail?"

"Aye," Felton said. "They're delicious."

"Ewww," Lili said.

"They're not real tails." Felton laughed. "Have you never had one, either?" he asked Tilli.

"Never," she said, unsure what to think.

They stood in line waiting to reach the front where a human family buzzed about a tent, cooking something. While they waited, Captain Bradnir walked by the line.

"Captain!" Felton called to the man.

Bradnir glanced about looking for the person who had called him. Realization dawned on him as he spotted Felton, a sweet little girl mounted upon his shoulders.

"Hello, Felton," he said. "Who are these lovely ladies with you?"

"Captain Bradnir, meet the Marigold ladies, Tilli and Lili," Felton beamed.

"How lovely to meet you," Captain Bradnir said, extending a hand to Lili. The girl giggled and shook the man's hand. "I take it you're the ones who've been keeping my favorite guard out of trouble in the Garome District."

"We try ..." Lili said, shaking her head and shrugging helplessly.

Captain Bradnir laughed. "Well, you let me know if he gives you too much trouble, and I can transfer him," the captain said with a wink.

"No!" Lili said, frantically hugging Felton's head and covering the dwarf's eyes. "You can't take him. We love him. He's the best guard there ever was. I would miss him too much."

"Oh, no," Bradnir retracted, waving his hands innocently. "I was only joking. I promise I won't take him unless we really need the help. And even then, it would only be for a little while at a time. Then I would send him back right away."

"Promise?" Lili asked.

"Promise," the captain said. He flashed Tilli an apologetic smile. "Speaking of, I do have some guards from other districts who came to help. I need to check on them and make sure they have everything they need."

"Very well. Nice to see you, Captain," Felton said.

"Nice to see you as well. Are we due for another report soon? I do always enjoy your visits."

"Soon," Felton said with a nod.

"Good. Well, you have a lovely family," the man said, stepping away. "I hope you have a wonderful time at the parade."

Felton's gut reaction had been to correct the captain and tell him they weren't his family. As the guard watched the captain slip through the crowd, he realized Tilli had also not corrected the man. Felton took Tilli's hand in his own, sliding his fingers between hers.

"We're almost up," Tilli said as they reached the front of the line.

"Good day to you," a teenage girl said. "Three beaver tails for you?"

"One will be fine," Felton said.

"Those are the beaver tails?" Lili asked, leaning over to see a man frying a large ovular piece of dough in some oil.

"Aye," Felton nodded. "They make it hot and fresh, then sprinkle sugar and cinnamon on it. You can also put some jam on it or—"

"Three beaver tails will be fine, thank you," Lili said to the girl.

The girl looked at Felton who chuckled. "How about two?" he asked, nodding toward Tilli. "She and I can share one, and one for the sprout growing on my head."

"Two coming up," she said, taking his coin and hollering to the others behind her.

Then the girl stared at him.

Felton's eyes glanced from side to side.

"Next," the teenage girl said, trying to peer around them.

"I think she wants us to move to the side," Tilli whispered into his ear.

"Oh," Felton said, sheepishly shuffling aside.

When the beaver tails came out, Lili attacked the fried dough as though she'd never eaten anything so good. Sugar and cinnamon fell atop the dwarf's head, and he quickly set her down to walk on her own so he could brush the crumbs from his hair.

Tilli offered him a bite, which he gladly took. "Mmmm," he said, cocking his scarred brow and nodding at Lili.

Lili's mouth was so full, she could only mumble and nod vigorously to indicate her approval.

Lili dragged them to a spot near the front of the crowd where they'd be able to see the whole parade. Dancers and musicians led the way, riling up the crowd. Jugglers and acrobats flipped and performed tricks. Felton and Lili gawked at another juggler dangerously flipping daggers. Tilli let out an exasperated sigh next to them.

A warhog cavalry unit approached, riding their menacing beasts. The hogs grunted and plodded along, their riders waving to the onlookers. Lili's mouth gaped at the enormous hogs, packed with muscle and sharp tusks. Felton caught sight of the red banner adorned with three tusks crossing a double-bladed axe and smirked, recognizing the 3rd Cavalry's emblem.

"Woohoo!" An elderly dwarf shouted nearby. Felton turned, and Tullen's face lit up with surprise at the sight of the guard. "What are you doing here?" the old barkeep asked.

"Came for the parade," Felton said, motioning toward the Marigold ladies. "What about you?"

Tullen excused himself as he pressed past onlookers. "You think I'd miss a chance to see my old unit in the parade?" he asked, laughing hoarsely.

Felton chuckled.

Tullen looked past the younger dwarf toward Lili. "You see that cavalry unit?"

"Uh-huh," Lili said, nodding.

"That's the best unit in all the warhog cavalry."

"Whoa," Felton said with a laugh. "Don't go telling the girl lies, now."

"No lies," Tullen said. "You know why that one's the best?"

"Why?" Lili asked, watching the cavalry with a renewed sense of awe.

"Because that's the one I was in," the old dwarf said proudly.

Lili's features scrunched as she watched. "What unit were you in?" she asked Felton.

"I was in the 7th Cavalry," he said, showing her the tattoo on his arm.

The girl inspected the emblem, a shield with a warhog head, the beast bearing its tusks with a 7 on its forehead. Felton made hog noises as she traced his tattoo. Lili laughed at the sounds.

"I think the 7th is probably the best," she said.

"No!" Tullen said, acting wounded. "What would make you say that?"

"If Felton was in the 7th, it must be the best," she said, as though it were a matter of fact.

"That's my girl," Felton said. "I see another beaver tail in your near future."

Tilli narrowed her eyes at him. He only shrugged. The guard couldn't help it; Lili's cuteness slew him.

They watched in silence as the 3rd Cavalry moved down the road and more performers bounded before the crowd.

Felton found himself watching the cavalry unit long after they'd passed. He caught Tullen doing the same. He placed a hand on the old dwarf's shoulder. "Does it make you sad to watch them go on without you?"

Tullen's shoulders bobbed with an obvious chortle. "No," he said contentedly. "I'm proud to be able to say I was one of them. Seeing them march on reminds me I was part of something bigger than myself, something that will endure long after I'm gone."

"Aye," Felton said under his breath.

Up the street, the crowd's excitement mounted. The guard could just make out a wagon with a bunch of dwarves in the back, waving to the crowd.

As they approached, time slowed for Felton. He watched the garvawk warriors as they waved to the cheering crowd. He should be up there. He should be going with them. He should …

"Felton!" someone called from the wagon.

He did a double take as he recognized the wagoner. It was Tobin. Felton laughed and shook his head. The halfling had told him Foredwarf Lotmeag was his brother-in-law.

A hand softly touched Felton on the shoulder, and he noticed that Tilli had pressed herself against him reassuringly. That was when he realized Foredwarf Lotmeag had called for Tobin to halt and had climbed out of the wagon.

Several dwarves handed down a pair of mugs to the foredwarf before filling all theirs from the flagon in the back of the wagon. Lotmeag strode to Felton, the crowd all around falling quiet to watch the unexpected display. Lotmeag handed one of the mugs to Felton and nodded to him.

"Garvawk warriors!" he shouted, his voice booming over the quieted crowd. "One for our brother!"

The garvawk warriors in the back of the wagon grunted in unison, and they all tipped their mugs back, drinking down the contents.

Tilli nudged Felton, spurring him to tip his own and down the ale. When he finished, he breathed heavily.

Lotmeag wore a wide grin and grabbed Felton's hand, raising it high with a victorious roar. The cheer was echoed by the garvawk warriors on the back of the wagon and, soon, by everyone in the gathered crowd.

Tobin spurred his wagon back into motion, the horses slowly pulling it along.

Lotmeag pulled Felton in for a hug and whispered, "Still no garvawk sign. I don't know how long we'll be gone, but I'll come by to see ye when we get back. I promise ye that."

"Be careful out there," Felton said, returning the embrace.

"Will do. Ye keep on the mend. That's an order," he added with a wink.

Felton bit at the inside of his cheek and nodded in affirmation, afraid that if he spoke, he might let loose the overwhelming emotion flooding him.

They watched the rest of the parade, Tullen pointing out all the interesting things he thought Lili should know. Felton didn't bother to correct any of the old dwarf's embellishments, deciding he could do so if Lili asked later. Tilli held his hand as they enjoyed the rest of the parade.

"Alright," Felton said finally. "I think I owe this one another beaver tail."

"Yes, please! With jam this time!" Lili chimed.

"Aye," Tullen said. "I ought to get back to *The Hungry Hog*. With the parade ending, I'm sure folk will be stopping in soon. You should come have dinner. On me."

"That's very kind of you," Tilli said.

"Oh, ma'am." He waved it off. "It would be my honor. I have greatly enjoyed my time with Felton."

"As have I," Tilli said with a smirk. "Seems he's even more popular than I knew."

Felton blushed.

"Can we still get another beaver tail?" Lili asked.

"Of course," Tullen said before Tilli could answer Felton's awkward pleading face. "I know where to get the best ones in Galium."

"Really?" Lili asked excitedly.

"Aye," the old dwarf said. "Make them myself."

"Alright," Tilli said with a laugh. "Lead the way."

When they'd finished dinner at *The Hungry Hog*, Felton chuckled at the softly snoring Lili on the booth bench beside him. Her sleep looked far more comfortable than his night passed out on a nearby table had been.

"She's worn out," Felton said, brushing the girl's hair from her face.

"It was a big day," Tilli said. "She got to see the best unit in all the cavalry."

"Aye—wait, what?" Felton realized what the woman had said and looked to her, unsure if *she* knew what she'd just said. As he spotted the teasing gaze on her face, a soft laugh rumbled through him. "Let me say goodbye to Tullen, and we can head back to the Garome District. Bound to be plenty of wagons still out and about after the parade."

Tullen embraced Felton and shook him with a fatherly pride. "I see you've been filling your cup with the good stuff then," he said, looking over to the Marigold ladies as Tilli picked up the snoozing Lili.

"Aye. I have at that."

"Good. Good," the old dwarf said, his eyes glossing at some distant memory. "You just remember to be grateful for them."

"I am," Felton assured him. "I still have the night terrors but not every night anymore."

"Good," Tullen said. "Just keep filling your cup."

"Aye," Felton agreed.

"And ..." Tullen said slowly. "Don't forget to visit me every once in a while, eh?"

Felton laughed and slapped a hand on the barkeep. "With flapjacks like yours, I can't stay away too long. Every time I have to report, I'll make sure to come by."

"Fair enough," Tullen agreed. "Now go catch those ladies before they leave you behind."

Felton took off after them, caning quickly through the tavern. He turned back over his shoulder and said, "It's my favorite thing to do."

CHAPTER 28
ENDORSEMENTS

The dragon's claw dug into the rocky clay, carving ruts and forming mounds of dirt that pushed up to Felton's ears. He heaved with all his might, grasping at the dragon's toe that pinned him to the ground.

"Mud and shale." He grimaced before shouting, "No! Run away!"

He flailed a hand wildly toward Lotmeag, who was busy cutting down goblin foot soldiers.

"Get out of here!" Felton cried as the dragon turned its great head toward the battle-weary foredwarf.

Felton beat at the dragon's toe, roaring in outrage. The dragon's foot twitched and pressed harder on his chest.

"No!" he cried, as amber flame rolled up through the dragon's breast and along its great neck. The dragon expelled a burst of flame that engulfed the foredwarf.

Felton woke up, heaving, on the couch in his aunts' apartment. His whole body was soaked with sweat, and his hands trembled. Tears poured down his face as his mind attempted to process, differentiating nightmare from reality.

He worked to control his breathing—in through the nose, out through the mouth—returning his heart rate to normal levels. The process was slow, but eventually he began to breathe normally again.

"Felton?" The query came as a whisper.

The guard groaned. He must have made a ruckus if he'd woken Aunt Cleary again. "I'm alright Aunt Cleary," he breathed. "Sorry for waking you."

"It's alright, deary. I'll put on some tea."

"No, it's fine. You can go back to bed."

He heard her start the tea in the kitchen despite his words.

"Night terrors again?" she asked as she came around the couch.

"Aye." He nodded quietly. "Different dreams, but the same thing every time. I find myself in some dangerous situation, which wouldn't normally bother me—been in many of those. Problem is, there's always someone else with me—someone in harm's way. Someone I want to save ... but I can't. I'm not strong enough. I'm ... too weak."

"I see," Aunt Cleary said. "You know, your mind is playing tricks on you."

"Aye," Felton agreed. "They're usually situations that make no sense. One of them had Tilli in it. Another had Sergeant Grisham riding a garvawk, which has never happened. This one had Lotmeag fighting goblin foot soldiers, no garvawks in sight. They all have minor things that should make them easy to spot as farces, but they feel so real in the moment."

"Why do you think you can't save them?" his aunt asked.

"I don't know ..." Felton said, letting his words fade. He rubbed at his knee. His face twitched as his scar itched.

"You know," Aunt Cleary said softly. "Words are mighty powerful."

Felton's chin raised as he eyed his aunt curiously, wondering where their conversation was heading. "I suppose so."

She smiled and continued. "Words have the power to breathe life or death. They can build or destroy. The question you have to ask yourself is: what kinds of words are you speaking over yourself?"

Felton thought for a moment. "I did forget to list the things I'm grateful for before bed tonight. I was so tired, I just passed out."

"I don't mean just those," Aunt Cleary said kindly.

"Well, what do you mean?"

"I think recognizing the things you're grateful for, no matter how small, is a great way to open your eyes to what life has to offer. But I'm talking about the words you speak over yourself. What do you say about yourself? What do you think about yourself? Where your mind dwells, the body follows."

"You mean throughout the day ..." Felton whispered, catching onto her thoughts.

In truth, Felton was not very kind to himself. He beat himself up regularly. He cursed at his knee. He looked at his cane with disgust. When he caught a glimpse of his reflection with the scar on his brow, he shook his head at the broken dwarf he'd become.

"I believe you have far more grand qualities than you give yourself credit for," Aunt Cleary stated bluntly.

"I ..." Felton started to speak but didn't know how to respond. His aunt's words had stunned him. He had only spoken or thought negativity over himself for so long, he'd lost sight of anything positive.

A flicker of a memory tickled his mind. The letter. Felton thumbed the couch cushion, knowing the letter still rested under it. Captain Bradnir had told him to save it for the right time. Maybe this was what he meant. Maybe Commander Qwen's letter could give him words to speak over himself and breathe life back into him.

As if she could read his mind, Aunt Cleary asked, "You going to finally read that letter?"

Felton lifted the edge of the cushion and retrieved the letter. It still had the wax seal Captain Bradnir had placed on it. The guard rolled it in his hand thoughtfully.

"Maybe," he said quietly.

Aunt Cleary stood and squeezed him in a tight hug. "Nephew, I want you to see as much good in yourself as you see in those around you. I want you to see what the rest of us see in you."

"Thanks, Aunt Cleary."

"You're welcome. Get the tea yourself?" she asked.

"Aye."

"Drink some tea, count your blessings, and get some rest. Read that letter in the morning light, will you?"

"Aye," he said again.

"I love you, deary."

"I love you, too."

Felton sat on the couch for a long time, rolling the letter in his hands, thinking on what his aunt had said. He thought also on the negativity he'd let seep into him. His whole life he'd been a positive force. All through his training, he'd never had any doubts about himself. He'd never doubted that if he worked hard enough, he could accomplish anything. He knew he would be selected to the garvawk warriors years before he had been.

What had changed?

Felton glanced at the cane leaning against the couch. His gut reaction was to curse the thing, but he checked himself. How could he spin his thoughts to consider the crutch in a different light? It had helped him in his healing process. It had been instrumental in helping him get as mobile as he had … A bitterness rose inside, but he breathed it down. That last thought might take longer to accept.

He summoned his courage, for it took great courage for him to venture back into the realm of sleep where he had no control. As he did, he trusted those who had spoken good over his life.

I'm grateful for Aunt Cleary and her care. I'm grateful for Tullen and his wisdom. I'm grateful for his guidance. I'm grateful for Commander Qwen, he thought, as he held the letter tightly.

He continued to list blessings until sleep took him once more.

The next morning brought a bright and sunny spring day. Birds sang happy tunes and flitted about. Felton couldn't help but smile at their beauty as he walked toward the Garden of Garome. His cane swung lighter in his hand with each step.

He walked through the gateway and into the lush garden, green and bright in the full swing of spring. Felton didn't immediately see Tilli or Lili and expected that the Marigold ladies were somewhere deeper within the great garden or in the greenhouse. The day was too nice for them to be tucked away in the cottage.

They were probably busily working on some task. The thought brought a smile to his face. He resolved himself to help them when he was done, but for the moment, he headed toward a bench that sat next to one of the dirt paths.

Felton glanced about to see if Templeton were anywhere to be seen. With the better weather, the tortoise had reemerged from his blanket nest in the house and begun to venture into the garden to nibble from the various plants he liked. Felton had still never seen the tortoise move anything more than his head, munching happily on his leaves before eyeing the dwarf as the guard passed.

With no sign of Tem, Felton settled himself onto the bench and produced the letter from his pocket. He breathed in the morning air, feeling the warm sun on his face. He listened to the birds playing and singing. He heard the swish of leaves rustling in the spring breeze. The whole world teemed with life around him. He made a mental note to add that to his gratitude list.

After he sat there for a long time, he opened his letter.

My Dear Captain Bradnir,

Please accept this letter as the highest recommendation on my behalf for full consideration on the character and quality of Felton Holdum, former member of the 7th Cavalry and garvawk warriors of Galium.

It is with great sadness that I do this, for there is no warhog rider I would rather keep than he. I have known Felton for many years and have found him to be of a quality higher than any other I have ever commanded. His inclusion and selection to the garvawk warriors was not a fluke, nor was it a surprise. I can say with all confidence that he was, and I believe still is, the best of us.

Due to unfortunate circumstances, he sustained injuries during the Battle of Galium and lost his garvawk, leaving him a warrior without a place among warriors. I have no doubt that he will prove to be among your best if you should give him a chance with the city guard.

Felton works harder than anyone I've ever known, but that is not the quality I believe to be the best representation of his character. I would suggest his best quality is that he serves with great pleasure and kindness. He does not only seek to climb through the ranks or become the best of the best. Instead, he seeks to raise the bar and bring those around him up. I witnessed him countless times in training as he took young riders under his wing.

It is this quality, I believe, he does not currently see in himself. Felton has spent his entire life focused on serving people as a warrior. I believe, given the chance, he will surprise everyone—most of all himself—with his great kindness and attitude toward serving others. It will only be a matter of time before he learns what that looks like.

So, my dear Captain Bradnir, accept this letter as a complete endorsement for Felton's character, and further—if I may be so bold—as an admonition that it would be foolishness to pass him up. I, myself, would have brought him back on if I could have.

I have no doubts, wherever Felton ends up, he will only make the place and people around him better.

With honor and glory,
Commander Qwen
7th Warhog Cavalry

Several teardrops splattered on the parchment, and Felton quickly wiped them away, hoping not to smudge the ink. He rolled the letter back up and clutched it close to his chest.

Commander Qwen's words had pierced him. Her faith in his ability to overcome his struggles and, even more, to make the people around him better moved him.

As he thought of his interactions with the people he'd met in the Garome District, his gut reaction was that they had made him better. Though, he remembered Lana Smith thanking him for speaking with Waen and encouraging the boy. He recalled the joy of Enny Miller, utterly shocked by her first pie contest victory. Felton had only been one judge, but Enny had thanked him time and again. He thought of Tilli and how grateful she was that he brought so much joy to Lili. And to her ...

Felton started to believe that maybe—just maybe—he had done some good in the Garome District.

A loud rustling forced Felton to wipe his face and stand quickly, pretending he hadn't been crying.

"I was just sitting here for a mome—" His words seized in his throat as he turned face to face with Tem.

The tortoise stood on the pathway, eyeing the dwarf in a showdown.

Felton stood rigid, wondering how he'd let the tortoise sneak up on him. "I'm not afraid of you," he said, though his voice quavered. He gulped down his fear and stood as tall as he could.

Templeton faced him, unmoving, his eyes locked on the dwarven guard. The tortoise appeared to be blocking his path toward the rest of the garden, where Tilli and Lili would be working. The notion struck Felton as funny.

"I don't know why you're guarding this place. I'm pretty sure I'm the guard around here. Who's the real guard in the garden?"

Templeton didn't move; he only stared with unwavering eyes.

A gasp caught Felton's attention. Tilli and Lili had just rounded some bushes, carrying potted plants. Tilli watched the showdown with worry, while Lili laughed.

"Are you alright?" Tilli called to Felton.

"It's alright. I'm not afraid of ... yipes!" Felton cried as he turned back to the creature. Tem stood directly in front of him. The tortoise's great mass had moved so quickly and silently, the dwarf nearly fell over in shock.

"Felton ..." Tilli said slowly, placing the potted plant on the ground and moving toward them.

The guard's eyes bulged as the tortoise's long neck inched his face closer to the dwarf's.

"Listen," Felton said slowly, as his chin began to quiver. "If you want to be the guard of the garden, I'm sure we can work that out. I just don't want any trouble. Maybe we could even be frien—"

Tem's bald green head started rubbing into Felton's long brown beard. The tortoise clicked his tongue and seemed to vibrate with joy as he pressed his head into the dwarf's beard.

"What in Finlestia?" Felton murmured.

Lili let out a great guffaw. "He likes you!" she squealed. "I knew it."

Soon Tilli was also laughing at the display. "I think he likes your beard."

"Aye ... I can see that." Felton let out a nervous chuckle of his own.

"Hey, Tem," Tilli said as she came over to meet the pair. "You just want to show Felton you love him as much as we do?"

Lili ran over and sprawled across the tortoise's great shell, hugging him.

Tem continued to butt his head against Felton, nuzzling him for a long time. Eventually, Felton worked up the courage to pet the tortoise's bald head, which Tem accepted happily.

"See," Lili said cheerily. "Nothing to be scared of."

He wondered how he'd ever been afraid of the tortoise. Tilli seemed to understand his thought and smiled at him as she shrugged. "I suppose if Tem likes you, we might have to keep you around for a while. Seems like a raving endorsement to me."

CHAPTER 29
PRETTY TOUGH

Lili giggled.

"What are you doing?" Felton asked, arching an eyebrow and glancing at her.

"No peeking," Lili said, putting her small hand on his face.

Felton smirked and leaned back on the bench while Lili completed her work. The girl giggled again as she pulled at the braid she'd been working into the side of Felton's great beard. Though he normally didn't braid his beard, he knew many dwarves who did. Lili had gotten the idea in her head that he needed a braid, and Felton found it increasingly difficult to say no to the little girl.

"There," Lili said, stepping back on the bench and tilting her head as she inspected her work.

"How do I look?" Felton asked.

"Pretty," Lili said with a laugh.

"Pretty?"

Felton stood and walked over to a fountain so he could see his reflection. He pulled at the braid in the side of his beard. It was a little braid and looked odd by itself. At the end of the braid, Lili had fastened a little flower like the ones he put in her hair. He smirked at the reflection.

"What do you think?" Lili asked as she ran to him. "Pretty, right?"

"I don't know ..." he teased. "You think it makes me look tough? I am a battle-hardened veteran, after all."

Lili bit at her lip, scrunched her face, and bobbed her head from side to side. "Maybe ...?"

Tilli rounded the path and grinned at the sight of the pair.

"What do you think, Mama? Does he look pretty or tough?"

Tilli laughed. "Oh, very tough," the woman said as she strode toward them. She leaned in and placed a hand on Felton's cheek and whispered, "And so pretty." She kissed him on his other cheek.

Felton chuckled.

"Is it alright if I borrow Felton for a little bit?" Tilli asked her daughter. "I want him to help me with something in the greenhouse."

"Sure!" Lili said excitedly. "I'm going to climb Big Barth today!"

Tilli stopped in her tracks. "Oh no, you don't."

"But Mama, I can do it. I've been practicing on all the other trees. And I've grown so much since last time. I know I can do it."

"Lili, I don't want you to get hurt."

"I won't, Mama. I promise!" Lili said.

Tilli sighed. "I might as well let you two learn how to juggle daggers," she grumbled. "If you can't reach the low branches, you leave it alone. Fair?"

"Yes, ma'am!" Lili said, running off.

"And be careful!" Tilli yelled after her. "That girl, I swear ..."

Felton laughed. "The way she climbs around on the walls and other trees, you'd think she was a squirrel."

"Yeah," Tilli said, shaking her head. "Come on, I've got something I want to show you."

When they reached the greenhouse, Tilli led Felton to a wooden table with an empty clay pot sitting atop it.

"Here," she said, leaving him standing next to the table. She grabbed a bucket and stepped back beside him. "Take some of this soil," she said.

"Sure," Felton agreed, scooping the soil from the bucket and placing it in the empty pot.

"You're going to want to pack it down a bit to make sure the soil won't lower too much when we water it," Tilli said, showing him with her own hands.

Felton mimicked her example and pressed the soil in before scooping more into the pot.

"What are you planting in this one?" he asked.

"I'm not planting anything. You are," she replied with a grin. Her wide blue eyes lowered as she pulled a small pouch from a pocket on her apron. "You're going to plant these," she said, opening the pouch so Felton could see the tiny seeds inside.

"Oh, I don't know ..." Felton hemmed. "I don't have the green thumb like you."

"That's alright," she said. "I'll help you."

She poured the contents into his massive hand. The tiny seeds were more like pointy black and white slivers in his palm.

"What are they?" he asked curiously.

"These are special seeds," Tilli said, drawing closer to him. "And they're a surprise. I picked them up from Harley's in Crossdin, just for you."

"Really?" Felton asked, touched by the gesture, even though he had no idea what the seeds would grow into.

"Let's plant them," she said with a shy smile. "I meant to help you plant them immediately after the last frost, but with the tavern reopening, it's been a busy start to the spring."

"Aye," Felton agreed. "What do I do?"

Tilli pushed her finger into the top of the soil, creating a divot. "Place the seeds in here, and we'll cover them."

Felton did so and brushed soil over the top as she instructed.

"Let's scoop some water in there to start them off right," Tilli said, crossing to a barrel of water, spooning some into a ladle, and then pouring it gently over the soil in the pot.

"Now what?" Felton asked, looking at the pot as if something should already be happening.

"We tend it and help it grow." Tilli laughed. "I thought we could put this one under the glass bubble outside to give it the best chance to grow."

"Fair enough," Felton agreed. He grabbed his cane and hoisted the pot into his other hand.

They reached the glass bubble, and Tilli lifted it on one side so Felton could slide the pot beneath the covering that inspired the construction of the greenhouse.

"We'll check on it every few days to make sure it has everything it needs—maybe add water if necessary. I think it will love the conditions under the bubble as it starts to grow."

"As it grows into what?" Felton asked, popping his scarred brow.

Tilli opened her mouth to respond but shifted. "Very clever," Tilli said pursing her lips. "Nice try. Almost got me to—"

A bloodcurdling scream deep within the garden pierced the spring air. Felton launched to his feet, throwing his cane to the side as he sprinted through the garden.

"Lili!" he called as he ran. "Lili, are you alright?"

He ran the paths he'd hobbled so many times before, his goal being Big Barth. Heart-wrenching cries pressed him forward even faster. When he saw Lili's dusty form at the foot of the tree, Felton slid next to her and lifted the little girl into his arms.

"I'm here, Sprout. I'm here," he said to her. "Where does it hurt?"

"Everywhere, Papa!" Lili cried, burying herself into his chest.

Tilli slid beside them. "Lili, love, are you alright? What happened?"

"I fell, Mama," the girl said through her sobs.

"Oh, love," Tilli said, smoothing the girl's hair.

"How did you fall, Sprout? Did you hit your head?" Felton asked.

"No," she blubbered. "My arm."

Felton did his best to inspect her arm as he cradled her. "Alright," he said holding her close and letting her cry it out for a moment. He could get a better look at her arm in a minute, but he had to make sure she hadn't hit her head.

The three sat in a close embrace, Felton rocking Lili softly. After a long time, Lili squirmed and turned her face away from Felton's chest so she could speak.

"I broke my promise," Lili said. "I'm sorry, Mama."

Tilli huffed out a laugh. "Lili love, it's alright. I know you didn't mean to."

"I didn't," the girl said as she sniffed.

"Hey, Sprout," Felton said, gingerly shifting her. "Can you show me which arm you hurt?"

"This one," she said, pointing to her left arm to show him. "Ow," she moaned.

Felton issued her a compassionate smile. "Looks like you broke your arm."

"I did?" Lili asked, her eyes growing wide and her frown drooping into her quivering chin.

"Aye. I've seen it before," Felton said. "One of the toughest warhog riders I ever knew broke his arm during training. He cried like a baby. Way more tears than you. You must be really tough."

"As tough as you, Papa?" Lili asked, sniffling.

Felton's own chin began to quiver. He knew he wasn't Lili's father and could never replace the man. The love with which she called him that touched something within him. He didn't have the heart to correct her, nor did he want to.

He looked at the girl's glassy blue eyes and said, "Way tougher! And much prettier," he added with a wink.

Lili giggled despite her tears. Felton thought there might not be any better sound in all of Finlestia.

Chapter 30
Wheels In Motion

A bell jingled above his head as Felton carried a crate filled with jars into the Millers' storefront.

"Just a moment," Arth called from the back of the shop.

Felton proceeded to the counter and began pulling out the jars and bottles labeled for Enny Miller. Some of them he'd come to know—rosemary and thyme and parsley—while others were new to him.

Arth Miller rounded a wall and met the guard at the counter. "Mister Felton, how nice to see you. Need some flour or—" He stopped as soon as he saw the bottles and jars that Felton was unloading on the counter.

"Just a delivery today," Felton chimed.

"I see that," Arth replied, inspecting the growing number of jars his wife had requested from Tilli. "Enny has been talking about this for several days. She's been trying all sorts of new pie recipes. Wants to win the pie contest again this year," he said, shaking his head. "Says it was her 'ingenuity' that got her the win last fall."

"*That* was a very good pie," Felton said, reminiscing. His mouth began to water as he could almost taste the memory. "I think she'd have a good chance to win if she made the same kind this year."

"Aye. That's what I've told her. She won't hear of it. Says it has to be 'new and fresh.'" Arth leaned over the counter and looked both ways as though his wife might be lurking somewhere. "Between you and me, I think she's taking it a little too serious. I've eaten more pie in the last month than any dwarf should."

He stepped back from the counter and slapped his belly. Felton couldn't be sure, but the miller did seem a little rounder.

"Any of them turning out good?" Felton asked with a laugh.

"A couple ..." Arth mused. "But some of them are getting wild."

"Sounds tough, having to eat homemade pies every day," the guard teased.

Arth gave him a flat look. "I'm hiding at the storefront to avoid another pie for supper. Said I'd be having supper at *Roey's* today. You care to join me?"

"I've got a couple more deliveries to make, but that sounds great."

Arth looked over the crate. "Miss Tilli is too kind. I wish she would let my wife pay for all this."

"Ha!" Felton laughed. "I've been telling her people would be willing to pay for the herbs and tea she gives them."

"Aye. I have no doubt."

"She's even told me she dreams of one day opening her own shop. '*Tilli's Herbs & Tea,*' she'd call it."

"Has a nice ring to it," Arth agreed.

Felton nodded along. An idea struck him. "Hey, Arth ..."

"Hmm?"

"You still haven't found a renter for the storefront attached to your building over on the side here?"

"I haven't," Arth said, rounding the corner and tugging thoughtfully at the bottom of his red beard. "Haven't bothered to renovate it since old Jenbo moved out to Crossdin."

"Aye ..." Felton said quietly, the wheels of his mind spinning. "What would you think about me buying it from you?"

"Hello, Mister Felton!" Laen Smith hollered and waved wildly as the guard approached *Roey's Tavern*.

Felton would have returned the exuberant wave if he hadn't been carrying the empty crate in both hands. It wasn't terribly heavy since it was empty, but it was awkward. "Hello, Laen," he responded.

Laen beamed and stood straighter, inhaling deeply and puffing his chest. Felton braced himself.

"Castle Brick tourney happening on Finsday!" the boy hollered. "Coin purse prizes and more! Best drinks and eating you can get at any tavern three districts over!"

Felton winced. Even though he'd braced himself, the boy's volume was still jarring. "Thanks for the information," he said.

"You're welcome!" Laen yelled.

Felton shook his head in amusement at the boy's enthusiasm as he entered *Roey's Tavern*. Several tables were already filling with the supper crowd. The glow of the lanterns made the tavern warm and inviting, even though the last light of the day still poured through the windows. Felton maneuvered around tables with ease, lifting the crate carefully as to not bump anything.

He strode to the bar where Roey was wiping down a section, prepping it for the lucky patron who would be sitting there soon.

"Hello, Roey," Felton said kindly. "I've got Tilli's crate. She asked me to bring it by when I was finished helping her with deliveries."

"That woman," Roey said with a smirk. "She's in the back right now, but if you'd like, you can leave the crate behind the bar here." The halfling tavern owner motioned toward a spot near a barrel.

"Actually," he started to say as he walked around the bar and placed the crate in the spot she'd instructed. "I was wondering if I might talk to you about Tilli."

"Oh?" Roey raised an eyebrow and pursed her lips expectantly.

"Aye. You know Tilli pretty well."

"I've known her for years. She came to work for me here at the tavern when her husband passed away."

"Aye," Felton said, stroking his brown beard. Tilli's past was not where he intended to go with the conversation.

"I haven't seen her this happy in all those years," Roey said, stepping toward him and looking straight in his eyes.

"I ..." Felton smiled. "That's good to hear," was all he could muster.

"I think it's quite fortunate that the Garome District got you for our guard."

"Thank you," Felton said. He hadn't always agreed with the sentiment and hadn't felt as though he'd gotten to do much in the way of the traditional work of the city guard. However, Felton had certainly found himself more and more entangled in the community.

He shook his rabbit trail thoughts away and refocused the conversation. "I just wanted to ask if you've ever heard Tilli talk about dreams outside of being a barmaid?"

Roey laughed. "Sweetie, all the time. That woman knows more about plants than anyone I've ever met. You know she has been single-handedly responsible for some of the best changes to our recipes? Not to mention the teas she brings. Folks looking for something other than ale and water know we have the finest tea around."

"Aye ..." Felton said, stroking his beard again. "Has she ever mentioned *Tilli's Herbs & Tea* to you?"

Roey laughed again. "Only a thousand times. I've encouraged her to go for it. She always has some sort of excuse, though. 'Not enough money to get a storefront.' 'Not enough help at the garden.' 'Lili's too little.'" Roey leaned in conspiratorially. "You know what I think is the real reason? I think she's afraid to do it by herself. Losing a spouse is a hard thing. One day you do everything together, working toward common goals; then the next, your partner is gone, and you have to figure out how to do things all alone."

"Aye," Felton replied. He didn't know the exact feeling, but he thought it similar to how he had felt when he no longer had his brothers and sisters in arms working next to him. How many times had he gone on missions where he had to rely on the riders beside him? They supported one another and worked together toward the same goal. When he got injured, he faced that mission alone.

Felton shook the notion away. He had not been alone. That had been a lie he'd believed.

Aunt Cleary and Aunt Gael had been with him the whole time, supporting him along the way. And before them, Healer Gembeck had been by his side the whole time he was in the healing ward. Commander Qwen had helped him in the way she could. Captain Bradnir had given him a chance when he didn't have to. Felton was more than grateful for old Tullen's kindness. And then there were all the folks of the Garome District who had welcomed him with open arms, even though he hadn't been warm or approachable himself.

"Do you think you could help me with something?" Felton asked. "Something for Tilli?"

Roey flipped the rag onto her shoulder. "Sweetie, I would do anything for that woman. What'd you have in mind?"

A wide grin crept across Felton's face.

CHAPTER 31
NEW SEASONS

Tilli watched him as Felton stared at the sprouting plant in his pot. Felton had never grown anything before. As he gazed upon the growing leaves, he was speechless and overwhelmed by wonder. He recalled the tiny slivers of seeds he and Tilli had planted. From those, this ... this ...

"What is it?" Felton asked the woman kneeling beside him.

Tilli smirked. "You'll have to wait a little longer to find out."

"Still not telling?" Felton bemoaned.

"Don't want to ruin the surprise," Tilli said, planting a quick kiss on his cheek.

"Alright, alright," he surrendered.

"Maybe another couple of weeks," she said sweetly.

"A couple of weeks?"

Felton thought the timing rather humorous. He'd enlisted the help of Kinson and Warner and Waen to help him renovate the storefront attached to the miller's shop. Arth himself offered to help as well, still spending extra time at the shop to avoid more pies.

The guard took one last look at the plant; it was so tiny, so fragile, and yet it seemed bright with life. For some reason, it made him emotional. He turned to find Templeton had snuck up on him. The tortoise headbutted Felton's beard, rolling his bald green head in the thickness of it.

"Okay. Okay." Felton laughed and petted the tortoise's long neck with one hand. He rubbed at his glossy eyes with the other. "I'm fine, Tem, really."

Tilli snickered as she walked toward the greenhouse. She turned over her shoulder and asked, "What was it you have to do today, again?"

Felton tried to remember what he'd told her. He didn't want to lie to Tilli, but he also wanted to keep his secret project a secret. *What was it…? Oh, right.* "I'm helping Arth Miller today." It was enough truth to keep his secret and avoid a lie.

"Oh, right. I thought I saw Warner and Kinson over there the other day. Arth must have found someone to rent the storefront next to his, eh?"

"I don't think so," Felton said. In truth, none had rented it. The guard had bought it off the miller.

"Hmm. Maybe he's just renovating it to make it more attractive for a renter."

Felton didn't say anything. For the life of him, he couldn't come up with a response that wouldn't be a lie.

Tilli laughed. "Maybe I should go by and ask how much he's renting it for—"

"No!" Felton said, quicker than he'd meant. "I mean … no bother. I could ask him while I'm there."

"Well …" Tilli stammered. "I probably wouldn't be able to afford it anyway. Most of the money I make at the tavern I use to feed us and keep the garden. Plus, I can't be in three places at once. Couldn't tend the garden and work a shop and work at the tavern."

"Aye …" Felton said. "But you've got Lili and me now."

Tilli blurted a laugh.

"What? I can help with things," the dwarf continued.

"Yeah. That's true. You are very helpful," she said, patting the side of his face. "Lili …" She paused and sighed. "That girl is more set on breaking another arm than helping with something like a shop."

"Still climbing the walls?" Felton mused.

"Probably climbing one right now."

Felton chuckled. "She's been awfully helpful with tying labels on the jars. Her little bows are getting quite good."

"She only likes to do that when you're the one helping," Tilli teased. "That girl is happy to do anything with you."

Felton's smile stretched from ear to ear. He went to work, watering some of the plants as Tilli checked on others. They worked in silence for a while, neither needing to say anything as they went about their tasks.

The guard's heart thumped in his chest as he worked up the courage to say what he needed to. He loved Tilli. He wanted to support the woman and help her make her dreams come true.

"You know," he said, returning the watering ladle to the barrel. "It's alright to be afraid sometimes."

"What?" Tilli asked with an incredulous smile.

"I was afraid before."

"Of Tem." The woman laughed. "Lili and I could tell, even when you denied it."

Felton chuckled and shook his head. "That's true. But look how much Tem loves me, now that I've gotten over that fear."

"He probably loves *you* more than anyone," she said. She rotated her hand under her chin to form an invisible beard. "Though, I think you have an unfair advantage."

Felton rolled his eyes and smirked. "That's not what I'm getting at."

Tilli grabbed a shovel from the corner and stood it in front of her, leaning her chin on it. "What is it you're getting at?"

Felton took a deep breath to make sure the words came out right. "All I'm saying is, it can be scary to embark on a new season when you don't know what it looks like. Especially if you feel like you're alone. But you're not alone."

"I know," Tilli said, her blue eyes falling on him with genuine affection.

"When I first came to the Garome District, I had lost everything I'd spent my entire life working toward. The only thing I was ever any good at was being a warrior. It was the only thing I'd ever known. And when I couldn't be that anymore, I found myself in a new season. A season that was scary, one I'd never walked through. One I couldn't see the path through."

"One you were forced into," Tilli said.

"Aye," Felton agreed with a nod. "But I've found so many beautiful things in this season. Things I never dreamed I would discover. I found that even though I thought I was alone, I wasn't."

"You're a dreamer," Tilli said with a smirk.

Felton shook his head and downcast his eyes. A hand on his chin lifted his face.

"It's one of the things I love about you," Tilli whispered.

Felton smirked back at her. "I just want you to see your dreams come true."

"You're too sweet for your own good."

"I was thinking the same of you."

"Ah," Tilli said. "But your sweetness surprises folks. You're supposed to be a big tough warrior. On the inside, you're as sweet as Enny's pecan pie."

Felton laughed. He suddenly remembered he was supposed to meet Arth and the others at the shop on the main street.

"Oh!" He started. "You've reminded me, I have to go."

"Well, get a move on then," Tilli said to him. "I'm never going to get enough work done to open my own shop if you're here distracting me all the time."

Felton stopped and turned to roll his eyes at her. Tilli responded with a wink.

CHAPTER 32
JOY OVER JUDGMENT

Waen helped Felton slide another metal rack into place. The teen stepped back and surveyed his design as a whole. The wall was lined with metal racks, custom-built to hold Tilli's preferred bottles for housing dried herbs. Kinson had been kind enough to craft several of the bottles for them to test with the boy's design. The racks were spiraled black iron, which contrasted elegantly against the whitewashed shiplap wall.

Felton patted the teen on the shoulder, even though his gangly frame stood taller than his own. "Good work, lad."

"Thanks," Waen replied, looking around the little shop.

The interior resembled nothing of the old tackle shop. The walls were artfully redone, and every square inch of space had been rearranged. The beams above them were stained with a dark hue, another beautiful detail.

They had replaced two of the beams while fixing the roof. They weren't sure how much smoke damage the place had taken, but they didn't want another incident like the collapse of the roof at *Roey's* under the heavy snow. They erred on the side of caution and replaced the ones they didn't have a good feeling about.

Kinson had replaced the windows, making the shop bright again. They had hung canvas cloths to keep the inside a secret from prying eyes. The glasswright also worked with a local carpenter Felton hadn't met to create stunning cabinet doors that allowed viewers to see inside through panes of glass.

The place had taken them a couple of weeks to renovate—each of them working on tasks before or after their daytime job requirements. Felton was immensely grateful for their persistence and willingness to sacrifice for the secret project.

Numerous times, his compatriots had brought in another item they thought would be good for the shop to have, surprising him with their thoughtfulness. The guard offered to pay them for their work many times, but none would accept more than an occasional supper or ale at *Roey's*.

As he looked over the place—the final rack in its proper position—Felton could finally imagine it filled with Tilli's jars and bottles and baskets of flowers and sacks of seed. He could see it all so clearly, and nothing in the world excited him more.

"Looks good, lads," Kinson said, closing the door behind him quickly as he entered. The old dwarf carried a wide object covered in canvas cloth.

"Oh, no," Felton said. "Not again. What have you got this time? I thought everything looked just right."

Kinson snorted. "Aye. Aye. But Warner and I have been working on something we didn't tell ye young'uns about."

"Oh? And what's that?"

"Help me take this cloth off, lad," the old dwarf said, beckoning Waen.

The teen helped pull the canvas away from what appeared to be a metal frame with loops on top. As Waen helped Kinson swivel the object, the boy gasped. They held it up so Felton could see the face of it. The piece was an artfully crafted stained glass sign. The black iron had been crafted to make letters and floral patterns, rimmed by a square frame. The flowers were meticulously filled with colored glass, making the sign a breathtaking sight as the light poured through. The sign read: *Tilli's Herbs & Tea.*

"Kinson ..." Felton said, barely able to speak. "It's beautiful."

"Aye," he said with pride. He turned to Waen and said, "Yer Pa is quite the artist."

"Yes," Waen agreed.

Felton thought he saw a new light in the boy's eye, as though he were seeing his father's skill for the first time.

"I'd say you both are," Felton said, stepping closer for another look.

"I think it'll look beautiful hanging above the door out front," Kinson said, his gravelly tone sounding softer somehow.

"Aye," Felton agreed. "Can we hang it and keep the canvas over it?"

"We can tie some twine around it to keep it covered," Kinson replied.

"Good. If I can get some help from you both one more time tomorrow, we can pull this off."

The old dwarf and the teen boy nodded their agreement. Felton patted them on the shoulders, grateful to have such good friends.

After they hung the sign outside above the door, Kinson returned to his shop, while Felton and Waen locked the store. The afternoon was warm and bright, a lovely day in the Garome District. Felton chuckled as he looked down the main street.

"What is it?" Waen asked.

"You're a smart lad," Felton said, squeezing the boy in a side hug.

"Sometimes," Waen said with a grin.

"Look at this place."

Waen followed Felton's gaze and realized what the dwarven guard was referring to. The cobbled street was flanked on either side with shops run by Garome locals. Ornate brackets stretched out from many of the buildings, holding baskets which swung lightly in the breeze. Flowers cascaded radiant colors from the baskets. Birds flitted overhead, completing the wondrous scene.

"You know," Felton admitted to the teen, "when I met you the day you were preparing those brackets, I didn't get it. I couldn't see the purpose for them. I thought it was a waste of time."

"And now?" Waen asked, not looking away from the scene.

"I get it," Felton said. "Even if the purpose is merely to bring joy to the onlooker, is that not purpose enough?"

"Ma always says that bringing someone joy is one of the greatest gifts you can give."

"That's because your Ma is smart, too. You get it honestly."

Waen grinned. They stood for a long moment, taking in the landscape of their home. Finally, the teen asked, "Mister Felton?"

"Aye?"

"You remember the first day you stopped by the smithy to speak with me?"

"Aye."

"Well ..." Waen paused, chewing on his lip. "Well, that meant a lot to me. We were still new to the district, and I was worried folks would judge us because we're not dwarven smiths. But you were so kind and didn't give it a second thought."

"In fairness," Felton said, "I was new to the district, too, and I thought everyone would judge me because I lost my honor when I could no longer serve with the garvawk warriors."

Waen's face scrunched, and he looked at the shorter dwarf. "I never thought that at all. I've always thought that showing kindness is one of the most honorable things anyone can do."

"I suppose," Felton mused with a nod and a stroke of his beard.

"That makes you one of the most honorable people I've ever met—at least in my book."

"Thanks, lad," Felton said, a flood of emotions coursing through him.

"Anyway, I better get back to the smithy to help Pa."

"Aye," Felton choked out.

Waen sauntered off. He turned back to look at the dwarf as he continued to walk backward down the street. "And, Mister Felton?" he called back.

"Aye, lad?"

"I'm so glad your leg got better."

"Thanks, la—"

Felton's words dropped right out of his mouth. His fingers rolled as if he were feeling for something that should have been there. Where was his cane? And where was his pain?

The guard watched the wise young Waen walk down the center of Garome's beautiful main street. The dwarf's face revealed a mixture of confusion, shock, and utter joy.

CHAPTER 33
ONE STEP AT A TIME

Aunt Cleary dished out a heaping pile of dinner on Felton's plate. He absently rolled and unrolled the strange flat bread Bend had sent home with him. It was indeed flatter than the flat bread he'd made before, and Felton assumed the baker had called it a "bendtilla" because of the guard's "flatterbread" joke. The round white circle was the strangest bread he'd ever seen, but it was no less delicious than anything else the baker had concocted.

Felton had spent most of the day attempting to figure out where he'd last seen his cane. The guard's eyes narrowed as he put the pieces of the puzzle together. His best guess was that he'd left his cane somewhere in the garden. *But when?* he wondered.

He had racked his brain to pinpoint the exact time. The conclusion he came to was he'd ditched it when Lili had fallen out of Big Barth. He'd been so worried about her and had raced to her aid. It was the first time he could remember running after his injury. In all honesty, he couldn't remember feeling any pain in his leg since the incident.

Felton made a mental plan to look for the cane—not that he needed or wanted it anymore. Rather, a curiosity filled him with the need to see where it ended up.

"What's the matter, deary? Too spicy?" Aunt Cleary asked.

"Oh, no," Felton said, quickly shoving a bite into his mouth.

"He's just excited about tomorrow," Aunt Gael said.

"That's right," Aunt Cleary cooed. "Everything you've been doing for Tilli is so sweet."

"Thanks, Aunt Cleary," Felton said, then tried to change the subject. "Supper is delicious."

"Look at him blush," Aunt Gael said, poking his cheek. "He always gets so rosy. Your father was the same way when we teased him."

"Well, I think Tilli's going to love it, deary. It's about time she gets paid for everything she does. I know my spices and herbs cabinet isn't the only one in the district she fills."

"Aye, that's true," Aunt Gael agreed.

"And it's clear she makes you happy, too, deary. Last time she stopped by, she told me how much Lili loves you, too."

"Sweetest girl," Felton agreed. "Though you ought to stop teaching her how to shark folks in games," he scolded Aunt Gael.

"The girl has the gift!" his aunt argued.

"Aye," Felton grumbled but smiled. "That she does."

His aunts stared at him for a long time. Felton glanced from one to the other as he chewed his food. Finally, he asked, "What?"

"Well, deary ..." Aunt Cleary paused as though she were trying to be careful with her words. She started gingerly, "As much as we love having you, and you know you're always welcome—though I'm sure a proper bed would be better for you to get some proper rest ..."

"Aye ..." Felton prompted her to go on.

"Are you going to marry that woman or not?" Aunt Gael asked bluntly.

"Whoa!" Felton said, waving his hands in front of him. "One step at a time. If you want me to move out, that's fine. I can find an apartment in the district. To be honest, I wasn't sure I'd be here long enough to need one."

"Oh no, deary. That's not it. We just love how happy the Marigold ladies make you. When you first arrived … your sorrow was …"

"Terrible," Aunt Gael finished.

Aunt Cleary nodded uncomfortably.

"I'm sorry for that," Felton said. He looked to Aunt Cleary. "You've suffered through wakeful nights with me more than anyone. I never meant to bring that to your doorstep."

"Deary," Aunt Cleary said with more directness in her voice, "no one blames you for having seen what you've seen. As much as we can't truly know what you've been through, we *have* watched you grow since being here."

"Aye," Aunt Gael said. "You're a lot more pleasant now."

"Thanks …" Felton said, accepting it as a compliment rather than a comment on his less-than-pleasant presence when he'd first arrived.

"We just think," Aunt Cleary continued, "if someone brings that much joy to your life, you should do everything you can to keep them in your life."

"I …" Felton stopped, processing their words. He could easily say he loved Tilli. He'd never before felt the way he did when he was with her. He loved everything about her. "I just want her to know how much she and Lili mean to me. I wanted to help her dream come true."

In a surprisingly gentle gesture, Aunt Gael placed a hand on top of his. "Felton, when people love each other, that's exactly what they want to do. They build each other up. They work together to fill each other's lives with joy. It's a beautiful thing."

Aunt Gael pulled something from her pocket. She held a closed fist out in front of him, turning his hand with the one she had placed atop his own. She placed the small item into his hand, and Felton's face scrunched.

"Did you win this off someone at the Tavern?" he asked.

"No." Aunt Gael slapped his hand in mock offense. "That was the ring your uncle gave me years ago when we got engaged."

Felton's mouth fell open. "Aunt Gael, I can't take this. If Uncle Gendor gave this to you—"

"Nonsense," she said. "He was the only one for me. Not every woman loses their husband so young as Tilli. I had many good years with your uncle before he died. If I had been younger, perhaps another dwarf would have caught my fancy—"

"That's not the point," Aunt Cleary said. "The point is, if you find that kind of love, no matter when you find it, you should try to keep it."

Felton sat quietly for a long time. Just like Tullen had explained, Tilli filled the guard's cup with love and joy—and Lili, too. As much as he was grateful for that, he hoped even more that he filled their cups with the same. Felton brushed at the scar on his eyebrow as he was acutely aware of its presence. "But why would a woman so beautiful as Tilli want to marry a beat-up dwarf like me?"

"I don't think you remember how pretty I was compared to your uncle," Aunt Gael said.

Felton laughed.

"Love goes beyond such things," Aunt Cleary said.

"Aye," Aunt Gael continued. "Everyone comes with faults and weaknesses. Love isn't blind to those things; love persists nonetheless. You choose to love regardless of the weaknesses. You choose to love because you're better together."

Felton nodded and stroked his beard as he processed their words. His fist closed around the ring, and he put it in his pocket. Aunt Cleary's smile widened.

"I'm not going to ask her right away," Felton said, trying to temper his aunts' excitement. "One step at a time."

"We're just happy for you, deary."

"I know," Felton said, with a smirk. "Just ... one step at a time."

CHAPTER 34
MARIGOLD

Tem watched Felton as the guard quietly walked through the garden on his way to visit the Marigold ladies. The dwarf had one small detour to make first. He glanced about, looking for any sign of his cane.

Felton thought back to the day Lili had fallen from Big Barth. Retracing his steps proved more difficult than he'd anticipated. His memory of the day was a little fuzzy. In the moment, he'd had no space in his mind for anything other than Lili's safety. He hadn't even realized he'd ditched his cane until Waen mentioned it.

It dawned on him. He and Tilli had been looking at his plant under the glass bubble. His cane must be somewhere near there.

Felton scoured the area, searching high and low as Tem watched him curiously. The guard didn't think the stick would be so difficult to find. When he finally spotted the cane, he merely smiled as he realized why the task had been such a challenge.

His cane leaned against a bush that grew spindly vines of flowers. If he hadn't been so intent in his search, he never would have seen it. The wooden cane appeared to be embracing its resting place, accepting the flower vines.

Felton's lip peaked on one side. *Thank you*, he said silently to the cane as he decided to leave the aid to the flowers. He then turned onto the garden path and proceeded to find his favorite ladies.

Lili bounced excitedly next to Felton as he pulled his potted plant from under the glass bubble. The guard's mouth fell slack, and his shoulders dropped as he stared in wonder. Tilli lowered the glass bubble—once he removed the plant—and stood by with a giddy expression.

Felton's plant had grown and blossomed into something more beautiful than he'd expected. It was a flowering plant. A globe of orange blossoms grew with lacy foliage. At first, it was hard to tell as the petals rippled around each other, but Felton thought he counted five elegant orange petals with rounded tips.

"Shave me," he murmured under his breath. "It's beautiful."

And the scent ... the flower smelled earthy, almost spicy, with a hint of citrus and pine. Felton inhaled the alluring and refreshing aroma.

He couldn't help himself and laughed as he carried the plant to the bench and sat to gaze upon it. How funny it seemed to him that only a couple weeks earlier he would have thought the flower useless. Yet here it was, bringing him a wondrous joy he never would have expected.

Lili climbed onto the bench next to him, hugging him and looking upon the flower. Tilli stood behind the bench, affectionately rubbing his shoulders.

"Do you like it?" she asked.

"Aye," Felton breathed. "May be the most beautiful flower I've ever seen. What is it?"

"Well, that's what the surprise is."

"What?"

"It's a marigold."

An emotional tidal wave crashed over him.

A marigold? he thought. He saw the Marigold girls in a whole new light. How apt was their name? How much like this rich flower that brought such wonderful joy to him were the pair who'd opened their hearts to him?

Felton's chin quivered under his bushy beard as he fought back welling tears. He set the pot in his lap and pulled Lili into his big arm. With the other he reached up and held Tilli as close as he could, breathing them both in. He held them there in the warm spring sun, never wanting to let go.

"Thank you," he whispered. "You two have changed my life. I love you both dearly."

"We love you, too!" Lili chimed, nuzzling deeper into Felton's side and squeezing with all her might.

"It was very difficult to keep it a secret," Tilli said. "I had to watch everything I said, trying not to spoil the surprise."

Felton barked a laugh. "I know the feeling."

"Oh?" Tilli asked, eyeing him.

"Aye," Felton said. "Would you ladies like to go on a walk with me?"

"Sure!" Lili said, jumping off the bench as though she were about to fly.

Tilli joined him around the bench and asked, "Where are we going?"

"Do you trust me?" Felton asked, extending his hand.

Tilli narrowed her eyes suspiciously, but she couldn't hold back the grin that grew across her face. Her slender hand grasped his, and she said, "I'll follow you anywhere."

CHAPTER 35
THE BIG SURPRISE

As they walked up the Garome District's main street, Felton shot a look to Waen, who sat at the front of the smithy. Seeing the dwarf ushering the Marigold ladies with their eyes closed, the boy leapt to his feet and ran to the bakery.

Good lad, Felton thought.

"Where are we going?" Lili whispered next to him, her face contorting as she tried to peek without him noticing.

"Ah," Felton said, clicking his tongue at her and gently squeezing her hand, "no peeking now."

The little girl's face scrunched, but she whispered back as though Tilli couldn't hear her. "You can tell me. I won't tell Mama."

Felton chuckled, and he thought he heard Tilli muffle a laugh.

"Patience, Sprout," Felton said.

He led them by their hands, holding them close to him on either side. Waen ran past, shooting a nod to the guard as he sprinted in silence. Felton shook his head in amusement. As he watched the blacksmith's boy run ahead toward *Roey's Tavern*, Felton found himself oddly content.

The spring day brought a comfortably warm breeze. The hanging bowls of flowering plants swayed from their hooks, lovely in the sunlight. It struck the guard as strange that he hadn't recognized the beauty of the place before spring came.

As they neared the storefront attached to the miller's, Felton's heartbeat quickened. A nervousness bubbled inside him. He'd spent so much time and effort working on the shop for Tilli. What if she didn't like it? What if she was upset at him?

"What is it?" Tilli asked, not opening her eyes. Felton hadn't realized his pace had slowed.

"Uh, nothing ..." Felton said quickly. "Almost there."

He led them up the two steps that led to the door of the storefront. The sweet chime of a bell rang out, scaring Felton half to death. Warner and Waen must have made the addition without him knowing. Though it startled him, he was thankful his friends had thought of it. He certainly hadn't.

Felton carefully navigated them through the door. "Stand here," he said, leaving them in the middle of the room. "Don't open your eyes yet!"

He hurried to the windows and pulled away the canvases they'd used to deter prying eyes. As the guard pulled down the first canvas, he locked eyes with a surprised Kinson, as the elder dwarf set his ladder. They exchanged unspoken gestures, the glasswright indicating he was preparing to uncover the stained glass sign. Felton bade him wait but laughed as he saw others gathering outside. He waved them off, trying to get them to hide themselves.

Felton pulled down the canvas from the other side of the door. The spring sun poured through the windows, bathing the place in warm light. Felton stood in awe for a moment. With how secretive they'd been with the project, he hadn't seen the place in the full light of day. The little shop was bright and beautiful, primed and ready for an herbalist to move in.

He grinned as his eyes fell upon the Marigold ladies standing in the middle of the shop. Tilli waited patiently, her eyebrows arching as she listened for Felton's movements. Lili's face was squeezed into funny wrinkles as she looked around through squinted eyes. The guard smirked, knowing the girl still had no idea what she was looking at, despite her best efforts.

Tilli turned toward his footsteps as he approached them, her eyes remaining closed. "Is this some elaborate scheme you've concocted to finally entrap me and put an end to my criminal endeavors?"

Felton smiled broadly, feeling the tightness of his skin as it wrinkled around the scar on his face. He grabbed Tilli's hand and said, "Go ahead, open your eyes."

"What have you brought us to—" Tilli's words fell away.

"Whoa ..." Lili said as she fully opened her blue eyes.

Both ladies' mouths fell slack. Tilli squeezed Felton's hand and covered her mouth with her free hand. Tilli and Lili slowly spun, surveying the cozy shop, taking it all in.

The shop was bright and cozy. The white shiplap walls were clean and beautifully accented with the black iron racks Warner and Waen had designed and built. *Tea* was painted on one of the side walls in big ornate script, while *Herbs* labeled the opposite wall. Beautifully stained tables and cupboards were neatly placed with baskets on top. The main counter held the beautiful glass cupboards where special herbs could be housed.

"What ... what ..." Tilli couldn't seem to find her words.

Felton eyed her, unsure what her shocked face meant. *Does she like it? Is she overwhelmed? Is she upset?* The last question came to him as tears began to stream down the woman's cheeks.

"It's ... uh ..." he stammered. "Well, we tried to think of everything an herbalist would need in a shop. None of us are herbalists ourselves ..." He chuckled.

"You did all this?" Tilli asked, her chin quivering.

"Aye. Well, I had help—Kinson and Warner and Waen. Even Arth Miller helped with some things. And ... well, I know it's been your dream to have your own herbs shop and—"

Felton's words were cut off, his lips smashed against Tilli's as she kissed him.

A chorus of snickers outside drew their attention.

"What was that?" Tilli asked, her eyebrow popping.

Felton shrugged his shoulders and chuckled. "Well, everyone is excited about this."

"Everyone?"

"Aye," he said, pulling her toward the front door. "There's one more surprise."

"Another surprise?" Lili squeaked, popping up from behind the counter she'd been inspecting. She ran to catch up to them.

When the trio exited the shop, they noticed the gathered crowd that hid poorly off to either side. Kinson stood atop his ladder, right next to the door.

"Hello, Miss Tilli," he said cheerfully.

"What in Finlestia are all of you doing here?" Tilli asked as Aunt Cleary and Aunt Gael led a crowd of townsfolk around the corner and into view.

"We all wanted to be here for the moment, deary," Aunt Cleary said.

"What moment?" Tilli asked as she spotted Warner and Lana Smith strolling up with Bend to join the gathered crowd. It seemed everyone in the Garome District came out for the occasion. Even Templeton had made it and stood near Aunt Gael.

Felton wondered how the tortoise had gotten there so quickly but soon dismissed the notion. Tem was a strange creature the dwarf would likely never understand.

"The big surprise!" Laen hollered over the crowd.

"I think everyone knows about it now," Roey said, shushing the boy. A ripple of amusement rolled over the crowd.

"Are we ready?" Kinson asked from atop the ladder.

Felton pulled Tilli close and whispered, "Are you ready?"

"I ..." Tilli hemmed.

Felton squeezed her hands in his. "I'm here with you; just say the word."

Tilli bit at her lip, her big blue eyes glassy as she stared at him. She didn't need words; she simply nodded.

"Aye," Felton called up to Kinson. "We're ready."

Kinson cut the rope and pulled the canvas cloth away from the sign. The spring sun shone through the stained glass sign, dazzling the onlookers. Gasps of awe sounded from the crowd.

"Wow ...," Lili said, grabbing her mother's hand.

Tilli pulled herself closer to Felton as tears streamed from her eyes.

"Tilli's Herbs & Tea!" little Laen's big voice boomed over the crowd.

The crowd erupted into laughter and applause. Folks cheered and whistled, clapping with fervor.

When they finally settled down, everyone inched closer, trying to get a glimpse of Tilli's reaction.

"Everyone's staring," Lili whispered.

"I see that," Tilli replied. "What now?" she asked Felton.

The guard realized he hadn't thought that far ahead. He'd been so worried about how Tilli would react, he hadn't given any thought to the awkward crowd.

As if Aunt Cleary sensed the tension, she strolled to the front of the crowd, standing at the bottom of the steps to the shop.

"Deary," she said to Tilli, "I'd like to be the first customer at *Tilli's Herbs & Tea.* I have benefited from your herbs for many of my recipes."

"Aye, and not just her," someone shouted from the crowd.

Others laughed. Felton agreed. Many had enjoyed a meal with the abundance of flavors from Tilli's herbs through Aunt Cleary's generosity and hospitality.

"And I'd like to be the first to put in a bulk order," Roey piped.

Tilli appeared caught between some unseen tension. "Roey, I—"

"Don't worry," the halfling waved her off. "I've already hired someone to help me."

Tilli huffed a disbelieving laugh. She shook her head as she looked over the crowd. She cast a glance back toward the shop and its gleaming empty shelves.

"Well, I guess I won't be able to sell you anything until I move all my herbs to the shop." She offered with a shrug. "May take a little while. Some of you have seen my house." Several folks chuckled.

"I don't know if you noticed," Aunt Gael said, "but you've got lots of folks with empty hands standing around, willing to help."

Affirmative nods and spoken agreements rolled through the gathering.

"Aye, deary," Aunt Cleary agreed. "We're here to help. You're not alone."

"No," Tilli whispered as she turned her hand over, inspecting Felton's in her grasp. Her eyes settled upon him, and she said, "No, I'm not."

CHAPTER 36
NEEDED

Felton brushed his hands together and heaved a breath. He slapped the top of the wooden table and wiped his brow with his forearm.

"This where you wanted it?" he asked Aunt Gael.

"That'll do," she said, inspecting its distance from the other two tables Felton had placed in the designated area for the Castle Brick tournament. He thought Aunt Gael a little too eager to shark unwary visitors.

Aunt Cleary added, "That's lovely, deary. Thank you."

Felton gave each of his aunts a kiss on the head before strolling away.

The Garome District was abuzz, preparing for an influx of visitors. The city wanted to hold a memorial celebration to commemorate the honor of the defenders who fought during the Battle of Galium.

An aide from Castle District had visited to appraise the area. He praised the Garome District for its beauty and hospitality, and the district had been chosen as the location for its quaint charm.

The first day of summer was only days away, and the district still had plenty of preparations to make. Not a soul sat idle. Everyone seemed intent on showing the world how great their cozy little district was—and they would certainly get the chance to do so.

Not only was King Thygram Markensteel making an appearance, but ambassadors from other cities around Tarrine were coming to partake in the festivities as well: royals from Whitestone, elves from Loralith, and more. The district's excitement was palpable.

Felton thought they were selected because of the beauty of the place with its flowers in full bloom. Not only did the hanging flowers look lush and bright, but folks had begun to roll out great flower beds and pots around the main street with Tilli's help, making it even more vibrant.

Merchant tents had been erected all about the square in front of *Roey's Tavern*, as folks prepared to sell wares to visitors. Felton passed a gathering of folks where Enny Miller was organizing the pies they planned to serve during the festival.

The guard thumbed the ring in his pocket, a habit he'd developed in recent weeks. He wasn't sure when he had started carrying the ring his aunt had given him, but he regularly fiddled with it in his pocket. Each day that passed, his courage and certainty grew. He would give it to Tilli soon. He just wanted to find the right time.

Tilli and Lili were setting up a small table outside the front of their shop as Felton strode toward them. Tilli smiled at his approach, while Lili raced to greet him.

Lili skidded to a halt, her eyes widening as she gawked at the sky. A great shadow swooped by, and Felton grabbed the girl, drawing her into the safety of his arms. He glanced about for dangerous flying creatures. *Wyverns? A dragon?*

To his surprise, he spotted a garvawk and rider.

The panther-like creature glided in and landed in the middle of the square, roiling its wings before tucking them tightly to its body. Lotmeag Kandersaw slipped from the back of his garvawk and whispered to the creature. The garvawk sat straighter. Stone crept along her tail and hind end, slowly overtaking the sleek coat of black fur. One of the Miller boys gasped as the garvawk glanced in his direction before her head turned to stone.

Folks that had, moments before, been carrying out tasks in preparation for the celebration stopped and stared at the foredwarf as he approached their local guard.

"Felton," Lotmeag said, greeting him with an outstretched arm.

"Foredwarf Lotmeag," he replied, straightening himself and releasing Lili from his smothering protection.

"It's good to see ye."

"And you," Felton said, grasping the outstretched arm. "Though, the celebration isn't for another few days."

"Aye," Lotmeag said, glancing about. "Looks as though it'll be a lovely celebration."

"Aye," Felton said. "I was glad to hear you arrived home safely. Would love to share a drink and hear some tales from Kelvur when you have the chance."

"Agreed," Lotmeag said, peering around as though he were looking for someone else. "It was an experience I will not soon forget."

"I can imagine," Felton said, a small pang of guilt pricking his chest. While his brothers had been far away and fighting, he'd been in the beautiful Garome District.

"Ah, there they are," Lotmeag said.

"Who—" Felton began to ask but knew as soon as he turned. Commander Qwen and Sergeant Grisham hopped down from a wagon. Captain Bradnir led the way, walking toward Felton and Lotmeag.

"What is this?" Felton laughed, greeting the others.

Many folks from the district had moseyed within earshot to watch the unexpected arrival of guests, wondering what news they bore.

"Well," Lotmeag said, nodding to the others. "We all wanted to be here. Captain Bradnir has filled me in on all the good work ye've been doing here in the Garome District." Lotmeag paused and nodded proudly as he looked around. "Seems a beautiful place."

"Aye," Felton said as he glanced about, smiling to many of his friends and the people he believed made the place special.

"He also mentioned ye seem to have healed up quite nicely," the foredwarf continued, inspecting the guard.

Felton adjusted uncomfortably but remembered he hadn't carried his cane in a long time.

Pride and gratitude battled for dominance within Felton. The captain's confidence meant a lot to him. He'd grown fond of the human captain. Felton had reported to him the week prior. The dwarf enjoyed their time together, plus the visits allowed him time with Tullen at *The Hungry Hog*.

"You can't take him," Lili said to Captain Bradnir, wrapping Felton in a protective hug.

"Oh, Lady Lili," the man said softly, "didn't I already tell you I wouldn't take him from you?"

"Yes," Lili said tentatively.

"Aye, but what's this all about then?" Felton asked.

"Well ..."

"Who are all your friends?" Tilli interrupted as she joined them. "Hello again, Captain," she said with a nod to Bradnir.

"Miss Tilli," he greeted her.

"This is Commander Qwen and Sergeant Grisham of the 7th Warhog Cavalry," Felton introduced them. "And this is

Foredwarf Lotmeag of the garvawk warriors. You remember him from the parade."

"Yes," Tilli said with a smile. "So nice to see you again."

"Nice to meet ye properly, ma'am," Lotmeag said to her.

"What are you all doing here so early? The celebration isn't for a few more days, though I'm sure Roey's got some rooms ready for you."

"I do," Roey called from nearby, breaking any illusion that the folks of the Garome District were not listening.

"Aye, well ..." Lotmeag said, straightening and turning to face Felton. "We all wanted to share the good news together."

"What good news?" Tilli asked, but Felton already guessed what the foredwarf was going to say.

"We've gotten reports of garvawk sign, and we're going to put together a *glendon* team to capture it." Lotmeag beamed. "As I told Mister Felton before, I'd let him know first thing. If ye'd like to join us on the *glendon* team, the garvawk is yers, and ye can come back to Bannett Hall and rejoin the garvawk warriors."

The world slowed around Felton. This was the moment he'd been waiting for—the very offer he had hoped for. All those difficult days he'd walked with the cane, thinking he'd never be able to rejoin his warrior brothers. All those nights he'd sat on his aunts' couch, fearing to fall asleep.

On those long nights, all he thought about was getting back in the fight, waiting for the day his foredwarf would call upon him. He experienced the night terrors still, but they'd become less frequent and more sporadic. Tullen's thankfulness exercises helped. Knowing that he'd see Tilli and Lili when day came gave him something to hope toward.

"Oh." The word came out of Tilli's mouth as a whisper.

Felton recovered from his stunned shock. He couldn't say why he was so surprised. How many times had he dreamed of this moment? As Lili squeezed him, it dawned on the guard that his shock was not about the invitation but his hesitation.

The Garome District's only guard gazed across the eavesdropping neighbors he'd come to know and love. Their faces were bright and filled with excitement for him. They appeared genuinely thrilled that he was getting the opportunity to rejoin the garvawk warriors—something they knew he'd wanted fiercely.

When his gaze landed on Tilli's downcast countenance next to him, he turned and took her hand.

"Tilli ..."

The woman bit her lip and mustered a proud smile. "I'm so proud of you," she said through a lump in her throat.

"Tilli ..." he said again.

She shook her head, pressing her lips together, forcing the smile forward and her tears back. "No, really, it's—"

Felton gently gripped the nape of her neck and pulled her in for a kiss. A couple of tears escaped her eyes, rolling down her cheeks and dripping from her chin. The dwarf guard shook his head and chuckled. He turned to Lotmeag and said, "Foredwarf, with respect, I would like to decline the honor."

"What? No!" Tilli said, her voice hoarse. "Felton, you've done so much for us here. You've helped me accomplish a dream I was too scared to embark upon on my own. I want you to follow your dream, too. I won't be the reason you turn away from that dream."

"Tilli," Felton said, "you are my dream, and I'd follow you anywhere."

The woman gnawed at her lip. "Even if you don't get to go on wild adventures to distant lands? Even if it's just a walk through the garden? You're sure?" she asked, her blue eyes disbelieving.

"As long as I get to be with you," Felton replied.

"And me?" Lili piped, hugging him tighter.

"Aye," Felton laughed. "And you, Sprout."

"Are ye sure?" Lotmeag asked, but the foredwarf's tone and smile suggested that he didn't expect the guard to change his answer.

"I am where I'm needed, where I belong," Felton said with a nod. He motioned toward Captain Bradnir and then waved his hand wide over his eavesdropping neighbors. "That is, if the good Captain and the people of the Garome District will allow me to continue serving as their guard."

"We will!" Laen bellowed, sending everyone into laughter. Numerous others affirmed the boy's statement with calls of their own.

"Seems you've made quite the impression around here," Lotmeag said.

"Aye," Felton agreed, a broad smile splitting his brown beard. "They've made quite the impression on me, too. Let me show you around before the celebration happens."

"Oh," Lili started. "Can we show them the garden?"

"A garden ye say?" Lotmeag asked, meeting the girl with equal enthusiasm.

"Yeah! We've got all sorts of plants in bloom right now!" Lili said, grabbing the foredwarf's hand and leading him away.

Tilli laughed as she leaned into Felton's shoulder while they strolled toward the garden.

"Have any spinach?" Lotmeag asked.

"Loads!" Lili said.

"Why spinach?" Felton asked.

"While we were sailing across the Gant Sea to Kelvur, the ship's cook made this orcish dish with spinach in it," Lotmeag said.

"An orcish dish?"

"Aye." Lotmeag shrugged. "Got a taste for some orcish cuisine while we were traveling."

"Sounds like we really need to have that drink so you can catch me up on the journey," Felton said with a laugh.

"What sort of dish do orcs use spinach in?" Tilli asked, as they walked down the flower-lined main street of the Garome District.

"An orcish dish with eggs," Lotmeag said. "They called it an omelet."

Tem walked slowly beside Felton as they strode along the garden's path. The warmth of the sun danced through the tree leaves, teasing summer's approach.

The guard fiddled with the ring in his hand. Its green stone glittered in the sunlight as he twirled it between his fingers. The celebration would happen the next day, but after everything Felton had been through, he didn't think he could wait another day.

"What do you think?" Felton asked the massive tortoise. "Think she'll like it?"

Tem said nothing, of course, but the dwarf was pretty sure the slow bob of the tortoise's head was an affirmative nod.

Felton smiled as they walked. He glanced toward his cane, completely covered and overgrown with foliage, having become one with the garden. How different this walk through the garden compared to his first visit. He strode easily, walking with no visible injury. Tem, who he'd originally thought to be warding him away, walked alongside him contentedly.

The dwarf's heart thrummed in his chest, his nerves sparking. He didn't know what Tilli would say when he asked her to marry him, but he hoped more than anything she'd say yes. He had no idea what the new season would bring, but he was excited to find out.

Felton believed whatever sprouted from the seeds they'd sown, they would tend its blooms well together.

A Note from the Author

Thank you for reading *Guard in the Garden*! I hope you had as much fun exploring Galium's quaint Garome District as I did writing this book. If so, please leave a wonderful review. Reviews are the lifeblood of indie authors like me. The more positive reviews we have, the more likely it is that others will pick up the book as well.

A lot went into this book, and I've had some great encouragement and love from folks along the way. I especially want to thank Brittany, Crystal, and Joy for helping me make this book a reality.

And now to a more serious topic ...

I endeavored to write a book that delved into some rather deep and delicate subjects while remaining approachable and hopeful. Writing about such things as PTSD, loneliness, depression, and hopelessness in a fun fantasy world was no simple task. In truth, many of Felton's struggles are far too real, and I'm afraid to say, often under-recognized. I, myself, have wrestled with many of these since my time in the military ended. But, as is the way with literary art, fiction with a dash of magic can open up unique avenues for sharing things that are difficult to discuss otherwise.

I am not the only one.

Millions of veterans who have fought for freedom and justice have found themselves in very similar circumstances. It is not an embellishment to say that leaving the military is one of the hardest things a warrior can do. When you're still enlisted, like-minded and mission-focused brothers and sisters surround you and have your back. They'd take a bullet for you, and you would do the same for them. The bond, formed under the stresses and rigors of training and war, forges in blood and is strong as steel. When you are removed from that, isolation crashes into you like a tidal wave. Despite the best intentions and empathy of caring friends, those who have not served simply do not completely understand.

Let me be clear—this book does not include all the struggles or difficulties veterans face. Nor would I suggest this book contains a cure-all for the various intricacies of healing veterans. Every one of us wages our own personal battle. However, I would implore you as the reader ...

Friends and Family of Veterans:
Be there! The veteran you love has deep and difficult battles waging with them; ones that you cannot understand unless you have served yourself. That does not mean you can't be there for them. Check in on your veterans. Share with them joy, passion, and excitement. Give them your love in word and deeds. Be cautious not to let words fall flat. Follow through and show them your love with your actions.

My Veteran Brothers and Sisters:
Show up! Every. Single. Day. Never back down, never surrender. Surround yourself with love, joy, and gratitude. There is *more.* Find your new mission. There are many to choose from. Do not isolate yourself. When the darkest days are upon you and you feel all alone, reach out to someone who will shine some light into your life.

If you find yourself in a situation where isolation is overwhelming and you feel like you're drowning, or you just recognize you could use some extra support, know you are not alone. Below I've listed a few resources, should you need to call upon them.

US Veteran resources:
Veteran Crisis Line: Dial 988 then press 1
Vet Center (Readjustment Counseling): 1-877-927-8387
Wounded Warrior Program: 1-877-832-6997
Vets 4 Warriors: 1-855-838-8255

Canada Veteran resources:
Veteran Crisis Line: 1-800-268-7708
Wounded Warriors Canada: 1-888-706-4808

UK Veteran resources:
Veterans UK Help Line: 0808 1914 2 18
Veterans Gateway: 0808 802 1212

Australia Veteran resources:
Lifeline Australia: 13 11 14
Open Arms: 1800 011 046

I wrote *Guard in the Garden* for myself and friends I know who have struggled with similar things. Though I trust it will have a great impact on others as well. I hope it was an equally enjoyable and impactful read for you. If you know someone you think would benefit from this book's message of hope, I would be grateful if you'd share it with them.

Never give up. Ever onward!

ABOUT THE AUTHOR

Z.S. Diamanti is the award-winning author of the *Stone & Sky* trilogy, an epic fantasy adventure and *Guard in the Garden,* the first book in the *Fables of Finlestia* cozy fantasy series. He went to college forever and has too many pieces of paper on his wall. He is a USAF veteran of Operation Enduring Freedom and worked in ministry for over 10 years. He and his wife live in Colorado with their four children, where they enjoy hikes and tabletop games.

You can get the *Stone & Sky Preludes Series* of stories for FREE at zsdiamanti.com

Connect with him on social media: @zsdiamanti

CONNECT

A Cozy Adventure!

Read the next book in

Fables of Finlestia

ORDER NOW!

WANT MORE FROM THE WORLD OF FINLESTIA?

JOIN THE
GRIFFIN GUARD
TODAY!

JOIN Z.S. DIAMANTI'S

OFFICIAL READERS LIST

AND GET EXCLUSIVE ACCESS TO NEWS,
SHORT STORIES, EVENTS, AND MORE!

Good reviews are vital for Indie Authors. The importance of reviews in helping others find and take a chance on an indie author's book is impossible to overstate.

If you enjoyed this book, would you help me get it in front of more people by taking a minute to give it a good review?
I can't tell you how thankful I'd be.

Check out this link for the best places to review this book and help me get it to more readers who love good books just like you and me!

www.ingramcontent.com/pod-product-compliance
Lightning Source LLC
Chambersburg PA
CBHW021040310726
48969CB00006B/1733